Gordon K. Jones

PREDATORS AND PREY

BookLand press

Copyright © 2022 by Gordon K. Jones

All rights reserved. No part of this publication may be reproduced or transmitted in any form or by any means, electronic or mechanical, including photocopying, recording or any information storage and retrieval, without the written permission of the publisher. Names, characters, places and incidents are either the product of the author's imagination or used fictitiously, and any resemblance to actual persons living or dead, events or locales is entirely coincidental. All trademarks are properties of their respective owners.

Published by
BookLand Press Inc.
15 Allstate Parkway
Suite 600
Markham, Ontario L3R 5B4
www.booklandpress.com

Printed in Canada

Front cover image by Bodysport

Library and Archives Canada Cataloguing in Publication

Title: Predators and prey / Gordon K. Jones.
Names: Jones, Gordon K., 1954- author.
Identifiers: Canadiana (print) 20220223629 | Canadiana (ebook) 20220223645 | ISBN 9781772311655 (softcover) | ISBN 9781772311662 (EPUB)
Classification: LCC PS8619.O53255 P74 2022 | DDC C813/.6—dc23

We acknowledge the support of the Government of Canada through the Canada Book Fund and the support of the Ontario Arts Council, an agency of the Government of Ontario. We also acknowledge the support of the Canada Council for the Arts.

PREDATORS AND PREY

For my sister, Judy, and my late mother, Minnie,
who love and loved animals.

Chapter 1

Trent Corbett sat in his office, took a bite of his toasted bacon and egg sandwich and stared at the laptop screen in front of him. The image, not the first of its kind he had seen, enraged him. Before him was a Facebook post, one which was shared many times over the site. It was a picture of a big game "trophy hunter" sitting with his rifle on top of his kill, a beautiful adult lion. The usual comments followed under it, condemning the hunter.

"Look at the asshole!" he mumbled. "Sitting there so proud with a big shit-eating grin on his face. He thinks he's so brave, but look at the rifle he's holding. That piece could hit anything from two thousand feet away. So brave. Hell, he was totally safe! Poor beast never even heard the shot."

A knock on his office door interrupted his rant. "Come in," he said as he closed his laptop.

The door opened, which let in the sounds of the talk and clatter of the restaurant's breakfast kitchen on a weekday morning. Sandra, the manager of his restaurant, Corbett's, leaned in. "Hey, Trent. We're getting a little slammed. We could use you."

6 GORDON K. JONES

"On my way."

Trent left his office and checked the kitchen first, to ensure they weren't getting behind on their orders. Things were running fine there, so he headed to the front to see where he was needed most. His servers had almost everything under control, however, more people were coming in, which was starting to create a backlog by the door. He headed over to sort it out.

As he neared a booth located halfway along a window, he overheard the four men who occupied it talking. One was showing a picture on his phone to the other three. Trent eavesdropped as he approached.

"Look at this beauty. Apparently, he was two football fields away when the guy dropped him."

"What a shot!"

"That head's going to look great on his wall."

"Do you know what I dream of? The four of us going to Africa together for a hunt. I can see us each coming home with a different game head to mount. Oh man, wouldn't it be great!"

"Me, I get to bag a rhino!"

Trent stopped at the table. "Hey, guys. So, what're you all talking about?"

The owner of the phone turned it in Trent's direction so he could see the picture. Trent bent slightly to have a look. It was the same picture he had been looking at in his office.

"We're saying how great it would be to do what this guy did. Shit, though, look at all the comments under it from those bleeding-heart pussies. 'He's a murderer. He's evil. God's going to get him.' Hell, the man's an ecological hero. He's thinning the herd, feeding the villages, helping their economy. Screw those whiney-ass little dip shits."

"Of course, you know everything you said is mostly incorrect," Trent interjected. "You should try doing some research. Read about what this is all really about rather than drooling over pictures these murdering assholes post, you jerk."

"Jerk? Who the hell do you think you are? Where's the owner? I want to complain."

"The owner? Now, that would be me. I'm the one who owns this establishment." Sensing their discussion might escalate to something more than a verbal one, Trent straightened and unconsciously crossed his arms. Even though he was just five foot nine, he presented an imposing figure to the men. It had been six years since his honourable discharge from the military, and even though his body had softened somewhat, he still owned a muscular frame.

"Establishment? This place! It's a dump!" The man drained the last of his coffee, "why don't you stop giving us lip and go fetch some more coffee for us? Oh and see what's holding up our breakfasts while you're at it. We've all got important jobs to get to."

Trent looked to the counter where one of his best servers stood and called out, "Chelsea!"

Chelsea, dressed in the restaurant's uniform of a mint green short sleeved top with a black dress to the knees, stopped what she was doing and went over. "Is there a problem?"

"No. Not at all. I need you to go and cancel their orders. These men have to leave." Chelsea nodded and headed to the kitchen. Secretly, Trent hoped their meals weren't already on the grill, as he didn't want to lose the cost of the food.

"You're throwing us out?"

"I am."

"Hey buddy. This is a free country. We have freedom of speech. Who the hell do you think you are to-"?

"I already told you. I'm the owner of this place and yes, you do have freedom of speech." He pointed to the door, "Out there."

"And if we don't?"

"There are two plainclothes detectives having breakfast in here right now. Regulars of mine. I'd be more than happy to call them over and have them charge you with trespassing."

"Come on, guys," said the phone's owner. He drained his coffee, wiped his mouth with a napkin, and dropped it on the floor. "We're out of here."

"Excuse me," Trent said when the men stood, taking a position between them and the door. His hazel eyes, usually more on the green side, turned to dark brown as was always the case when he became mad, a trait of hazel eyed people. "You haven't paid for your coffees."

"You just threw us out."

"Yes. And you had four coffees. Nine dollars please."

"Fuck you!"

"Let me explain. If you leave without paying, I'll have you charged with theft. I don't think your boss at that very important job of yours would appreciate having you coming in late after being arrested. Oh and so you know, I've made charges like this stick before."

The man's face was red and his hand shook slightly as he reached into his jacket for his wallet. He pulled out a ten, crumbled it up and threw it into an empty coffee cup. "I want change!"

Calmly, Trent reached into his own pocket, counted out four quarters, and placed them in the enraged man's hand. The customer clenched them and brushed against Trent's shoulder as he stormed by him with his buddies close behind.

Chelsea returned with a cloth to get the table ready for the next customer. "What on earth was that all about?"

"There was a difference of opinion. Turned out I was right and they were wrong, so they had to go," Chelsea shrugged and began to clean the table when Trent stopped her.

"I charged them for the four coffees they drank." He reached into the coffee cup, pulled out the ten-dollar bill, ran it through his fingers to flatten it, then gave it a quick inspection before handing it to her. "Here you go. Could you ring it up on the till? No change. There's no need for you to lose a tip because I have a disagreement with a customer."

◆ ◆ ◆

It always felt good after a day at the restaurant to walk into the house, kick off his shoes, grab a beer and flop into his favourite chair to watch the news. That first sip of beer always tasted so good. He was comfortable and relaxed, however after a few minutes he found his serenity begin to slip away.

Once in a while, perhaps every couple of months, a sense of anguish would wash over him. It didn't matter how he felt minutes before, and it always seemed to come over him when he was alone and had time to think. Again, it was happening. He felt himself sliding down that same slope, one which took a hard look back at his life. Although successful in business, when he looked at the overall picture of his life, he felt he never accomplished anything of great importance with it. There was nothing he ever did which could benefit man, beast or the world.

Even back in his younger days, Trent wanted to make a difference. He joined the army with the thought he could bring order to a world he considered had gone mad. What drew him in was the dream of criss-crossing the world, defending righteousness and justice, freeing the oppressed and toppling the oppressors. He didn't even mind having his long, light brown hair buzzed short by the company barber, although now it was longer and swept back with no part.

It never occurred to him at the time he enrolled that being in military meant he might have to kill people in the process. It should have been obvious to him, but until he was handed a rifle, it was something he hadn't thought about. He remembered holding it and praying it was something he would never have to use.

Once the army discovered what an excellent shot he was, they trained him as a sniper. He was surprised after being sent into hostile territory that not only could he kill, but he could do it without regret. With his keen eye and training, he could drop targets from over a mile away. He was trained to think of those he shot as targets and not people, which made it much easier for him and other snipers alike.

Trent killed because he had to. He was a small cog in a much larger machine. It was his job. Kill for the current operation. Kill so his people could attack. Kill to give his comrades a better chance of not being killed.

After six months in the field, he began to realize he hated fighting. Hated the military. He started thinking of the enemy in his sights as people, not as targets or an enemy willing to kill him and his friends. Soon he began to hate taking out a target. None of it felt justified to him. It was something he was required to do. He received absolutely no pleasure from it.

A news story on the TV snapped him out of his thoughts.

"*Violence reared its ugly head in an affluent neighbourhood in Columbus, Ohio, this afternoon*", the male personality behind a news desk stated. "*John Gertz, owner of a string of plumbing supply stores, was returning home from a trip to Africa. While there, he had posted pictures on Facebook and Instagram showing him with his 'kill', a giraffe he shot from long range,*" Trent straightened in his chair, his attention captured.

"*A group of approximately twenty masked protesters who somehow discovered when his flight was due to arrive back in Columbus, were waiting for him outside of his home.*"

The shaky image on the TV, obviously shot from a phone, showed a BMW slowly approaching a driveway. As it attempted to pull in, it was forced to stop by the small mob. Shouts of *"Killer! Where's the head? It's not going onto your wall, butcher! Murderer!"* could be heard.

Trent leaned forward as if he was trying to better absorb the story. He saw Gertz's car lurch forward and knock down a couple of people who were standing in front of it blocking the driveway's entrance. Their screams as they hit the ground inflamed the crowd. Quickly, the car was surrounded, the crowd violently rocking it from side to side. Many grabbed rocks from the garden and tried to smash their way through the car's windows.

In the background, the flashing lights of a single police car could be seen approaching. Before it arrived, the trunk of the Gertz's car was forced open and its contents flung about. As the squad car pulled up, Gertz's car was tipped onto its side. The police car skidded to a halt, causing the protesters to scatter before the two uniformed officers could jump out.

"The suitcases and bags which were in Mr. Gertz's trunk, including four long range hunting rifles, were stolen. The victim had kept his seatbelt on and was not injured in the attack. There were no arrests made and currently no named suspects. Police feel this is the work of an animal rights group. (No kidding, Trent thought with a snicker) *No person or group has stepped forward to take credit for the attack. Anybody with information are asked to call police."*

Trent thought for a moment, then smiled as he leaned back in his chair and took a sip of beer. "Hmm, you guys might be onto something. You even made it on national TV and probably scared the shit out of every asshole trophy hunter out there. In fact, I think you may have pointed the way for me. Showed me the path.

"Maybe it's about time I do something. I could sit here and be angry or I can take action. Oh yeah, it's right here in front of me. It's time for me to do something. Those poor animals need protecting. They need me. I have to get out there and start defending them. It's time for me to contribute and make it a safer world for them to live in! And I know just how to do it."

Chapter 2

Usually, Trent would enjoy sleeping in on a day where he didn't need to be at the restaurant until noon. This morning, after his new "call to arms" he was out of bed early. After all, he now felt there was more purpose to his days than running a successful business and feeding the public. Starting that morning and every morning after, the moment he opened his eyes to start his day, he was on a mission. A moral mission.

It was a little past eight when he locked up his restaurant for the night and walked the few blocks to Silver Taps for a couple of enjoyable beers and supper. He'd been going there every Wednesday night for years. Now as he was about to embark on a quest which would quickly grab local, maybe even national headlines and, for sure, the interest of the police, he knew there was no way he could make any changes to his normal routines.

As he walked, he thought back to what he accomplished so far that day. The first thing he did was to fetch his .300 Winchester Magnum Sniper Rifle, also known as a .300 Win Mag, from his closet. It was a dangerous looking weapon, the same make and model of the one he used as a sniper in the army.

The army taught him the importance of his rifle. A rifle was a soldier's best friend and guardian, words which he took to heart. When he was discharged from the military, he was not allowed to take his weapon with him. It was something which surprisingly bothered him, even though he had reached the point where he hated using it. For the next couple of months, he found it hard to sleep without it. So, he went out and bought another. From that night on, even though it sat unused in his closet, there was no further issue with Trent's ability to sleep.

He smiled as he looked at it lying on his living room coffee table and thought, *I wonder if I can still do this blindfolded?* Although it took him twice as long as it once did, when he disassembled the rifle, then put back together again, it was in excellent working order.

"You still got it!" he said, congratulating himself. He spent the rest of the morning with the rifle disassembled, meticulously cleaning and oiling every single piece.

It was a slow afternoon at the restaurant, which gave him plenty of time to spend in his office researching big game hunters on his laptop. He was amazed at how easy it was to compile a fairly extensive list of trophy hunters from the web. *What an arrogant bunch of rich, braggart, attention craving bastards,* he mused. *Makes this so easy for me!*

He opened Facebook and began to research each name. After only a few minutes, he came across one, which made him sit up straight in his chair. Robert Able. It was a perfect way to start. Able wasn't shy about bragging about his kills online, posting pictures of him standing on or beside the dead animal. What stood out most for him was Able lived in Coe Hill, a small community only 30 miles outside of Lansdowne, about a 45-minute drive away.

Able's most recent post, from the day before, showed a picture of him kneeling beside a beautiful dead zebra in South Africa. The man wore a big smile on his face, with the animal's head resting on his knee. Underneath, he tagged his friends when he wrote how it was a difficult hunt and would tell them all about it when he arrived home on Friday.

Trent stared at the man's smile as anger raged up his spine. One line in particular made him seethe: *I can hardly wait till my little daughter's older so I can teach her how to shoot and she'll be able to share this joy with me.*

He slammed his laptop shut and shook for a moment, "Goddamn murderer. Friday's only a couple of days away and, boy, do I have plans for you when you get back. Hopefully your daughter will learn a lesson too when you're laying dead on the ground. Too bad I won't be able to have my picture taken resting your dead head on my knee."

Trent was aware what he was going to do, now that he was again back in society, was considered murder. As a sniper in the army, it was called *justified kills*. It was cold blooded murder and Trent knew it. As much as he hated it, he continued as ordered, doing so without feeling. To Trent, what he was about to do was more a justified kill than any he had done in the past, and he was excited by the prospect.

When he reached Silver Taps, he grabbed a seat at the bar like he always did and seconds later, Larry, the owner and bartender, was there to serve him.

"Hey, Trent," Larry said as he tossed a beer mat down in front of him, "How's the restaurant business been this week?" Larry always liked to compare notes.

"Not bad. A couple of busy days. Business has tapered off a little. How about you?"

"Down a bit, but you know, it's summer and people are away."

Trent made a mental note of it. He would be travelling on a Friday of a summer's weekend, one which was supposed to be beautiful. The drive to Coe Hill might take him longer.

"Yeah, I guess that's it. So, do you have anything new and interesting on tap?"

"Two this week, but one's a lager. I know that won't interest you. There's a new brewery out of Orlando which specializes in British style ales. I happen to have their British bitter on tap right now. Keg was just tapped a couple of hours ago, so it's nice and fresh."

"British ales from Florida?"

"Yeah. Seems New York and Orlando are the two American cities visited most by Brits and I guess this company wanted to take advantage of that."

"Great. I'll have a pint."

While he waited, a woman entered the bar and took a seat two over from him. She placed her purse on the empty seat between them and gave him a little smile. Her attention then turned to the displays behind the bar. When Larry returned with Trent's beer, she ordered a glass of pinot. Trent smiled at her answer when Larry asked if she would like a six or nine ounce pour. "Nine, of course. I'm looking for more than just a tease." Larry chuckled as he turned to get her wine.

Trent picked up his glass and took a moment to breathe in the ale's aroma. Satisfied, he took a sip and savoured it for a moment before swallowing. He smiled and placed the glass back on the beer mat.

"Most men, I've noticed, don't take such care with their beer. They dump down their glass in five or six swallows," the woman observed. "You taste yours like it's a fine wine."

Trent was surprised. Nobody ever mentioned it to him before.

He turned to answer and for the first time was able to take in more than a fleeting glance of her. She was in her early to mid thirties. Her deep brown, bordering on black hair, with purple and red streaks running through it, nicely framed her captivating face.

She wasn't thin, nor would he consider her overweight. He liked her full-figured curves and soft feminine features. Her skirt was hiked up a little by the chair, revealing a tattoo of an old-fashioned clock surrounded by roses, with an hourglass within them on her left thigh.

Trent smiled. "I love craft beer. Tasting an ale is as much the same experience as tasting a wine. A properly made beer has layers of flavour in it. Some people say they don't like beer. It's like saying you don't like wine. What particular style of wine don't you like? Well, beer's the same way. What don't you like? Lagers, pilsners, blonde ales, stouts, cask ales, IPAs, saisons, sours ... I could go on."

He stopped himself. "Oh, I'm sorry. Here I am on a rant and I haven't even introduced myself. I'm Trent. Trent Corbett and you are?"

"Maya Livingstone."

"So, what do you do, Maya Livingston?"

"That's stone. Livingstone. Don't worry. Many people make the same mistake. I'm in inventory control, 'just-in-time delivery'. You know. That kind of crap. Our company moved here from Hartford a few weeks ago, so I'm the new gal in town. How about yourself?"

"Me? I run Corbett's, a few blocks from here."

"Are you the manager?"

"No. The owner."

She bounced a finger off her forehead, "Of course. Sorry, I'm usually a little brighter than this. Trent Corbett, of Corbett's ... Restaurant, Diner, Eatery. What exactly is it?"

Trent chuckled, "None of the above. I didn't want to call it a diner as it has that 'greasy spoon' connotation to it. Café' sounds too much like a coffee shop. Restaurant was too plain. I couldn't decide what to call it, so I went with Corbett's and let everyone else figure out what it is. When I'm talking about it, I do call it a restaurant. Have you been yet?"

"No. I'm a vegetarian. I find most places don't have much for us non-meat eaters to choose from unless it's strictly advertised as vegetarian or a vegan place. No offence to your establishment, of course."

"Of course. No offence taken. I've tried to offer a better variety of vegetarian selections before, but we had to throw out too much. To me, it seems the type of person who goes to my place is someone looking for comfort food, which usually involves meat or cheese. Still, I should have one or two."

Larry came by, slid a napkin in front of Maya, and set her wine on it. He took a moment to interrupt to ask if she needed a menu, which she did, so he reached under the bar and pulled one out for her.

Maya took a moment and ran her eyes over the two-page menu. She looked over to Trent, "Do you eat here or do you just drop in for a beer or two after work?"

"I'm a weekly regular, not a barfly. It's a nice break coming here for supper after work on a Wednesday night. I have the menu pretty much memorized. Tonight, I'm going with their schnitzel. It's really delicious."

When he saw her screw up her face, he realized what he said, "Oh, damn it, sorry! That was stupid. And you just finished telling me you're a vegetarian. Where's my brain?"

Larry came over and gave her a couple of recommendations from which she chose the vegan bangers with garlic mashed potatoes. With a smile, Larry turned to Trent, "And for the barbarian?"

"A person has to watch what you say around this guy. He's got damned good ears. I'm sure he's able to eavesdrop on conversations from the other end of the room,"

"You weren't exactly whispering, you know."

Trent turned to Maya before he gave Larry an answer. "Before I order, do you have a problem with people eating meat in front of you?"

Maya shook her head no. She appreciated his gesture.

"Glad to hear it. Schnitzel for me Larry and hold the wisecracks."

Larry nodded and left, which gave Trent the chance to turn his attention back to Maya, "So how long have you been a vegetarian?"

"About twelve years. How about you? Ever thought about becoming one?"

"The idea is definitely a noble one and I do have a bit of admiration for vegetarians and vegans and the fact they practice what they preach, but for me, no. I can't see myself ever going that way."

"Why?"

"Why? Hmm. Good question ...

"First off, I love the taste of poultry, beef, pork, or fish. There are so many excellent ways to prepare them. Man needs protein and meat is the protein I crave. I don't go for any of the exotic stuff, though, like ostrich, alligator or any of the game meats. If an animal has to die to sustain me, let it be from a short list of creatures and let the others live free."

Maya thought it over for a moment. "It's a reasonable answer. Not one I could live by, or support. So, what's your view on hunting?"

My God, she's killing me, he thought before answering, "Many people need to hunt for food. Certainly, the aboriginal people. It's part of their culture, which we've never had a right to interfere in. You need to also think about the northern communities closer to the arctic, where vegetables are scarce. It's always been their only source of sustenance."

"Alright. I'll agree with what you said about the First Nations people."

"I also believe in most states and Canada, hunting does help to keep the population down so none of them starve. I'm on the fence about it, though. The more I think about it, the more I lean towards being against hunting period. Now, hunting for the thrill of the kill, don't even get me going on that. Those rich bastards who fly over to Africa to kill a lion, giraffe, elephant or any of those other beautiful animals to get their jollies ... well, if there's a hell, let them all end up there."

"You know, I think this is the first time I've sat down with a guy who eats meat, who I've wanted to get to know better," Maya said, looking directly into his green hued, hazel eyes. She moved the bag, which was on the chair between them, and slid over.

They talked through supper and enjoyed a few more drinks. He found Maya extremely easy to talk with. She was funny, interesting and as they got to know each other better, she became a little flirty.

After they paid for their respective meals, they stood up to leave. It was then that Trent noticed she was as tall as he was. It was unusual for him, as any woman he'd been out with in the past was usually a half foot shorter, not that being shorter than he was what he was looking for in a woman. It was the way it seemed to have always worked out. Of course, he hadn't been out with her ... yet.

He glanced downward. Her skirt was a couple of inches above her knee and hid much of her tattoo. "I noticed your ink when you were sitting."

"You mean this?" She lifted her skirt to reveal most of it.

"Why the clock?"

"The antique clock shows the time I was born. The hourglass is a reminder how time's always moving. Have to live life. The roses, well, I love roses." She let her skirt drop.

"I like it. Like the thought."

"Thanks."

Usually Trent finished his Wednesday with two beers and supper, all of which took an hour. In the couple of quick hours he spent eating and talking with Maya, he consumed five. Spread out over that amount of time, it had little effect on him when he stood to leave. He and Maya paid their tabs at the same time and headed outside together.

As they made their way through the door, Trent spotted a taxi a block away. "Do you need a cab?"

"Yes. Not knowing my way around and starving after work, I grabbed one at the office and asked him to take me to a good spot. Sure glad he brought me here." She stepped closer to Trent, put her hands on his shoulders and her lips against his. Even though he wasn't expecting it, he most certainly enjoyed it.

When they were done, she stepped back and raised her arm to hail the cab. Then she turned back to Trent. "Is your phone handy?"

He nodded and reached into his pocket.

"If you give it to me, I'll punch in my number."

He was happy to comply.

The taxi pulled up. He opened the back door to let her in. She stepped forward to get in and, with the door between them, leaned forward, kissing him one more time, then climbed in. Before closing the door, she looked up at him. "Better not forget to call."

Then she closed the door, and the cab pulled away from the curb. Trent's eyes never left it until it had travelled a few blocks before disappearing around a corner.

Chapter 3

For the first time in his life, Trent was excited by the expectation of killing another human being. It was amazingly easy to find Robert Able's address online. He found the 3D Google maps satellite view to be a useful tool in searching for a place ahead of time where he might possibly be able to set up and be out of sight as he waited. A spot which provided a clear line of fire to his target.

As he drove along the highway, his cruise control set to five miles an hour over the speed limit, instead of thinking about the task ahead, he thought about Maya. Trent definitely wanted to see her again. He found her an amazing person, yet was unsure if starting up with her would be a hindrance or bonus for him. After all, he would have to keep his newfound purpose in life hidden from her.

Perhaps it was only a onetime encounter. No, not with the kiss they shared. There was too much in it and it wasn't from the few drinks they enjoyed together. He now had her number and knew he must call. If she came into his life, it would cause some issues with what he wanted to do, no, needed to do with his life. A relationship would be something he would need to balance if he went forward. He smiled as he decided he would give her a call either that night or the next at the latest.

The past couple of days for Trent were busy ones, and it helped how he already had those days off from the restaurant. His first stop was to a large sporting goods store outside of town, where he would be merely another faceless hunter with money to burn on buying a new toy. While there, he bought range finder binoculars, which would greatly assist him with hitting his target on the first shot. Years of experience taught him how to adjust for any wind or breeze. He also picked up a noise suppressor, which wouldn't silence the shot but muffle the sound considerably and reduce the muzzle flash.

There was an abandoned farm north of the store, which sat on two hundred secluded acres. It was perfect for checking out his newest gadgets, calibrating the scope on his rifle and getting the rust off his skills with an hour's worth of shooting.

He remembered back to the smell of the gunpowder after a shot, the feel of the recoil and the sound of the bullet as it blew a hole through the target and, with a thud, burrowed themselves into the hay bales behind. Where before in sniper training, it was a tedious, necessary practice, now it became an activity which filled him with joy. Trent was quite proud it only took a little over half an hour until he could fire three consecutive rounds which landed within a single half square inch spread in the middle of a target set up two hundred and fifty yards away. He walked away from the farm with a huge grin.

His attention returned to the job at hand when he turned onto the final couple of roads to an abandoned auto repair shop on a rarely used dirt road. The building was halfway up a hill, about a half mile from the Able house. He parked along the side of the building, out of sight of the road. With his gear bag, he climbed a pile of barrels onto the edge of the flat roof. After a quick inspection, he thought the roof looked firm enough, so he crossed over to south side of the building and sat.

With a satellite map of the area in hand, he grabbed his binoculars and checked out the locale. He ended his sweep by zooming in on the Able house. He smiled. It was perfect, as there was a totally unimpeded line of fire to his target's home and driveway.

He took his time to set up. After he confirmed the distance with his new toy, he checked the wind and made the required adjustments. Satisfied, he raised himself up onto his elbows to take another check by sweeping the target area with the rifle's scope. He rose to a sitting position and took a swig of water. Now came the hard part. The wait.

There was only one flight arriving from Johannesburg that day and Trent figured, no hoped, Robert Able felt like heading straight home.

In the past, he could be patient. It came with the territory. As a soldier, he could spend days sitting in the heat, hidden by boulders on the edge of an outcrop of a dusty plant-less hill without bother. Not now. Every heartbeat, as fast as they pounded in his chest, he felt and heard. His body would tense and he would tightly grip his rifle each time a car came down the road towards the house. When he realized it wasn't Able, he would let go of the rifle stock and swear as it passed by.

"I guess you're not in any rush to die, are ya?" he muttered.

The words were barely out of his mouth when he spotted another vehicle driving towards the house, only this time it turned into the drive and parked. He drew his eye away from the scope and checked the trees around him. Then he looked through the scope to the trees in the Able yard. The leaves barely moved. Quickly, he made a final adjustment to his scope to allow for a drop in the wind.

24 GORDON K. JONES

"Come on! Get your ass out of the car. You're home, damn it!"

The trunk of the car popped and a few seconds later, the passenger's rear door opened. Through his scope, Trent took a close look at the man who climbed out. A quick double check with the Facebook picture he brought with him confirmed it was his target, Robert Able.

Trent kept him in his crosshairs as Able rounded the car to the trunk. His back was to Trent as he lifted the lid. For a moment, a wave of indecisiveness came over him. He took his eye off the scope and lifted his head, *Damn, do I shoot him in the back? Something seems wrong about that. Come on, man. You've done this so many times before and without a thought. What in hell's wrong with you? From this distance, front or back, who cares? The giraffe he murdered never saw it coming. Asshole here shouldn't either. Jesus, for all the good in the world, just do it!*

His eye went quickly back to the scope, and the idea of shooting Able in the back was now a moot point. Able pulled his gun bag from the trunk and turned so Trent could see his face clearly. Instinctively, Trent's finger squeezed the trigger. A small burst of flame and a muffled report erupted from the gun's muzzle. An instant later, he saw his bullet violently rip a hole in the gun bag, swinging it backwards and almost out of Able's hand.

Able looked at his bag, then up the hill in Trent's direction. He should have run, ducked or taken cover. Instead, he stood frozen with a puzzled look on his face, contemplating what had just occurred. Trent took the moment to make a quick adjustment and two seconds later, fired again.

This time the bullet found its mark. It struck the right side of Able's chest with a small burst of blood and fabric. The force of the bullet's strike sent Able back against the bumper and the partially closed trunk lid.

"Damn it!" exclaimed Trent, who knew a hit to a man's right side didn't guarantee it was a kill-shot. Once again, he took aim. Able's body was falling forward after bouncing off the trunk, so when Trent fired for the third time, he saw the top of Able's head explode. The body pitched sideways and fell like a jellied heap into a garden decorated with flowers and plastic bunnies.

"A death well-deserved," Trent stated with a quiet satisfaction which filled his soul. He sat up and methodically unscrewed the scope and noise suppressor from his gun, packed his gear, and climbed down to his car. All the way back to the city, he cranked the tunes in his car and happily sang along. He could hardly wait to get home and turn on the news.

Chapter 4

Trent arrived home. He was torn between sitting and watching all the local newscasts or doing something to celebrate. Finally, he decided he was on too much of a high to sit still. Feeling the need to get out and do something, he picked up his phone and gave Maya a call.

Ha. Even though I've been out of circulation for a while, I was still smart enough to get her number before she left, he thought, forgetting it was Maya who offered her number to him.

"Trent Corbett. I saw your name come up on my phone. It's been a few days. I was wondering if you were going to call or if you were using that stupid three-day rule."

It caught him a little off guard. "No, no, I've been quite busy. If I wasn't, I would've called the next day. I was wondering if you felt like going out and getting some supper. There's a vegetarian restaurant which opened recently across town and it's getting good reviews. I was wondering if you would like to try it out?"

As much as Trent would've preferred to enjoy a nice juicy steak to celebrate his day's work, being with

Maya won out. He made sure the cards would be stacked so she would say yes.

"Vegetarian? Will you be okay with it?"

"Sure. I can skip meat. Well ... for a meal or two anyway. I wouldn't want to make a habit out of it like you do."

Maya laughed and said she thought it was a good idea, much to Trent's delight. An hour later, they were sitting across from each other sharing a bottle of Riesling at the new Market Garden Table.

"So. What have you been up to the past couple of days? You had them off, didn't you?" Maya asked as she opened her menu.

He was ready for the question, remembering he told her on the phone he was too busy to call. "I needed to go out of town to visit a few suppliers. When you have your own business, sometimes your days off are not your days off."

If only she knew what I was really up to, what would she think? he thought as he talked. "And you?"

She explained how her days were busy setting up her workspace at the office and coming home too tired to do any unpacking. A soft chuckle escaped her when she heard a stomach rumble. "Is that you?"

Slightly embarrassed, he bowed his head slightly as he nodded.

"You must be hungry. I know I'm starving."

They both became silent as they looked over the menu. Once Maya found something she wanted, she closed hers and looked over to Trent. "See anything you'd like?"

"Hmm. The Mushroom and Ramp Tagliatelle sounds interesting. 'Wild mushrooms and Ramps." He looked up and saw her quizzical look. "Ramps are wild leeks. They taste something like an onion or garlic. I haven't been able to determine which." He looked back down and continued, "in a pesto sauce topped with parmesan. Sounds like something I've never had. I love mushrooms and you can't really go wrong with pasta. Think I'll get that."

Janine, their server, came around and took their order. Maya ordered a non-chicken chicken dish. Trent understood the concept of tofu. He didn't like its texture. Although he hoped she wouldn't offer him a bite of hers, he was looking forward to his dish.

"After you called, I cleaned up and changed out of my grubby work clothes. I was about to turn off the TV and head out when I saw this thing on the news," she said, pausing to sip her wine. "It happened a few hours ago up in Coe Hill."

"Coe Hill? That's the high-priced town a little east of here." It was hard for Trent to not sound excited. He hoped his tone came out as curious.

"They said there was a professional hit done on some businessman there."

"What? What do you mean?" This time, there was no restraint. No acting in his reply. He was truly shocked at how the news media misinterpreted his shooting.

"They said some big wig business guy was shot and killed in his driveway as he was returning home from a trip. Apparently, the dead man had some suspected connections with organized crime."

Trent was stunned. *Organized crime! Give me a fucking break. It was supposed to be clear to everyone he was killed because of his hunting trip and not a mob hit. Next time, I'll need to make it clear why they died.*

He hoped he held his expression in check. "Wow! Wonder what he did to get himself knocked off?"

"They said he was getting home after a hunting trip in South Africa when he was shot." She paused, her face turning serious, "He killed a beautiful zebra on his trip. He even bragged and posted pictures. Bastard! I don't feel one bit sorry for him."

"That's a little harsh!" Trent said, feeling he needed to play devil's advocate at the moment.

PREDATORS AND PREY 29

"Maybe so, but it's the truth. It was on the TV. They showed the Facebook post of him with the zebra. If there's a hell, I hope he's there right now. Damn, murdering son of a bitch."

As much as he would have loved to blurt out he was the one responsible and why, Trent kept it suppressed. "You know Maya. I agree with you. Like I said the other night. I don't believe in killing an animal for the sake of killing. Personally, I'm with you on this. I think the world's a much better place without him."

Maya reached across the table, took his hands, and looked into his eyes. "For a meat eater, you're one hell of a decent guy."

Trent found his pasta underwhelming and made a mental note of how to modify it. If successful, he could add it as a vegetarian dish for his place. As they left the restaurant, she took hold of his hand.

Once they were outside, Maya explained she would invite him over except for the mess of boxes, scattered furniture and unhung pictures propped against the walls around her new place. When Trent offered for her to come over to his place to share a bottle of wine, he was slightly surprised and happy when she agreed.

They hailed a cab and the moment they were inside the side door of his raised bungalow, she took hold of him, hungrily pressing her lips to his. It was a long while since Trent had been with a woman and with Maya's passion and eagerness, thought it might be the same for her.

Then a thought, a reminder, flashed into his head. His rifle! The one he used that morning was leaning up against the side of his sofa with the extra clips and a box of bullets still sitting on the coffee table. She couldn't see it. She couldn't know he owned it.

Maya stopped for a moment and took a small step back. Her hands still rested on his shoulders. Trent noticed a couple of buttons on her top, had somehow become undone, revealing more than a modest amount of her cleavage.

She took a breath and when she spoke, it came out soft and slightly panting, "You told me you have wine, but I have a question. Do we want some before or after?"

"How about in between?"

She grinned and placed her left hand against the side of his face as she kissed him. When she was done, she grabbed his hand with her free one. "I love the way you think. Lead the way."

Trent was glad he was holding her right hand. This way, he would be between her and the living room entrance on their way to the bedroom. Still, there was a chance she would see them. In the kitchen, before they passed the living room, he stopped, turned her towards him, and kissed her passionately. She responded in kind and he was able, with their lips locked together, to back her down the hall to the bedroom.

Quickly, he worked out a game plan. When they were done, he would suggest they have their wine in bed. After she agreed, she would maybe, maybe not, head for the bathroom, which was between the bedroom and living room. When he went for the wine, he would grab the rifle, stow it behind the couch, and quietly throw the rest of the stuff into the end table drawer. That way, if she wanted to have the wine in the living room, the gun wouldn't be an issue.

The plan worked to perfection, except he had to wait until after their second time to execute it. Maya was fun, playful, daring, and enjoyed stretching boundaries with him. She was all he wanted of a woman in bed and hoped she felt the same about him. She wasn't leaving which was a good sign.

He wore a contented smile as he carried in the bottle and two glasses. It had been an exciting day for him and an equally exciting night. Sitting beside her with the sheet only covering their waists, he was fully content. Exhaustion began to sweep over Trent's body as he sipped on his wine.

PREDATORS AND PREY   31

His eyes were about to close for the night when he heard Maya ask, "Falling asleep?"

"No," he lied, doing his best to fight the wave of tired which abruptly fell over him. "Why?"

"I was thinking about that shooting."

Trent's eyes popped open. Any other subject and he would have made his plunge into the wonderful state of slumber. The shooting, though. His shooting, he was ready to hear about. He rolled onto his side to face her. "What about it?"

"I've always found murders fascinating. It's almost like I study them. When I read, it's almost never fiction, but true crime and always murder. It's far more fascinating than anything which could be made up."

"Interesting."

"The more I think about that shooting today, I don't think it was mob related."

"Really? Why?"

"Because organized crime does it hush hush unless they want to make a statement. Then it's done close-up. More of an execution. This guy was shot at long range by somebody who knew he was returning from a hunting trip. Did you hear about the animal rights group, the one which attacked a hunter a week or so ago?"

"Uh-huh."

"Maybe, just maybe, it gave some animal rights guy the idea to kill instead."

"Or animal rights girl."

"Glad to see you're all about equal rights," she grinned. "Anyway, whoever did this, it sure wasn't a mob job."

He was so tired, he became worried he might say something to make her suspicious of him, no matter how irrational it sounded. "You could be right. Interesting idea, but you know, I really need to get some sleep."

His eyes closed involuntarily, and he felt her kiss his cheek. He could smell the aroma of her hair when she placed her head on his shoulder. A smile came across his face as sleep took over. If Maya had those thoughts, others might too. He hoped they did. In the future, he would need to ensure the point would be made shockingly clear.

Chapter 5

Despite being almost twenty feet up in a tree, Trent felt steady and secure perched on a thick branch, with his back leaning against its trunk. In his recon of the area, he found it was the only accessible place for him to have a decent sightline to his target. It was three weeks since his first shooting and in about fifteen minutes, he planned to have his second successfully completed.

As he waited, he reached into his pocket and pulled out a folded sheet of paper. On it was a picture from a Facebook post, showing his target holding a long-barrelled rifle and laying against a dead lion, the man's latest kill from a few months before. Scrolling down, he saw there were many more from other previous hunts. Trent discovered how to use his cheap photo program to paste a cartoon talk bubble rising from the animal. In this one, the lion was saying, "I pulled the trigger on you while you ate, the same as you did to me! Now, we're both dead!" On the bottom of the page was printed, The Predators Predator. Trent smiled as he looked at it, then folded it along its original crease and slid it back into his shirt pocket.

Trent had decided there was no need to strike when these murderers returned home from a hunt. He could do it anywhere, as long as it was with the highest probability of not being caught. If he could shoot the big game hunter while they were doing the same activity the animal was doing when they were murdered, their death would resonate with the press and public so much more. After all, publicity was what he wanted. He wanted people to cheer every hunter's death.

During his research, he read the lion this bastard assassinated was shot while standing over an animal it had killed and was feasting on. This son-of-a-bitch was going to die while he ate his own lunch.

The week after his first kill, he changed his days off to help Maya unpack and put her new place in order. He was surprised and happy at how fast they became close. It felt natural and right. The following week, his days off were spent scouting Elm Grove, a small town two hours north of the Lansdowne and north of his first kill. It was where he found this hunter and his next target. The man was a member of a local group of trophy hunters, all within driving distance of Lansdowne, which gave Trent a long list to choose from.

During his scouting, Trent found a tree at the edge of a wooded area, set back behind some bushes, at the western edge of a park in the middle of Elm Grove's business area. There were a couple of trails, one about fifty feet from his tree, which cut through the woods. From what he saw, people tended to stay in the open area during their lunch hours and not wander through the trees.

Finally, the moment Trent had been waiting for arrived. In the days when he was scouting the town, he watched W. Charles Howell, CEO and founder of the Charles Howell State Bank, leave the bank at the same time every day. He would cross the street to the park on the other side where he ate his lunch on a bench under the shade of a

PREDATORS AND PREY

large oak tree. The tree he chose to take his shot from was at the opposite end of the open space of the park.

"Right on time," Trent whispered when he saw Howell leave the bank. With a book tucked under the same arm which held his brown bag lunch and the other shielding his eyes from the sun's glare, he crossed the road, walked across the park and settled himself onto the same bench where he ate lunch every day.

Trent was about to move his rifle into position when he heard the sound of somebody below talking. He froze and listened. Carefully and slowly, he looked down. Below him was a man and a woman, both in their late thirties, hidden from the rest of the park. Soon, they became quiet and embraced in a heavy, passionate moment.

"*Oh, for Christ's sake. What? You couldn't have found another place for your damned rendezvous?*" he thought. There was nothing he could do but stay quiet and impatiently wait.

"I have an idea," he heard the woman say in a gasping voice. "My mother's away."

"Oh, yeah?"

"For two weeks. We can use her place. Nobody will suspect."

"I like it. If my wife calls, I'll tell her I was down in the vault with no reception."

"Okay. Give me a five minute head start and I'll meet you there." She began to walk away into the woods, then stopped and looked back. "The side door will be unlocked. My old bedroom is the second one down the hall." Then she skipped off like a schoolgirl into the woods.

Oh shit! Five minutes? I might not have five minutes. Hormones, though, took over, and the man waited for only a minute before he left. Trent turned his attention back to his target.

Howell was finishing up. He folded his plastic sandwich bags, put them into the brown paper bag, which he also neatly folded and slid into the pocket of his suit jacket. Trent checked to the left and right of him and couldn't see any innocent people who might take the bullet should he miss. He turned his ball cap backwards on his head. It was time to get to work.

Up went the rifle. A slight breeze came along and rustled the leaves. Trent's fingers adjusted the scope one last time to compensate. He wanted a perfect first shot, not like the last time when he was forced to take hurried second and third shots. One bullet. One victim. Just as he did in his past life.

Howell was in the crosshairs. After taking a single deep breath, Trent let it out slowly. He focused on his heartbeat. Between beats, he pulled the trigger.

His timing could not have been more perfect. It wasn't planned, however, that the muffled crack of the rifle was drowned out by the town hall bell, chiming on the half hour. Blood erupted from the left side of Howell's chest. His body snapped back like he was kicked by a horse and when it came to rest was slumped against the back of the bench with his chin to his chest. From where he sat looking through the scope, Trent thought Howell looked like a man who suffered through a tough morning and fell asleep on a beautiful day ... unless a person noticed his bloodied shirt.

Quickly, Trent slid his rifle into its bag, zipped it closed, and clambered down to the ground like a young boy. He recovered the bullet casing, pinned his printed page to the tree and, as casually as possible, walked off in the same direction the cheater took. When he reached his car, he popped the trunk, tossed in his bag and slammed it shut.

He was about to round the car when he heard a man's voice behind him, "Your timing is impeccable."

"What do you mean?" Trent asked with his back still to the man. He turned, horrified to find himself talking with a cop! *Shit! Keep calm. Keep calm*, he thought as he faced the officer.

PREDATORS AND PREY

"Your meter was expired. I was just finishing up writing a ticket on this one and in another ten seconds would've started on yours."

Trent forced a smile. "Looks like I got back just in time then."

"For some reason, this is usually a good street for me. People parking here love to try to time it perfectly. You know, not give the town one more dime than they need to."

"I put in all the change I had. Must be my lucky day. Maybe I should go out and buy myself a lottery ticket," Trent replied. His smile became easier to wear as he realized he stood blocking the officer's view of his rear license plate.

The officer chuckled and walked past Trent's car without a look at the front plate. Trent climbed into the car, buckled up and waited until the officer passed the lights at the "T" intersection. Thankfully, the meters for the cars ahead of him were paid up, so there was no need for the cop to stop and ticket. Trent pulled out and, not wanting to take a chance on passing the cop, turned left at the lights and did his best not to speed off.

"Damn it, Trent. You've still got a lot to learn about this shit." he grumbled and slammed his fist against the steering wheel. "That's if I'm not finished already."

As he drove, he ran and reran the conversation with the officer over and over again in his mind. He looked at all the different scenarios he could come up with and how he might deal with each. It made the two-hour trip home, a long and torturous one.

◆ ◆ ◆

Trent sat upright in his chair, watching the news about his shooting. As the newscaster spoke, the image behind changed from a scene of yellow police barrier tape around the edge of a park to a sketch of a man's face. *"This is the police artist's rendering of a man who the authorities are calling a 'person of interest'". The man was seen placing a suspicious looking bag into the trunk of his car around the time of Charles Howell's murder. The suspect was not apprehended because, at the time he was spotted, the homicide had not yet been discovered."*

On his way back to the car, Trent had turned his ball cap around so it rested properly on his head. While he was talking to the cop, it seemed the shadow from the brim hid a fair amount of his facial features. To Trent's relief, the image was exceptionally generic and could be of almost any white male. He let out a sigh as he began to relax a little.

The newscaster continued, *"Elm Grove's police chief, Avery Johnson, a twelve-year veteran of the town's forty-five hundred resident six man police force, had spoken to this man while on patrol and suspects the man was from out of town. Once again, the crime hadn't been reported at the time Chief Johnson spoke to the suspect."*

Trent leaned closer to the TV to concentrate better when the newscast switched to an interview with the cop he had spoken with, *"This town is small and I've been on the force for a long time so I pretty much know the faces of everyone who lives here. I've never seen this man before. Also, from evidence found around the scene of the murder, we are of the opinion this murder was planned."*

The reporter looked shocked and pulled the microphone back, *"Planned? Charles Howell was a well-loved and upstanding citizen of Elm Grove. He donated vast amounts of money and his own time to community organizations. He sponsored teams in every one of town's children's sports leagues. He also funded the creation and upgrade of many of the town parks. Why would you suggest his was not a random act?"*

"The shot which killed him was done at a long range. It was obviously a shot that only could be successfully made by a professional."

Trent laughed, "Long range? Professional? Hell, it was a little over a hundred and fifty yards. That's nothing!"

Next came the piece of news Trent was waiting for, *"We believe he was killed either by a deranged crazed animal activist or at perhaps hired by a group of animal radicals."*

"How did you arrive at that conclusion?" the reporter asked.

"We found what might be described as a 'calling card' from the murderer. It was pinned to what we believe was the same tree the killer took his shot from. A poster with a picture of Mr. Howell with an animal he killed while on an African safari. I'm sorry. I can't comment any further."

The newscaster finished the story with a vague description of Trent's car, a silver four door Chevrolet, license unknown, which could be any one of millions on the road. Trent slumped back in his chair and let go a sigh of relief. His surprise meeting with Chief Johnson didn't seem to yield any bad consequences for him. He was lucky, and he knew it. W. Charles Howell may not have dodged a bullet that afternoon, but Trent had.

"Shit. I never thought there would be such a steep learning curve to this business. I gotta be a lot more careful when I hide the car," he mumbled as he switched off the TV.

It was almost time to head out over to Maya's for pizza. He liked how they were at a stage in their relationship where they could easily order in. Not only was it cheaper, neither needed to dress up before heading out to eat. They could relax. There were no decisions after a date about whose place they would end up at for the night. Tonight, obviously, he would be sharing Maya's bed. They also could talk freer and Trent had a good idea what the main subject of conversation would be that night. He looked forward to her thoughts on his noon hour kill.

GORDON K. JONES

♦ ♦ ♦

Avery Johnson walked over to Julie Burke's desk and placed the plastic evidence bag with the pin and paper which Trent purposely left behind in front of her. On a small-town police force, every member performed multiple duties. The same went for Julie, a woman with her light brown hair cut professionally short so she could keep it tucked under her cap, with bangs long enough to let down at night. She barely met the minimum height requirement for the force. She started her mornings on patrol, which were usually quiet, then the rest of her day handling whatever came along.

"You looked great on the TV today, AJ," she complimented. She picked up the bag and examined the contents. "Glad I was back here to see it."

"I hated every minute of it."

"How many chances do we get in this place to be on TV? You were relaxed and professional. I was proud of you."

"Thanks. I appreciate it," AJ answered, wanting to change the subject. "Could you send this to up to State Forensics for a full work over? Couldn't find any prints on it myself, but then I really didn't expect to. Hopefully, they can pick up DNA or something which can help."

For a moment, he froze. He snapped his fingers, "Hey Julie! Wasn't there a long range killing over in Coe Hill that happened only a few weeks ago? It was being investigated as a mob hit."

"Hold on," Julie said, holding up her hand to stop him from heading over to his desk. AJ was a great cop and although he knew his way around a computer, she found him agonizingly slow using one. It drove Julie around the bend having to wait when he insisted on looking information she could find in seconds. "I know the case you mean. Let me have a look."

It only took only a few taps on her keyboard to find what she was looking for. She gave it a quick read, then spun the monitor around so AJ could see it. "Here it is. Somehow, I don't think it's a coincidence."

AJ gave the screen a quick read, "No. Definitely isn't. Think I'll give them a call in Coe Hill and see what they have. In the meantime, could you do a search of our jurisdiction to see if we have any other African hunters we might need to warn? Oh, and when we get the slug back from autopsy, let's send it up to State. I'll get Coe Hill to send up theirs too. Wouldn't be surprised if there was a match."

"What are you thinking?"

"That it's quite possible we may have a serial killer on our hands!"

Chapter 6

Trent's next two kills went off without a hitch. The first he did in Beaconsfield, two weeks after his Elm Grove shooting. There, with a single pull of his trigger, he took out a hunter with a penchant for killing rhinos.

Two weeks later, he put a couple of bullets into a hunter in Brookfield, the same number the hunter needed to kill a giraffe. He hadn't planned on using two shots, though. Trent's first shot was supposed to be the kill shot. Instead, the bullet struck the hunter in his hip, dropping him to the ground. His past experience kicked in. He took a moment, adjusted his aim and as the man rolled over, squeezed the trigger one more time. He broke out in a grin when he saw his shot strike the side of the man's forehead, its force slamming the back of his head against the hard ground. His target's legs were twitching. Trent prayed the hunter suffered and was paralyzed with the same fear the giraffe would have felt for those last few seconds before a second bullet took their lives.

"Giraffes are so beautiful," he muttered under his breath when he was done. "How in hell could a person ever kill one?"

PREDATORS AND PREY

Trent felt quite comfortable with the rhythm he was in. Three kills over five weeks. A kill every other week. He was surprised by the pleasure which filled him with each kill. Never would he have thought how justifiable homicide could feel so good!

When Trent first took on this endeavour, he figured he might only find one worthy hunter in his drivable area and would need to find a way to travel incognito to get others. Lucky for him, he found a group of ten hunters in the surrounding area who called themselves the Tyndall County 10. After three of its members met the same fate as their prey, two of them having been left with the Predators Predator calling card, the remaining members of the group fully privatized their individual and group Instagram and Facebook accounts. They also removed themselves from Twitter. It didn't matter. Trent already had harvested all the information he needed for the giraffe killer and a few more. He would worry about the others later.

The coming weekend was his turn for a Saturday and Sunday off from the restaurant. He felt fortunate he could trust his manager, Sandra, with the brunch service so he could enjoy a normal weekend once a month. With his evening and weekend hours, plus Maya's regular weekday schedule, they hadn't enjoyed a full day together. Only nights.

Maya suggested a relaxing overnight stay at a Scandinavian spa resort would be a perfect way to spend their first full weekend together. Trent, of course, happily agreed and told Sandra he'd be taking the Friday off, too. He needed a relaxing break away from the diner and his extra-curricular activities. There could be no better way than spending Friday night to Monday morning together with Maya.

GORDON K. JONES

♦ ♦ ♦

The doorbell rang which sent the family cat scrambling for safety. As it slid around a corner, it almost took the feet out from under Lyn Mathews, who was on her way to answer the door. Quietly she cursed. After regaining her composure, she looked through the peephole before opening the door. "Ed. Please come on in. The rest are already here. They're in the study."

Ed Simpson stepped in and thanked her. As he had visited Walter Mathews dozens of times before, he knew those few words would be all the conversation he would have with Lyn. As usual, she left him at the entrance and walked off in the direction of the living room. He didn't mind as he knew the way to the study.

When the group first began to meet at their place regularly, Walter asked Lyn to drop into the study on occasion to see if anybody wanted something to eat or drink. He was surprised to have been met with a terse "No. I'm your wife, not your maid. You have money. Hire a bartender for the night if you're all too damned lazy to get up and get your own!"

And that was that.

Ed slid the study door part way into the wall, stepped inside, and slid it closed again. Three of the group, one man and two women, were seated comfortably in leather chairs, quietly talking among themselves while Walter and Spencer Maling stood at Walter's solid mahogany bar topping up their drinks.

"You know, I never thought our little group would ever have to hold an emergency meeting," Ed announced with a smile.

"Four of us are dead! All murdered. Christ, we've been to two funerals in the past three weeks and all you can do is be an asshole," Samantha Edgars said with venom as she glared at him.

"Sorry. Bad joke. My apologies," replied Ed with an open gesture of his hands before proceeding to the bar for a brandy. He took the bottle from Walter and almost filled his glass to the top, and downed about a quarter of it in one gulp. "You see, I figure I'm next on his list and excuse my language ladies, but I'm a really fucking unnerved about it."

"Why do you think it'll be you?" asked Walter. He was a little disgusted Ed would drink his expensive brandy like a beer, however, he kept quiet about it due to what he and others in the room were going through.

"Well, before I closed all my social media accounts, I posted about my trip to South Africa next month for an elephant hunt, the last I need to complete my 'Big Five'. Now I believe the bag of shit out there will put a bullet in me or my family before I get the chance to go."

Ed drained another quarter of his glass.

"One good thing is this maniac hasn't gone after any of our families ... well, at least not yet." chimed in Rebecca Farnsworth. She was seated in her chair in a form fitting dress with her legs crossed. One look at her would give the impression she was part of champagne society instead of a woman whose greatest joy was traipsing through the wilds of Africa with a rifle slung over her shoulder, hunting big game.

"Yes, thank God for that," Samantha replied. "What about those notes this killer's leaving behind?"

There was some grumbling around the room as Samantha reached into her purse and pulled out a page from a newspaper. "I know it sells papers and brings in viewers reading the notes this bastard's leaving behind, but doesn't the press realize they're romanticising him?

"Did you see today's paper? People are starting to sell t-shirts with animal prints on them with some of his sayings, and those animal rights assholes are buying and wearing them. Listen to this!" Samantha put on her glasses and read, "There are five versions of the best-selling t-shirt on the market, so people can purchase the one with their favourite Big 5 animal imprinted on it. The Big 5 African safari animals are the lion, elephant, leopard, cape buffalo, and rhinoceros. Printed below the animal is: 'Revenge for the Prey!'" She looked up, "I saw a couple of girls today walking down the streets wearing them."

Rebecca cut in, "The press picked up on the nickname he puts on his calling cards. Now everybody refers to him as *'The Predator's Predator'*. What kind of bullshit is this? It's making him out to be a hero."

"Walt. Have you spoken to the police?"

"Oh yes. I was speaking with Connie Stapleton, the police chief here in Springhurst. She said the FBI has been called in but won't talk to any of us unless they initiate it. She told me all they know so far is the gun used in all the murders is a .300 rem mag, which is owned by every Tom, Dick and Harry out there and how they think the killer is from around here. Because of this last tidbit, she suggested we all hire bodyguards till he's caught, as they don't have the manpower to watch us and our homes twenty-four-seven."

"Bodyguards!" Ed retorted. "For Christ's sake. Every murder was done at long range. A bodyguard won't hear the gun going off until we're already dead on the ground."

"I know. I asked if they could put up more of a police presence in our neighbourhoods. She said they don't have the resources but would do their best to do drive-byes for Ed, Rebecca and my place whenever they could. It's the best I could do. The rest of you should talk to your own police chiefs. Hell. You'll likely will be told the same thing. Oh and forget the state troopers. I asked and was told to speak to our own local police."

"So. Where does that leave us?"

"Sorry to say. Looking after ourselves."

PREDATORS AND PREY

♦ ♦ ♦

Even though the Predator's Predator case was passed off to the FBI, Avery Johnson still followed it quite closely. On one of his office walls was a permanent map of his force's jurisdiction. Alongside it, he taped up another, larger map of the state, with red pins placed at the point of all four murders.

Many mornings, after he finished reviewing the night reports, he would make himself a fresh coffee, lean back in his chair facing the map and stare at the pins. The one sticking in Elm Grove bothered him the most.

"Morning, AJ," called out Ben Chambers as he walked through the open office door. Dressed in his uniform, he was a tall, lanky, blonde haired member of the Elm Grove police force. "Haven't you memorized that map yet?"

AJ took a sip of his coffee, shook his head and made a face. "Yuck. It's lukewarm. I hate lukewarm coffee. He set his mug on his desk, then looked at Ben. "I figure if I stare at it long enough, it might tell me where the next strike will take place."

"It seems to me you've been beating yourself up about Howell's murder. You have to stop it for two reasons. One, when you spoke to the suspect, nobody even knew a murder was committed and two, he might not be the guy."

"He was the only stranger I saw in town that day."

"And you likely missed a few dozen more. It's the fact you spoke to this guy which makes made him stand out in your mind."

"Ross Barker and his wife, Irene, were in to see me yesterday."

"Isn't one of them part of the *Ten*?"

"Ross is. They came to see what protection we could offer them. Told me it's what the rest were doing. He didn't need to say it, but they're all worried. I guess every one of them feels they may be next."

"Yeah. Any one of them could be too. I damn well wouldn't want to be in their shoes. That's for sure."

"I promised we would do our best to swing down their streets as much as possible, but as we have a large town and small police force, I couldn't say how often." AJ took a sip of his now lukewarm coffee. He screwed up his face and set down the cup. "There was nothing much else I could tell them. I know you're right. I'm not responsible for letting that guy drive off or getting his plate number. I'll be damned, though, if I'm going to let this thing go until the bastards caught, no matter what."

AJ snatched up his cup and walked over to the coffee machine, emptying the remainder of his cup into a large planter as he had done before many times, although it was something he would never do in front of Julie. He knew better. After pouring himself a fresh cup, he strolled back to his chair, fell into it, then returned to staring at the map. He sighed, took a sip, then abruptly sat bolt upright. "Ben. Grab some white pins and go over to the map."

"Why?"

"Just do it. I have a hunch."

Ben did as he was told. Once he was in position, AJ read off a list of the six towns and communities where each of the surviving *Ten* lived. Ben stuck a pin in each. After they were done, Ben walked over beside AJ, who was now standing and together they stared at the map.

"Damn it. There it is," AJ softly said as though he were talking to himself.

"There's what?"

"The next hit. I know who it'll be." AJ approached the map and touched the red pin on Elm Grove. As he spoke, he touched each red pin in the order of their murder. "Every kill had a second purpose. He was working out the kinks for his next one by choosing the next town over. If I'm right and I'm damned sure I am, he'll head to Parkview Gardens next. Samantha Edgars and Spencer Maling live there. I'm not sure if he's ready to kill a woman yet or not. If he is, Ms. Edgars lives on the top floor of a condo. It would be too difficult to plan for this killer right now. He'd go for the easier one.

"I'll bet Spencer Maling is his next target!"

Chapter 7

A concerned looking blonde haired female broadcaster, her bangs almost reaching her eyebrows, sat behind a glass-topped desk intently staring into the camera as she described the live scene unfolding on the screen behind her. When Trent first began his quest, he only wanted to avenge the senseless deaths of African game animals, maybe even strike some fear into others who hunted them. Never did he think his actions would spark any form of activism. It was poetry to him to see how his idea, which originally came from seeing a protest on TV, now was sparking even larger movements.

The current story on TV, which he watched from his old favourite chair while sipping quietly on a beer, made him proud. The image showed a large, angry crowd outside a city hotel. Signs waved. People shouted and chanted. Then, like a tsunami, they surged forward towards the hotel's main entrance.

Trent smiled as the camera zoomed in. He saw many people in the protest were wearing t-shirts with statements of *'Avenge my Death!'*, *'The Predator's Predator Stands Up for ME'!*, *'Hunt the Hunters Down!'* and *'I (heart) the Predators*

Predator!' emblazed over a variety of different African animals. It was all he could do to restrain himself from going online, buying a t-shirt, autographing it and giving it to Maya.

As the broadcaster spoke, viewers could see police moving in, attempting to form a corridor for those attempting to leave the building. *"What originally started as a story about a murder in a small town has been growing into a nation-wide revolution, one which pits African game hunters against animal rights activists and conservationist organizations.*

"Right now, outside of this Indianapolis hotel, which is holding a hunting expo with an area of the show devoted to African game hunting companies, a large group of angry protesters are gathered. What are the estimated five-hundred protesters waiting for? Well, tonight a group of hunting safari companies are holding a special seminar promoting game hunting in Africa. It looks like the protesters are lying in wait for the hunters in attendance to leave.

"Wait a moment. It looks as if the attendees are about to emerge."

The camera zoomed into the hotel's lobby doors in time to show the police standing in front of them, facing the crowd, their batons held menacingly in front of them. When the doors opened, a group of around twenty people came through while the police forced their way forward. Obscenities were shouted. Rocks and bottles flew. The police kept moving forward but were overwhelmed by the numbers against them.

Fearing they might become surrounded if they moved forward any further, the police ordered a retreat, willing to surrender the ten feet they had gained through the crowd. More bottles and rocks flew, many striking the bruised, battered and scared hunters before they could reach the protection of the hotel lobby doors. The police were called in to manage a protest, not to quell what was quickly becoming a riot.

Finally, more police showed up in riot gear and shields. With them leading the way and the original officers protecting the group's rear, they parted the crowd and led the group to a bus before heading back to the hotel for another.

The broadcaster at the scene held a finger to one ear. *"The busses you see lined up here were ordered in by the city to take those trapped inside the hotel to undisclosed locations. From there, the show attendees were told to take taxis home. They've been warned to leave their cars as the police cannot guarantee their safety if they attempt to take their own vehicles home."*

Trent turned off the TV and headed to bed with a smile on his face. It was all coming together for him. The hunting community must be scared out of their wits. He heard during the broadcast how they demanded law enforcement agencies make more resources available to find, arrest and kill if necessary, the person responsible, which of course, would be him.

Animal rights groups cheered the *Predator's Predator* and flooded social media with their supporting comments, all of which he loved. It was really, though, the fulfilment he experienced while planning and executing a kill, knowing he was helping make the world a better place, which filled him with the purest joy.

His executions were so well-researched and planned, he felt he could never get caught. He found it much easier to kill his subjects at home. During a work week, people ran on a schedule. With only a little surveillance, it was easy to pinpoint the time within minutes when they left for work or arrived home. For Trent, it felt quite poetic to kill his target on their own property, in the same manner as the hunter did when he killed the African prey in theirs.

Somehow, in all of this, he also managed to get the girl.

Life was certainly good for Trent Corbett.

Chapter 8

Maya rolled over onto her back where she stayed for a minute or two before turning onto her side so she faced Trent, who was also on his back, far off in a dream world. She tried putting her arm over his rising and falling chest and closing her eyes, but it was no use. Sleep wouldn't come.

Sighing, she carefully removed her hand and raised herself so she could see over him to the clock on Trent's side of the bed. It was the second time in her restless night she needed to do so, and she didn't like it. Although she was getting used to sleeping with him, which they did over the weekend and sometimes once or twice during the week, she always found it easier when they did at her place. As much as she loved sleeping with him, she found it was the little things she had a hard time adjusting to when she slept over at his place.

Simple things, like not being able to be able to easily see the time when she woke up in the middle of the night. Most people, when they did, rolled over and fell right back to sleep. Maya wasn't like that. When she woke during the night, she needed to know whether it was two thirty or three in the morning. There was no explanation why she couldn't get back to sleep unless she could guesstimate how many more hours of sleep she would enjoy.

She saw it was 3:31am. The last time she checked, it was 2:19, meaning she'd been tossing and turning for over an hour. It couldn't be because she didn't have instant access to a clock, as this was only the first time out of the many she stayed over where she suffered a bout of insomnia. Still, Maya vowed they would stop somewhere that day and buy a clock radio for her side of the bed.

Their alarm, Trent's alarm, was set to 8:00 am so they could get an early start on their weekend away together. She fell back onto the pillow where, wide awake, she stared at the shadows on the ceiling.

Frustrated, she got up, grabbed her phone from her nightstand, threw on her tank top, and headed to the kitchen. After grabbing her stainless-steel water bottle from the fridge, she went into the living room and dropped onto the couch. She grabbed the blanket, which laid haphazardly over an armrest, pulled it over her and turned on her phone.

At least she tried to turn it on. Maya quietly cursed when the phone, instead of lighting up and bringing in the outside world to her fingertips, remained dark, its battery dead. She tossed the phone onto the coffee table, making a mental note to plug it in before she went back to bed.

Damn it. I wanted to see the pictures of the spa where we're staying tonight. So now what the hell am I going to do? Just sit here?

She sat back and looked around the room. Trent's laptop sat closed at the end of the coffee table. Although she figured it was password protected, she slid over and flipped the lid open. To her surprise, it came alive. "Wow. No password? That's stupid," she muttered as the last page Trent was looking at came up.

PREDATORS AND PREY 55

In front of her was the spa's homepage for where they were booked. She clicked on the gallery section and scrolled through photos of the pool, massage room, hot tubs, surrounding wilderness and the various rooms. A smile crossed her face as she anticipated their first weekend away. It really hadn't been long since she first met him. So far, however, they hadn't experienced even a tense moment. He was strong, attentive, smart and, as much as he could carry a conversation, he also was a good listener.

"I think I really might have lucked out with you," she said quietly as she went through the pictures. She let go of the mouse to take a drink of water. When she leaned forward, she found the cursor was resting on a folder on the task bar, exposing the *File Explorer* page. A devious thought came to her. *Let's see what he's got in here.*

Many of the folders were obviously for his restaurant. Although she was most interested in finding pictures he kept saved, a folder named *Hunters* struck her curiosity. She clicked on it.

If looking at pictures of the spa soothed and made her drowsy, *Hunters* brought her fully awake. Her eyes widened with every click or scroll. Names, addresses, scanned images of Facebook pages showing hunters with their dead prey and particularly a spreadsheet with a column titled, *"Hunters Deceased"* and another *"Hunters to Die"*. The *"Deceased."* column listed all the recent murders which she had seen on the news.

"My God, Trent," she muttered. She didn't know what to think. What to do. For the moment, even though she felt she should get the hell out of there, all she could do was click and scroll, click and scroll, mesmerized by what she stumbled upon. She clicked onto another folder marked *"Recon"* and found photos of what she could only imagine were ones he took while staking out a target. She shuddered.

Trent rolled over onto his back, pulled the covers up a little more before he reached over and found Maya's side of the bed empty. *Must be in the bathroom*, he thought. When he looked out the doorway, he saw light filtering out into the hallway from the living room instead. He heard sounds coming from there, so guessed she was unable to sleep and was watching TV. He got up, stretched, and headed down the hall.

"Maya?" he called quietly in case she was asleep. There was no answer. When he entered the living room, he was stopped dead in his tracks by what he saw. "Maya, what the-"

On the couch he saw Maya in her panties and tank top, lying with her legs curled against her chest, her forehead covered in sweat. She shivered slightly.

"Are you okay?" he asked as he quickly crossed the room. There was no reply. He pushed aside his laptop and sat on the coffee table. Feeling he should do something, he leaned over to the end table, grabbed a Kleenex from the box, and wiped her brow. "Cold?"

He grabbed the blanket and put it over her. She never looked at him, instead seeming to stare off into the distance. "Do you need to go to the hospital?"

She shook her head, then spent a minute or so quietly staring across the room. Finally, she looked at him. "I'm alright. Sorry. I woke up after a really bad nightmare and came in here. Can't remember what it was about but it's still bothering me."

When he went to sit beside her, she shifted away. She looked at him with what seemed to be a little panic on her face. "I think I'm going to go home and try to get some sleep there."

"Sure. Want me to drive you?"

"No thanks."

A couple of hours later, she called to let Trent know she wasn't feeling well and to cancel their weekend.

Chapter 9

There was no sleeping when she arrived home. Four deaths. Four murders. All by the man she'd been sleeping with a few hours earlier. Luckily, she had heard his feet hit the floor in the quiet house and managed to exit the file, close his laptop and flop onto her side on the couch. The sweat and shivering came naturally from what she understood he was or could be.

She cradled her hot tea in her hands as she sat cross-legged on the couch. For the moment, there was no focus. Her mind was scrambled as it wandered and raced over a variety of topics. She took a sip from her cup, leaned back, and closed her eyes. Figuring she would never be able to sleep, she was surprised when a wave of tiredness washed over her out of nowhere. She uncrossed her legs, set her cup on the coffee table and fell onto her side. Hugging a small pillow, her mind worked to filter out the newspaper images of the murder sites. The photos of those he killed and Trent's 'To Do' list. In a couple of minutes, she fell to the mercy of her dreams, and although most were bad, her real nightmare awaited her when she awoke.

♦ ♦ ♦

When she finally opened her eyes, she reached over to the coffee table and instinctively picked up her phone as she always did. It was still dead. She sighed, lifted herself off the couch, and went to the kitchen to plug it in. She chuckled when the call screen lit up.

"So, if I call the police, do I call 9-1-1 or their regular number?" She laughed out loud. "It's not an emergency. Hell, he's not planning to shoot anybody today. He was supposed to be with me. So, what number would I call if I was going to call?"

She set the phone on the counter, dropped her head, and mumbled. "If I was going to call? Christ Maya, you are going to call... as soon as the phone charges."

Of course, she knew with the phone plugged in she could call right then. Instead, she ignored the idea, poured a cup of cold tea from the pot and placed it in the microwave.

Why the hesitation? She thought. *Damn girl, you know what's right and what's wrong. Hell, you know what's evil.*

The bell dinged on the microwave. She took the mug, blew across the top of it, and sat at the table. Her fingers tapped her chin as she thought. *Is he really evil, though? He's not randomly shooting people. I actually enjoy hearing about those bastards dying. They kill those beautiful beasts and he kills them. Isn't that an eye for an eye?*

Stop it Maya! He may be a great guy, but he's a murderer. He's shooting these people for all the right reasons, but still he's killing. Hell, he kills then goes out with me, totally relaxed as if nothing has happened.

Perhaps she spoke aloud to let it sink in. "Oh God, what do I do? Why the hell is this even a question for me?"

Chapter 10

Maya was glad when she called Trent to hear he hadn't yet cancelled the weekend. Although still uncertain how to proceed, she realized she didn't have to hurry. He was unaware she knew. If he was caught, she figured she might initially be implicated as an accomplice. She was confident authorities would accept her explanation that not only was she unaware he was the killer, she was horrified to discover he was. Besides, she could turn him in anytime. She laid her cheek against the headrest while Trent drove and enjoyed watching the countryside roll by.

After about ten minutes, Trent interrupted the silence, "You're awfully quiet. Way off in your own world."

Maya was pulled out of her trance-like state. She turned her head towards him and rubbed her eyes. "I was almost asleep."

"Sorry."

"No, I'm glad you brought me back. I was enjoying the view, then my mind wandered. Next thing I knew, my eyes were closing. That's when I heard you speak."

60 GORDON K. JONES

"So, where did your mind go?"

"A weird place."

"Oh yeah. Want to tell me about it?"

She didn't know if the time was right or if it was something she wanted to bring up over the course of the weekend. "I was thinking about the Predator's Predator thing."

"Really?"

"Yeah. Remember, I told you how murder fascinates me. How I love to study it?"

"Uh-huh."

"Well, I've been going over his spree and I think I see a pattern."

He gave her a look.

"I'm not sure where he's from, but I see a line forming with his killings. All the murders have been those of the Tyndall 10. I did some research and located the towns where they all were from and think I know who's next?"

"Really ... who?"

"Somebody in Parkview Gardens. Two of the ten live there. One's a woman and he hasn't killed a woman so far and something tells me he won't yet. That narrows it down to Spencer Maling."

Trent turned his head quickly towards her and was glad his reaction didn't send them off the road. He hoped he kept a lack of surprise on his face. He felt his hands start to perspire.

"Really?" he said, after taking a few moments to gather his thoughts. Did she somehow find out? No, he'd be in jail now for sure. Is she that good? After all, didn't she say she always took a great interest in murders? "Interesting hypothesis. How'd 'you arrive at that conclusion?"

"He keeps moving north. His first kill was in Coe Hill and he's been moving up the map town by town ever since. Now, if it were me and don't be afraid, I'm not the killer, but if I were the *Predator's Predator*, I'd break away from this plan. It's hard for the cops to find a pattern until three or four have been killed. Hell, if I've figured it out, I'm sure the authorities who've been trained in this sort of thing have too. No, if it were me, I'd break the pattern. I wonder if he's smart enough or maybe too determined to keep it to this Tyndall 10 group."

"So, you think it'll be the guy in Parkview Gardens?" Trent decided not to use his alter-ego's name and sound like he knew too much about this.

"Yes."

"Five bucks?"

"Make it ten. I want odds, though."

"Alright. Five to one, then. If it's that guy, you get fifty. Anybody else and I get ten."

"You're on." He changed hands on the steering wheel so they could shake. She settled back in her seat and again watched the hills, fields, and trees fly by.

Although she still hadn't figured out how to handle the situation, it seemed automatic for her to protect him, nudge him away from his bad choices. There was a part of her which wanted to turn him in but another seemingly larger part, which could justify what he does. Absolve him of his crimes. After all, she hated the killing bastards too.

Trent was a good guy. A decent guy. A guy she really liked. Until she decided whether to tell the cops, or tell him, the best she could do was to keep him safe.

Chapter 11

It was a little past eight PM when Paul Hayer, owner and president of *Across the Sea Travel* in Northcote City, held the door open to the hallway and said goodnight to his staff as they left after a full day's work. He stayed at the door for a moment and listened to their banter as they descended the stairs and headed out onto the street before he stepped back in and locked the door.

His eyes swept the office. The next day would be an exciting one for him. At noon, he would be having lunch with a real estate agent and signing a lease for a new office, a street level storefront in the middle of the business area of the city. It was what he strived for from the time he first opened the agency. Although most of his business now came via the Internet or by phone, he always felt it was important to have a physical presence. A street level storefront not only would give him one, but it would also encourage walk-in traffic. His staff knew nothing about it and he was sure they would be as excited about it as he was when he gave the announcement after the signing.

He always loved travel and throughout high school remained focused on the travel industry. His friends

PREDATORS AND PREY

laughed when he told them he was going for a two-year Tourism and Hospitality degree at a state college rather than trying to attend a quality name university. Two years of university led to five years as an agent, where he saved every last penny to open his own agency focused on overseas destinations.

'*Across the Sea Travel*' began with a small fifth-floor office, himself, a computer and a phone on a desk. His friends held visions of owning valuable companies where they would be leasing the entire top floor of a tall city building, while Paul's dream took him down to street-level. It took two and a half years before he could afford a sizable second floor office and a small staff. Now, three years later, his long-term plan worked out. In six weeks he would have the storefront he always wanted. Even the window lettering was worked out in his head.

He walked over to his desk by the street window and looked out. The one bad thing about the move was how he was going to miss the view. Finally, he would have his own private office, although he always enjoyed the sunshine which beamed through the glass and naturally brightened the room he was now moving from.

A couple of old friends from his high school days had become highly successful. It made him happy, as not only did he wish the best for them, but they also became his clients. Ones he looked after personally. Ed Simpson was one of them, and he had a trip coming up. Paul picked up the folder with his tickets and printed itinerary and flipped through it.

"So, heading over to South Africa for an elephant hunt, are you?" Paul said as he pulled out some papers from his desk.

He didn't like hunting and felt no desire to get close to nature in the wilderness. For him, a nicely manicured park was about as outdoorsy as he got. The commissions his firm earned making all the arrangements for a hunt, however, he loved. There was a six-hour time difference between South Africa and Northcote City, so he jotted a

64 GORDON K. JONES

note on the folder's cover to call the hunting safari company at nine the next morning to firm up arrangements.

Hayer stretched and turned to look out the window one more time. Rita, his wife, was on the evening shift at the hospital where she was a doctor and wouldn't be home until after midnight. Paul let his arms fall to his sides and stood, pondering whether to eat out or go home. At home, he could relax with a box of macaroni and cheese with hot dogs, which he'd enjoy along with a nice glass of chardonnay. He smiled, his decision made. Mac and cheese from a box, mixed with cutup hotdogs and a glass of wine, was too hard to give up.

An instant later, a bullet shattered the window and his world as it crashed into his chest. The impact sent him rolling backwards over his desk and onto the floor. He was barely alive and bleeding out fast.

◆　◆　◆

Trent no longer could see his target, so he lowered the sight from his eye. He knew it wasn't a clean hit as the bullet struck Hayer's right side instead of the left and landed lower than he would have liked. A gust of wind came up as he squeezed the trigger, which, even at the speed the bullet travelled, would've slightly affected its trajectory.

He cursed. Although he didn't like his job in the army, he took pride in his work. It bothered him when a bullet didn't strike exactly where he had aimed.

When he looked over the short rooftop wall, he saw there was some commotion on the street. People with their backs to him were pointing up at the broken window and many of them were on the phone, probably calling 9-1-1. Trent smiled as he noticed nobody was heroic enough to rush inside to see if anyone needed help.

He ejected the spent cartridge and pocketed it. After a quick cleanup of the area, he once again left behind his calling card before clambering down the fire escape.

The message he left was on an '*Across the Sea Travel*' ad for African safaris with a picture of a lion. Trent had worked his photo editing magic on it and superimposed a speech bubble coming from the lion.

Once on the ground, he adjusted the shoulder holster which held his revolver, so it rested comfortably inside his jacket and slung his rifle bag over his shoulder. As planned, he headed to an alley and walked through it quickly and almost stress-free with the knowledge that when he left the rooftop, nobody had yet discovered what he had done.

He reached an adjoining deeply shaded alley, which would take him to where his car was parked. After turning into the dim, littered passage, he spotted something ahead and stopped. He squinted his eyes to see through the gloom and saw about halfway along the passageway what looked like one person hunched over another. Inwardly, he cursed. Being seen in the area of a murder scene with a gun bag was not something which Trent wanted or needed.

With no other way to get to his car, Trent quietly made his way forward and saw a man bent over, loudly scolding a smaller figure, like a child or animal. The man was too busy dealing with the cowering figure that he didn't notice Trent standing there.

Although he couldn't make out what the man was saying, Trent didn't like the man's threatening tone. It also didn't sit right with him where this was taking place, hidden out of view from the public. He made his way down the alley cautiously, not wanting to bring attention to himself until he could better see what was happening.

In one hand, the man held a dog by its collar. It was a small whimpering dog who only came halfway up his knee. Trent flinched when he saw the man strike the dog with its own leash, causing it to yelp loudly.

Again, the enraged man screamed at the dog. Trent saw his hand come up again and was close enough to see a gash over one of the dog's eyes.

"Hey! That's enough!" Trent said in a voice filled with anger and menace.

"Fuck off and mind your own business," the man replied, lowering his arm and turning his head to glare at Trent.

"It is my business. I just saw you beat that poor animal."

The stranger let go of the dog's collar and stood upright with his hands on his hips. He was tall, barrel-chested and his bulging biceps made it obvious he worked out. His manner oozed confidence that his size, physicality and bullying attitude would back people down. He took a large intimidating step towards Trent. "So, what the fuck are you going to do about it?"

"This." In one quick motion, a revolver appeared in Trent's hand and another split second later the dog beater was on the ground with the final couple beats of his heart pumping blood through the hole in his chest. His faithful dog looked at Trent, then to his owner, and began licking the dead man's face, even though moments before, it was taking a beating from him.

Satisfied the man was dead and once the body was discovered, the dog would be looked after, Trent calmly holstered his gun and made his way out of the alley to his car. He headed home with his arm out the window and classic rock blasting from his car radio.

Chapter 12

Trent cracked a beer, flipped on the TV and sat in his favourite chair. His timing was perfect as the evening news had just begun with the lead story being of his exploits earlier that day. A male reporter stood in front of the building Paul Hayer's office was in which was now cordoned off by yellow police barrier tape.

"Two murders were reported late today in Northcote City and police believe the two are possibly connected. Early this evening, witnesses saw a window shatter on the second floor of the building behind me, which is the office of Across the Sea Travel. Several 911 calls were made to city police who quickly arrived on the scene to find Paul Hayer, president and owner of the agency, lying on the floor suffering from an apparent gunshot wound to the chest, still alive but in grave condition.

"Damn it!" exclaimed Trent, who pounded the seat of the couch with his free hand. "I knew I was off target. Shit!"

The TV showed a female reporter standing outside the doors of a hospital emergency entrance. *"Paul Hayer was brought here to Northcote City General, unconscious and*

68 GORDON K. JONES

unresponsive. He succumbed to his wound minutes after his arrival. On a sad and traumatic note, it was his wife Rita, a doctor on staff tonight, who received him when he arrived. I was told she stayed with him as they wheeled him to the operating room where he died before surgeons could operate."

"Good ... he's dead."

"Later, the body of another man who'd been shot twice in the chest was discovered in an alley only a few blocks away from the original crime scene."

"Shit, I thought I fired only once. Only saw one hole in him. Guess that's my old army training kicking in."

"Police feel the victim may have witnessed the shooter trying to escape, but it's possible that wasn't the reason he was shot. The man, whose name we're not currently allowed to divulge, was found with a dog on a leash attached to his belt. The dog had fresh welts and a cut over its eye. We're told the victim had been reported to the Humane Society on three separate occasions for cruelty in the past. Twice, the Society went to his home, however, the dog was never taken away.

"Police theorize that Hayer's killer, while fleeing the scene, stumbled upon the man striking the dog, whereupon he shot and killed him before making good his escape. If evidence supports what police suspect, tonight's crimes will have raised the Predator's Predator death toll to six. Back to you ..."

Trent flicked off the TV. He took a sip of his beer and slouched in his chair, and wondered what Maya would do if she ever found out.

◆　◆　◆

Maya was curled up on her couch, flipping between the various local news channels. The weekend she just spent with Trent was amazing, aided by the fact she could now, for the most part, accept his newly discovered activities. After their talk in the car, Maya managed to put it all out of her mind so she could relax and enjoy being with the man

PREDATORS AND PREY

she met at Silver Taps all those weeks before. Not the serial killer.

When their weekend was over and she was home, things for her became a bit more difficult to handle. Most of her brain argued with the small moral part which said, *turn him in.* It was a losing battle for the moral side, though, with the other claiming that what he was doing was morally justified.

There was also the worry. Every time Trent had a day or a morning off and she was at work, she pondered if he would take her advice and decide on a different target. She hoped, prayed even, he wouldn't treat their bet as a personal challenge. That he would be willing to lose ten bucks just to prove to himself he was invincible and couldn't be caught. As she always did, when the six o'clock news came on, she became glued to the set.

Unlike other nights, the lead news story was of a murder of a travel agent in Northcote City. She turned up the volume, concentrating intently on what was being said.

"Police told a Channel Six reporter they believe it would be too great a coincidence if both murders were committed by different individuals. They believe both killings to be that of the Predator's Predator. A note was found in the location where place police believe the shot which killed Paul Hayer originated from. Instead of being on a Facebook page like in the other murders, it was on an Across the Sea Travel ad where a lion is shown to be saying, 'You made money selling our murders. We killed you for free!'"

"Nice wording!" she commented.

"The second man police confirm as being Seth Morris, who was shot twice in the chest, the shots so closely placed they looked like a single hole. The man was suspected of beating his dog at the time he was shot."

"Good!" Maya declared, pumping her fists. "Bastard deserved to die!"

Her phone rang. It was Trent's ringtone. She turned down the TV and answered.

"Hey, it's me. Did you see the news? Looks like I owe you ten bucks."

She laughed, and in an instant, the moral side of her brain finally lost its fight. Maya was fully on his side.

♦ ♦ ♦

"I don't think they like me much at the FBI," AJ said as he hung up the phone.

"Why? Won't they play nice with you?" Julie kidded.

"You know, it's not like I'm a reporter. I'm a police chief, damn it. One of the murders was committed in our jurisdiction. I'm looking for some follow-up. A report, an update, or even the odd email to keep me apprised. I mean, is that too much to ask?"

Both Julie and Ben shook their heads but said nothing. AJ was a little unbearable and obsessed since Howell's murder. The FBI had been called in when it became apparent the murders were all connected. AJ hated their refusal to share information.

"I did manage to get them to admit they thought Maling would be the next one, like we did and-"

"You mean like you did."

"Anyway, they're as surprised he went after a travel agent as we are. I asked for a meeting with them and the chiefs of the cities and towns around to update us and was given a terse 'no'. I asked if they would have people at the funeral. They told me, quite forcibly, in fact, they know their business and to leave them alone.

"Then they told me to just worry about my own little town. Shit! They keep talking down to me like that and this country cop will go over and kick their high and mighty asses."

PREDATORS AND PREY 71

"They're FBI, AJ," Ben stated, "Supposed to be the best investigators in the country. Hell, they're bred to believe they're better than all the rest of us peace officers, whether it's small town or big city. Stop taking it so personally."

"Well, I do. One thing for sure, the funeral is this afternoon and I'm going to be there."

"Why? Do you think something's going to happen?"

"Probably not. I figure the FBI will surely be there and maybe, just maybe, they'll be gracious enough to allow me an audience with them. I doubt it, but it's worth the shot. And hey, you never know, a few of Hayer's big game clients will be there, which may prove to be irresistible to our killer."

◆ ◆ ◆

The next morning, Trent sat in his office at the restaurant with a plate of ham and eggs in front of him. He sipped his coffee, leaned back in his office chair, and flipped on the news on the small TV mounted above his desk.

He wondered how long he could keep Maya from finding out about his hobby. Would it be a good thing to let her in on his secret? They'd been together only a month and a half. However, he felt so close to her, especially after their weekend away. She seemed to know a lot which could help him. It would be great to come home after he was done, tell her all about it and watch the report together on the news.

The smile and fantasy left him. Who could accept being with a murderer, a serial killer at that? No, it was a secret he would always have to keep. The news came on.

"The killing of Paul Hayer in his Northcote City's travel agency office by the Predators Predator has seemed to ignite the passions of animal activists all over the country.

"By early morning, travel agencies around the country dealing in African hunting safaris found their Facebook and Twitter pages jammed with thousands of comments and unflattering pictures.

"In Illinois, a travel company specializing in African hunting expeditions was set ablaze. A few travel companies found their businesses broken into during the night, their equipment trashed and their customer files stolen.

Other safari organizations arrived at work and found their websites hacked. Several were severely corrupted. Many had their client information stolen. News of this generated hundreds of calls to each company, effectively shutting them down from running their day-to-day businesses. Clients, especially those planning hunting trips abroad, are worried about their and their family's safety.

"Others, when they logged into their websites to view details of their upcoming trips, found their information replaced with the same pictures which police found at various Predator's Predator crime sites. Some websites were completely shut down.

"Police and the FBI are investigating. With the mammoth scale of the attacks, they feel there is little they can do. We've been told if you are looking to travel, it will be a few days to a week before you will be able to arrange a trip anywhere online or by phone as many lines have been compromised. Travelers are advised to go in person to arrange for trips."

It was more than he ever dreamed of. The news of the killing of the travel agent had ignited the idea of sabotage in thousands of people simultaneously without any leadership, plan or coordination. Trent turned off the TV, smiled, and held up his coffee as a toast. Although he couldn't solve all the world's problems, he felt he was making great headway with this one.

Chapter 13

Paul Hayer's funeral was the sombre event funerals usually are, however, beneath the sadness and loss could be felt an undertone of bitterness, bewilderment and anger. Losing somebody was hard enough. Losing them to murder was much harder. Losing them to the whim of a serial killer made no sense to those who loved him the most. It was a community who would miss him.

AJ sat on the aisle in a pew at the back of the church with Detective Holister of the Northcote Police. Holister was working the Hayer murder until the FBI unceremoniously relieved him of it. Holister, his team and the city's Police Chief were treated in the same manner as AJ and Holister didn't take kindly to it either.

Like AJ, he too felt a need to be at the service and the cemetery. Being a detective, Holister never wore a uniform. AJ chose not to wear his, as he wanted to avoid any questions regarding the investigation. If the attendance at the church was any indication, Howell was a popular man in the community, as the place was full. The city was too big and Howell's funeral was too large for Holister to be able to pick out anybody he felt was out of the ordinary.

74   GORDON K. JONES

Although it was a beautiful day outside, inside the church, it was quite warm. AJ fanned his jacket a little. The temperature seemed to be rising. He was far more comfortable in his uniform Kevlar vest than he was in his old suit. When the service first began, AJ hoped for it to be a short one, instead, he and everybody else were forced to endure the heat for an hour. The doors behind him were kept closed due to the air conditioning, although AJ never felt its benefits.

Finally, the pallbearers were called up to deliver the casket to the hearse, and the congregation rose. They picked up the coffin and made their way down the aisle, followed immediately by the family. Paul Hayer's widow, Rita, despite her slightly smudged mascara, seemed to be holding up well. In orderly fashion, the pews emptied row by row, falling in behind the procession as it passed.

When the pallbearers were about halfway down the aisle, the doors to the church opened and AJ immediately enjoyed the breeze which came through. It was cooler than the still air of the church, and he could feel it against the sweaty hair on the back of his neck. After the pallbearers and immediate family passed by them, AJ nudged Holister to butt in directly behind the family, which they quickly did.

Once outside, AJ and Holister covered their eyes and squinted as they tried to adjust to the bright sun. They stepped to the side to let others pass as the casket was loaded into the back of the hearse.

"So, what do you think?" Holister asked in a low voice and a grin as he did, "The Feds. Think they're blending in well?"

AJ chuckled, "They couldn't stand out more if *FBI* were tattooed on their foreheads. Black suits, white shirts and really, I thought they had better high tech than those cheap dollar store earpieces they have stuck in.

Both men dropped their heads and snickered. The earpieces the FBI agents wore included a clear curly wire running from behind their ears and down into their jacket. Most in the crowd wouldn't think to look, however, being trained officers, AJ and Hollister certainly noticed.

The cemetery where the deceased was slated to spend eternity was a little outside of the city, in the quiet of the country. AJ was always amazed at how some cities would immediately end and the countryside begin as if an invisible line was drawn in the earth. Cows were in fields on each side of the road, yet when he looked in the rear-view mirror, Northcote City still loomed large. A ten minute drive took the procession to the cemetery and crematorium. AJ saw the hearse come to a stop in the lane a little below an open grave situated on the crest of a small hill.

"Nice spot," Holister commented.

"Too bad he can't enjoy it more," replied AJ.

They parked and made their way with the others to the graveside, making sure to take their place behind all the true mourners. AJ noticed the black suited agents doing the same thing.

The grave-side service was mercifully short. After, many people went up to briefly give their condolences to Rita, who at the moment refused to leave the casket. People began to spread out as they made their way down the small hill towards their cars. As they filtered out, AJ took a moment to look around.

To the north of the cemetery, on the other side of the fence, cows lazily grazed. He looked to the south. A split-rail fence separated the well-manicured cemetery lawn from a wooded area where leaves gently rustled in the breeze. If one felt the need to be buried, not cremated, this was as pleasant a place to be put to rest as any.

AJ's head jerked around when from behind one of the trees in the wooded area he saw the flash of a gun muzzle followed almost immediately by the crack of gunfire. A split second later, he heard the sickening sound of a bullet's thud striking its target not far from him. He turned in time

76 GORDON K. JONES

to see a man lurch backwards from the impact and fall to the ground with a groan.

"Gun!" shouted AJ and Holister simultaneously. People screamed and dove to the ground. Others scattered in many directions. AJ noticed the Feds, guns in hand, hadn't moved from their positions. Holister reacted immediately and scrambled over to the victim.

"I saw the flash! It came from the trees," AJ hollered, pointing to the spot. Immediately, he broke into a run and headed towards it. The FBI followed at half speed in a covering fashion.

Shit, they'll never catch a suspect in flight that way. What assholes! he thought as he finally reached the rail fence. He cleared it with a single leap.

The shooter had taken position at the edge of the woods. AJ could see where he took his shot from. A bullet casing left behind was sitting on a bed of pine needles with a paper, his calling card, pinned to the tree. From the disturbed leaves which covered the ground, he could see the route the shooter took to escape.

There was no zigzagging or any attempt by the suspect to throw followers off his trail, so AJ made great time catching up. Ahead, he heard swearing, so he slowed down. Through the branches, he could see bright sunshine and a raised road, separated from him by a water filled ditch. Instead of charging into the opening, he stopped behind a tree at the edge of the tree line. Taking cover, he carefully looked around it in time to see the shooter, rifle in hand and covered in mud, clambering up the other side of the ditch and onto the road.

AJ called out for the man to halt, but the gunman ignored the command. In a running crouch, he raced to the protection of a silver Chev he left parked for his escape. There was a board which had been placed over the mucky water for the shooter to use but was flipped and ripped away from the muddy embankment. It was obvious to AJ how the board broke away from the opposite side, sending the shooter into the muck and green stagnant water which not only caused all the swearing, but slowed the man enough for AJ to catch up.

"Police!" he shouted after he produced his service revolver. "Drop your gun. You're under arrest!"

Two pistol shots originating from behind the car were the man's only answer. One bullet smacked into the tree AJ took cover behind, which felt a lot narrower than he would have liked, now he was being shot at. The other he heard whiz harmlessly into the woods.

"I'm not taking this shit from you, asshole. Drop your gun!"

The driver's door opened, and the gunman let two more bullets fly before trying to get in. Quickly, AJ stepped out from behind the protection of the tree to the edge of the ditch. As the gunman raised his pistol to fire again, AJ let go three shots of his own. The first shattered the passenger window. The next two sailed unimpeded through the open window. He saw his target jolt backwards and fall out of sight as both bullets struck.

Quickly, all became quiet except for the crashing footsteps behind him as the FBI made their way to the scene.

AJ dropped to a crouch, never taking his eyes from the car, his breaths coming deep and hard. He didn't notice any stirring from behind the car. Up until that moment, he'd been a small-town cop who never had reason to even pull his gun, let alone shoot. Adrenalin rushed through his veins. He found his hands a little shaky. He was thankful it took another fifteen or so seconds for the federal agents to arrive, as by then he managed to calm himself down somewhat.

"Is he dead?" one of the agents asked.

"Don't know. Haven't checked."

"Griffin. Farrington. Go check. Split up going around the car," ordered the same agent standing with AJ, flipping his hand towards the car as he spoke.

78   GORDON K. JONES

Must be the head asshole, AJ thought. He watched the two men approach the car and called out. "Careful! He has a handgun."

The agent turned his attention to AJ, "Why in hell did you have to shoot? You knew we were coming."

"You're right. You guys were so close behind I could feel you breathing right down my neck."

"I don't need any of your smart ass comments. "

"Screw you," AJ said, poking the agent in his chest with his finger, "I had no dammed idea how far behind me you were. My God, you guys drag your fucking asses. He was about to escape and he shot at me. Twice! What the hell was I supposed to do? Let the bastard escape. Kill me?"

Griffin called to them from behind the car, "Hey Johnson. I've got blood but no body. Looks like he made his way to the bush across the road."

With a last name like 'Johnson', AJ knew he would be sharing it with people. He hated sharing it with people he thought were total jerks.

"Good. He may still be alive," replied agent Johnson. "Okay people. Let's get up there and follow the blood trail. Slow and careful."

Agent Johnson turned and gave AJ an angry look. "Why the hell didn't you get up there to secure the suspect?"

"Not without back-up. I didn't see him drop his gun and wasn't about to check it out alone. I knew he'd be badly wounded and couldn't get far."

"You better hope he didn't."

"I hit him in the chest or gut with at least one shot. Maybe two. He won't get far."

AJ followed the others up to the car. When they got there, Griffin stood pointing his finger down towards a rifle which lay on the roadway.

Johnson surveyed the area. "Well, looky here. The suspect had himself a .300 rem mag. The town cop here said

PREDATORS AND PREY

he used a handgun when he shot at him and we saw a note pinned to a tree as we passed. An agent is keeping the area secured. Put it all together and you know, I think we've bagged ourselves that Predator's Predator asshole."

AJ shook his head. *Yeah. You bagged him!*

Chapter 14

Maya stood nervously on the sidewalk across from the restaurant, trying to decide whether to go see if Trent was there or to head home to wait for him. She heard the news of the shooting at the cemetery on her car radio and prayed it wasn't really Trent who'd been killed. He didn't answer his phone or respond to any of the texts she sent. To say she was worried would be a definite understatement.

Hell, he wouldn't do a brazen shooting like this. His others seemed so perfectly planned and executed. This one sure as hell wasn't, she thought. She looked at the ground, then at the restaurant, then at the ground again before deciding she couldn't wait and headed across the street.

It was the usual slow afternoon at Corbett's, with only a half dozen customers sitting at two tables, the same regulars which showed up for their breaks every weekday. Sandra was counting the till when she looked out the window in time to see Maya crossing the street.

"Hey, Chelsea. Come here for a moment," she called as she waved her arm to signal her. Chelsea stopped

PREDATORS AND PREY

wrapping cutlery in napkins for upcoming services and went over. "You've been asking why Trent has been in such an extra good mood lately."

"Yeah. He always in a good mood but, I don't know. Somehow, he's been extra happy the past month or so. You said he met a woman?"

"I did. And here she comes."

"The woman with the streaked hair in the skirt?"

"That's her. He doesn't like to talk much about his home life. I only found out about her a week or so ago. He wanted to switch our days so he could have the Friday of a weekend off. I was curious and pressed him to find out why. It took a bit of prodding, but finally he told me he had met someone and wanted a weekend away with her. This is my first time seeing her in person."

"How do you know it's her?"

"Trent showed me a couple of pictures."

"Hmm. I never really thought about him being with a woman before. I must say, I'm a little surprised its someone who looks, you know, hip and happening, and well, this is bad, but she's ... you know, a little heavy."

"You expected a model?"

"I don't know what I expected. She's not slutty or anything. I just thought maybe she'd be a little more straight, conservative, you know, suburban housewife-like. Not streaked hair and a short skirt."

Maya came through the door and did her best to hide the worry she felt radiated from her. She looked around hopefully, but didn't see Trent anywhere. When Sandra asked her if there was anything she could help her with, she prayed she would hear the right answer. "Yes. Is, ah… is Trent around?"

"Sorry. Not right now," Sandra answered. Chelsea turned and went to wipe down a table close by so she could hear. "He headed out a couple of hours ago. We expect him back anytime now."

"Damn," Maya muttered under her breath. Still, Sandra heard it.

"Would you like to have a coffee and wait, or leave a message for him?"

She thought for a moment. "Thanks. If you could let him know Maya was here, I'd appreciate it. Tell him I'll be at home."

"Sure, I'll do that."

Maya thanked her again and left. Her head was bowed as she tried her best to fight back the tears. In a haze, she crossed the street and walked around the corner to her car. She climbed in and sat staring straight ahead, her thoughts scrambled, lost.

Her mind was so unfocused it was a wonder she made it home without an accident, although she was unsure if she ran a stop sign along the way. As she turned off the car and prepared to get out, the phone in her pocket buzzed, bringing her back into the world. She pulled it out, looked at the screen, and quickly answered.

"Trent!"

"You sound surprised."

She fumbled for words. She wanted to scream. laugh or cry, but felt the need to hold it all in. When she did try to speak, nothing came out.

"Maya. You there?"

She laughed. "Sorry. I dropped the phone."

"I heard you were just here. Anything wrong?"

"No ... no. Everything's fine. I was wondering about ordering in tonight at your place?"

"Sure. Look, I have to go. Gotta deal with something at the back. See you tonight."

Three short beeps told her he had ended the call. Although she lost contact with him, she hadn't lost him to a bullet. Maya dropped the phone in her lap, put both hands and her forehead on the steering wheel, and began to cry.

Chapter 15

Trent pulled into his driveway and decided not to park in the garage. Maya's car was parked on the street and he was excited to see her. He was looking forward to pizza and whatever followed afterward.

He opened the side door off the driveway, stepped onto the landing, and called her name. There was no reply. He kicked off his shoes and climbed the stairs to the kitchen. Perhaps pizza wasn't going to be the first item on the agenda this evening. He smiled at the thought and called her name once more. Again, there was no reply. He heard a sound come from the living room, so he walked in.

There on the couch was Maya wearing only a tee shirt, his rifle resting on her knee. Her finger on the trigger. The barrel aimed directly at him. In front of her was his open laptop. He stopped, frozen in his tracks.

Seconds went by. Neither moved. The quiet was broken only by the sound of the ticking mantle clock.

Finally, Maya spoke, but not before she raised the rifle slightly and pumped a round into the firing chamber. It was the sound of the action which intimidated Trent the most.

"Something you want to tell me, Trent?"

Trent shifted uncomfortably, never taking his eyes off of her trigger finger.

"Come on. Don't stand there so quiet. You can tell me. It's all right here in front of me on your laptop. So, what do you say? I think it's time you told me."

"Told you what? You're interested in that crime story, so I started to track it."

"Bullshit!" She spun the laptop around so he could see. It was an excel spreadsheet he had of potential targets, the ones which already dealt with highlighted in red. It was superimposed over the Facebook page, showing his next target leaning with his gun against a dead leopard. "Well ...?"

He said nothing.

"God damn it, Trent! Look, I know. You're the one who's been doing all the killing and leaving behind the messages. I couldn't sleep the other night, so I got up to check where we were going to be staying and found this. I realize you couldn't tell me before. You needed to keep it a secret. But I want you to tell me now. Come on, admit it."

Still, he said nothing. Cautiously, he moved over to his chair, not once taking his eyes off of the finger which rested against the trigger. He remained standing. "So, what now?" He relaxed a little, seeing she never kept her barrel pointed at him as he made his way.

"Well ... now you're going to tell me you're the man they call the Predators Predator."

He knew she had him. "Okay, yes. You got me. I'm him. Now what?"

She let the barrel drop, so it pointed at the floor and put a hand to her chest and began to laugh. "Shit, I almost had a heart attack when I heard the news this afternoon. I thought you were dead! Scared the hell out of me."

"You thought I was the guy that was killed at the funeral?"

Her head dropped, and she wiped away a tear. "Yes. They said the Predator's Predator was killed in a

PREDATORS AND PREY

85

shootout with police. Then they said the dead man's name was Trent!"

"Brent."

"What?"

"Brent. The guy's name was Brent."

"Oh, for fuck's sake." She lifted her head and smiled while she wiped a tear from her eye, "I went totally blank when I thought I heard your name. I heard nothing else."

She tapped the empty space beside her. Taking her up on her invitation, he crossed the room and sat close against her side. He was still a little unsure of her until she handed him his rifle, which he lifted over the side of the couch and leaned against the wall.

"Why didn't you tell me when you found out?"

"I really needed time to figure out what was morally right for me. To turn you in or let you continue. In the end, I believe you're doing the right thing, but still I couldn't tell you."

He took her hand. "And you helped to protect me by sneakily steering me to another target?"

She nodded.

"You're one smart lady."

"I really like you. I mean, I like-like you. So much that I couldn't let anything happen to you. I feel so much better now that you know that I know."

"Are you with me one hundred percent? You're not going to change your mind, are you?"

"Hell no, just the opposite. With all my years of studying murders, I plan to be an asset."

"Good," he paused for a moment and thought. "I'm really glad you're with me, but you need to understand. I have a way of designing what I do for the skills I have. I know you want to help and one day, maybe, I'll need to ask for some, however, the most I can ask of you at the moment, is obviously, to keep this all to yourself."

"But-"

"No buts. At the moment, should I get caught, you can deny having any knowledge of what I've done. They'd have nothing on you. For now, I want to keep it this way. Keep you out of it."

"I think I understand."

"Good."

"Oh, one more thing. The name you gave yourself, the *Predator's Predator*? I think it's inspired."

Chapter 16

AJ stuck a yellow pin into the map on the wall to show the cemetery where he shot and killed Brent Olson. Originally, there were only red pins on it indicating where each hunter was killed. A day later, he added white pins to show where the rest of the Tyndall 10 lived. Then he decided on black pins to show where Hayer and Seth Morris were killed, as they were not part of the ten. He hoped he wouldn't need to add anymore colours in the future or even pins for that matter.

His eyes never left the trail of pins as he stepped backwards around the desk and settled into his chair. He sipped on his coffee while searching for anything the map might be trying to tell him. If it did hold any clues or secrets, it was keeping them to itself.

The door to his small office opened and Julie walked in with Ben close behind. It was seven thirty in the morning. Julie was finishing her midnight shift while Ben was coming on duty. Both looked tired, however, it was AJ who was rubbing his eyes.

Ben went to the coffee machine and poured a cup. He knew not to offer one to Julie, as she would soon be

88   GORDON K. JONES

heading home and straight to bed. Steam rose from the fresh cup AJ held. "Sounds like you had a busy day yesterday. Heard it first on the news, then followed the deets on our system. Hell, you actually got to the suspect before the Feds?"

"Yeah. The Feds are useless!" AJ declared. "And not one of them even thought to go check the victim. Good thing Holister did. So, there I am giving chase while they're busy dawdling behind in their two by two, three by three or whatever the hell their cover formation is these days."

"You sound pretty pissed," Julie commented. She was tired, but as much as her bed called, she wanted to hear what really happened out there.

"Well, yeah. First time I've ever been shot at. They were way behind me by the time I chased the asshole to his car. He shot at me and missed. I shot and didn't."

"What did the Feds have to say?" Julie asked.

"At first they were quite unhappy how I felt the need to defend myself. Then they gave me shit because I didn't storm the car after I shot without backup. The suspect managed to crawl off and, of course, by the time they got there, he was gone. It took a half hour to find him."

"Half an hour?"

"Yeah. Can't really blame them. He was pretty well hid. For some reason, the suspect never left a blood trail after getting off the road and managed to find an old fallen hollowed out tree trunk to crawl into. He bled out there and was dead by the time they found him."

"Guess they weren't very happy about that," Ben commented.

"No, they weren't." AJ took a sip from his cup. "After talking to the victim, it became easy to piece together. It turned out Olson, the shooter, owed a hundred and fifty grand to Henry Bishop, the fellow who took the bullet. No paperwork was ever signed. Olson couldn't pay it back or never had the intention to. We'll never know. Anyway,

PREDATORS AND PREY

Bishop threatened to take him to court. So, what better way to kill the problem than to actually kill the problem and make it look like the work of our serial killer?"

"Interesting. It might have worked if he hadn't just wounded the guy and you weren't there," Julie said. She got up from her desk and looked over at AJ, who looked especially tired. "You okay, AJ? You look like hell. Why don't you take the day off? I'll cover."

"No, but thanks. I couldn't sleep so I came in. Been staring at this damn map since five-thirty. Besides, I want to head down and check out where Olson lived. Ben will be able to look after things around here."

"If this guy has nothing to do with the serial killer, why go?"

"I don't know. You're right, this guy probably has no connection with the case. His place should be sealed off and thoroughly combed through by forensics. Still, for some reason, I feel the need to check it out myself. Maybe it's the old adage 'Leave no rock unturned' which was hammered into me during training."

Ben set down his cup. "So, where's this copycat shooter from, anyway?"

"Lansdowne."

◆ ◆ ◆

Trent opened his eyes and found his naked body pressed up against Maya. She too had fallen asleep, clothes free. He smiled as he slowly removed his arm from being wrapped around her. Not wanting to wake her, he carefully rolled onto his back without pulling his arm out from under her neck.

It was quite a surprise to find out she knew his secret. Even though she told him she was with him all the way, there was no way he could fully trust her one hundred percent. What if it only took a small argument with her to send her running to the authorities? Hell, what if they broke up? Then what? At the moment, though, the only choice was to take her at her word.

Last night after their discussion when they fell, entangled, into bed, she celebrated his knowing about her and still being alive in the most enthusiastic ways. Afterwards, he promised himself not to worry about it for the time being.

She rolled over and nuzzled his neck. There were many advantages for him not having to work until the lunch rush. Lying in bed with Maya late into the morning definitely was one of them. He kissed her forehead and sunk his head back into the pillow before he jolted up in the bed, remembering he wasn't the only one with a job to go to.

"Hey," he said as he gave her a gentle shake. "Don't you have to work today?"

Maya never moved as she answered in a groggy voice, "When I heard about the shooting, I was worried and left work early. I told them I had an emergency. I'll give them a call later to say everything's been looked after and I'll be in at noon."

"Good. It means we don't have to get up right away."

She lifted her head and pressed her soft lips gently against his, then fell back onto her own pillow. They laid in silence for a few moments before she rolled onto her side, raised herself onto her elbow while pulling the sheet up to cover herself, then looked at him. "Trent?"

"That's me."

"I know you don't entirely trust me. If the situation were reversed, I'd be hesitant, too. Like I told you last night, you can trust me. I plan to be a big help to you. You know I already have been. I guess only time and success will prove how committed I am to you."

He wrapped his free arm around her, much to her delight, and kissed her sweetly. "I believe we will be a great team." he whispered, not knowing if he believed it himself. Then he rolled her onto her back, pressed his lips to hers, enjoying how supple and moist they were while firing up both their passions.

And in that moment, all was right in both their worlds.

Chapter 17

Before AJ left the office for his drive to Lansdowne, he presumed there would be nothing at the Brent Olson house which would in any way be related to the Predator's Predator case. As expected, he was correct but felt better about going. It would have bothered him otherwise. As he explored the house, AJ thought deeply about the case.

At first, AJ really hated how the press latched onto the 'Predators Predator' label the killer had given themself, be it a man or a woman. Now, however, the term seemed to roll off his tongue. The more he thought about it, the more he felt those beautiful animals in the wilds of African shouldn't be hunted down and killed in cold blood just for sport. He was, of course, also against one human being murdering another for any reason and he was determined to stop this one particularly deranged psycho from killing any more.

He was hungry and decided to take the advice of the Lansdowne police officer who accompanied him into Olsen's house and, instead of trying a place nearby, drove across town to Corbett's. Luckily, he found a parking spot right in front of the diner, only steps away from the front door. He went in and was happy to find a seat in a booth by the window. Not only were window seats brighter, if he became bored leafing through his notes, he could look outside and people watch.

Chelsea walked over to where he sat, poured him a large glass of ice water, then placed a menu in front of him. "Would you like to start with a coffee?" she asked with a genuine smile. When he said he would, she excused herself and headed back behind the counter to grab the coffeepot.

One pot was freshly made, the other nearly empty. She dumped out the remains of the near empty one, gave it rinse and was in the process of making a fresh one when Trent came out of his office. He stood at the entrance to the kitchen and, like he always did after spending any time away from the floor, took a look around. His eyes stopped when he spotted AJ.

"Hey, Chelsea. I see we have the law here," Trent said as casually as he could, "Something you did?"

"Ha, I thought he was here for you."

Trent chuckled. *If she only knew!* The chuckle died when he looked closer and, although he could only see the officer from the back, he could tell it wasn't a Lansdowne cop. "He's not one of ours. Did you happen to notice who he's with?"

"His patrol car's parked out front. Let's see," she said, raising herself up on her tip-toes to look out the window. "Looks to be Elm Grove PD."

The colour left Trent's face as he took an unconscious step back so he was hidden from the cop's view. Chelsea didn't notice as she was busy pouring a cup of coffee from the fresh pot. He took a deep breath and did his best to sound nonchalant. "Elm Grove? Hmm, interesting. I wonder what he's doing here. When you go back, casually ask him what force he's with. Don't let on, you already

94   GORDON K. JONES

know. Simply ask him how he found out about us. It's not overly important but would be nice to know. Might help us bring in some more out of town business."

"I'll do that. Any comps for him?"

"Sure, why not? How about a free desert?"

Chelsea nodded and headed back to the table with the mug of coffee in hand. Not wanting to stay in view of the customer seating, Trent headed back to his office and closed the door behind him. He definitely wasn't comfortable with the idea of an Elm Grove cop being in his restaurant. For some reason, it made him nervous. He thought for a second, left his office, and stuck his head in the kitchen. "Tony. I slopped something on myself and I'm heading home to change. Let Chelsea know, would ya?"

"Okay." Tony the cook answered, never looking up from his grill. The staff knew Trent would never walk through the diner with a mess on his shirt, so leaving through the backdoor was not an unusual thing for him to do. Once outside, he followed an alley to the street to avoid the windows of the diner.

AJ saw Chelsea, her Champagne blonde hair, which was what it said on the bottle, tied back and bouncing a little as she approached his table with his fresh coffee in hand. She introduced herself as she placed it in front of him, then as she straightened, swept her bangs aside, even though they only came to her eyebrows. After the usual *'where are you from?'* and *'what brings you to our little establishment?'* questions, she stayed and chatted. He enjoyed her friendliness and outgoing personality.

After he was done, AJ leaned back, stretched, and looked around. He was impressed with the place. The coffee, food and Chelsea had been great. He definitely would stop in again if he were ever back in Lansdowne.

"More coffee, officer?" Chelsea asked when she returned to his table.

"Oh jeez, I love the coffee here, but no thanks. Just the bill, please."

PREDATORS AND PREY   95

"Well, I can't have you leaving me yet. How about a piece of our bumbleberry pie on the house? It's the best pie in the state, maybe even the best you've ever eaten!'

"Hmm. I don't know if I have the room."

"You sure will once you taste it," Chelsea commented as she turned and headed off to the kitchen. When she came back, she was holding more than an ample slice in her hand, "Go ahead. Dig in and tell me that's not the best pie you've tasted."

The pie came to him still warm with a combination of colourful berry filling spilling out over its crust. He dug in his fork for a taste. There was an explosion of flavour. It was tart, yes, but sweet at the same time. "Damn, Chelsea! You weren't lying at all. It's delicious! Never even heard of a bumbleberry before."

She smiled and gave his hand a pat. "So many people say the same thing, but there's no such thing as a Bumbleberry, officer."

"Really, no such thing? Oh and Chelsea, call me AJ please."

She smiled even more at the suggestion. "I'll do that, AJ. Bumbleberry pie, you see, is a combination of berries. Our head cook's from Nova Scotia, up in Canada. That's where the recipe comes from."

"Well, I'm glad he brought it down with him. Between you and the pie, it makes me want to come back again."

"You're so sweet," she said, touching his arm before she turned and headed back to the counter.

He paid his bill, leaving a generous tip behind, and headed to the door. Beside the door was a black-and-white photo of a man holding a coffee and what he figured was his staff at the time, each holding out a different plate of food. It was the man holding the coffee which caught his eye. He stopped to have a closer look.

AJ was always good at recognizing faces, something which was a big help in his line of work. The man looked as if he could be a younger version of the man he spoke

96 GORDON K. JONES

to on the day of Howell's murder. Framed under it was a news article with the same picture of the official opening of the diner. He made a mental note of the date on the article, the owner's name and the newspaper which published it before giving Chelsea a quick wave as he left.

It was a little over an hour before Trent returned. As he approached the restaurant, he checked to be sure the cop's car was gone. Satisfied it was safe to continue, he went in and checked with Chelsea to see if anything happened while he was gone. He purposely never mentioned the cop being there.

"Heard you slopped on yourself again." Chelsea joked.

"Yeah. I don't know how you guys do it, work a full shift without having to change a few dozen times."

"That's why it's best for you to stay in the office out of the way," Chelsea replied with a laugh. It wasn't really true as she and the rest of the staff, front and back of the house, appreciated how much he pitched in. Many owners they worked for in the past felt it was beneath them, feeling that was what the hired help was for no matter how slammed the place was.

"Oh, the cop who was in here," she continued. "Not only is he good looking, but he's also a hell of a good tipper."

"Great. I love to hear that. Well, the good looking part doesn't interest me, I like the big tipper part, though." Trent acted like he was going to turn and leave. Instead, he asked, almost as an after thought, "Did you get a chance to ask him about why he came here?"

"Sure did. He's with the Elm Grove P.D. I asked what brought him to our place and he said he was down here working a case and a town cop highly recommended us."

"Nice to hear we have a good reputation around town."

PREDATORS AND PREY

"You know," Chelsea continued, "I couldn't put my finger on it, but he looked so familiar. I've been racking my brains since he left, trying to think where I might have seen him. Then it came to me. You heard about the shooting yesterday at the cemetery in Northcote?"

Trent nodded.

"He's the cop who chased down and shot the gunman."

"No kidding? What a small world. A hero here, eating in our place. Wow!" he replied. His mind raced. *What case could he be working on down here in Lansdowne? Oh hell, relax. He only ate and didn't seem to ask any questions?* He forced a smile, "Did you comp him a desert?"

"Sure did. A big chunk of pie, which he absolutely loved. I wish I could have slipped him my number with it too."

Trent forced a smile

Great, he thought. *Having an Elm Grove cop around dating one of my staff. It's all I fucking need!*

◆ ◆ ◆

There was a lot going through AJ's mind as he drove back to town. First, he needed to confirm who was in the photo by the door, so he radioed the station.

"Five-one to station. Five one to station." AJ was aware there were only three cruisers for his small-town force of six and they all knew each other's voice. Still, he wanted everybody to sound professional. 'Sandy, this is AJ' didn't cut it in his mind. Neither did Car One, Car Two, Car Three. It was his idea to use 'Five One', 'Five Two' and 'Five Three' instead, five being the fifth letter of the alphabet, which was 'E' for Elm Grove. To him, it just sounded better, and as he was the one in charge, to hell what the others thought.

"Five One. this is station," Ben answered. "How did it go down there? Find anything interesting?"

"Not a thing at the house, but I may have stumbled onto something somewhere else. Before I get back, I need you to go online and dig up the September twenty-third edition of the Lansdowne Daily News. Damn, I forget the year, It's about the opening of Corbett's Diner. The owner at the time being Trent Corbett. I want the article, who the owner is now and any background you can provide on Corbett."

"Right, I'll get right on it."

"Thanks. It might prove to be nothing, but I've got a hunch it'll be worth looking at."

Chapter 18

The night was dark, wet, and extremely noisy. Gusting winds pelted the heavy rain against the windows. Overflowing water from the eaves troughs crashed in waves on the paved driveway. The tinny sound of raindrops pinging off the aluminium downspouts rattl-ed through the house. None of it distracted Trent from his research. Carefully, he flipped through all the paperwork Maya had pulled off the web for him regarding the Elm Grove Police Department.

Already she was being an asset. She found things he never would.

It was much worse than he expected. When he looked at the picture on top of the short pile, it filled him with massive anxiety. Police Chief Avery Johnson, the same cop he talked to the day he shot Howell in the park, stared up at him from the photo.

He winced, hesitated, then sifted through everything lying in front of him regarding the Chief, setting aside for the moment other members of the force. *Damn it! I couldn't have bumped into a parking cop or even a regular one. No, it had to be the guy in charge, a guy with all kinds of experience. Why him? Shit!*

Hmm, this is interesting, though. Johnson has always been a small town cop. Born and raised in Elm Grove and never wanted to leave. It could mean he doesn't have the training in murder investigations which a big city cop would have. A town cop also wouldn't have a homicide division. Big advantage for me!

He picked up another page from his desk. *Let's see. In the past, Johnson has been offered positions with larger city police forces but turned them all down. Must be a damn good cop to get those offers. Well, looky here. Howell's murder was the first one in twelve years for the town. Hmm, that murderer turned himself in right afterwards, so it looks like Johnson has no investigation experience.*

Why was he in Lansdowne and at my restaurant? He heard Maya come in through the side door at the same moment the answer jumped into his head.

She called out a hello, came up the short staircase, and headed straight to the kitchen. "I'm grabbing a beer. Do you want one too?"

"Sure," Trent answered. He grabbed the papers and moved over to the couch where he was joined seconds later by Maya, who handed him his beer.

They clinked bottle necks and took a sip, "So, was any of the stuff I found for you helpful?"

"It was. When I first looked at it I thought, 'holy shit I'm in big trouble'.

"Why?"

"The head cop, Avery Johnson. When I saw his picture, I nearly had a heart attack. He's the guy I was talking to that day when I was throwing my gear in the trunk."

"Oh shit."

"Yeah, it's what I thought. It really made me wonder why he showed up at the restaurant. Then I confirmed he was the cop who chased down and killed that bastard at the funeral yesterday. His name was Olson." Trent stopped to take a large swallow of beer.

"And?"

"Well, Olson lives in Lansdowne. It made sense for this cop to go down and check out his place for himself. He wasn't in town for me. He was here for Olson. My guess is afterwards he was hungry and ended up at my place. He told Chelsea one of our town cops recommended me. Hell, I never thought having a great reputation could get me in trouble!"

Trent laughed. Maya didn't. Wearing a worried expression, she pushed his shoulder. "It isn't funny. That town cop should have you worried. He can ID you. And don't forget the FBI. They have a team here looking for you. If he puts them onto to you, you're in big trouble."

"I'm not worried about the FBI. I was keeping two steps in front of them until you came along. Now with you, I'll be four steps in front. Seeing 'Andy of Mayberry' sitting in my place threw me off for a moment. He knows the area and the people. Thankfully, he doesn't know Lansdowne."

"Think he saw you?"

"No. No damn way he could've. I saw him first. He never laid eyes on me. I was lucky and dodged a bullet on that one. If he had seen me, it could have led to some huge problems, that's for sure. Right now, though, he still has no frigging idea who I am."

◆ ◆ ◆

The night was dark, wet, and extremely noisy. Gusting winds pelted the heavy rain against the precinct's windows. Overflowing water from eaves troughs crashed in waves on the street's sidewalk. The tinny sound of raindrops pinging off the aluminium downspouts rattled through the room. None of it distracted AJ from his research. Carefully he flipped through all the paperwork Julie pulled off the web for him regarding Trent Corbett.

It was much better than he expected because the first thing he saw when he set the file on his desk was the

102 GORDON K. JONES

picture which stared up at him from the top. Trent Corbett. The same person he talked to the day Howell was murdered in the park.

AJ went through everything in front of him, looking for things which might work for or against him. *Hmm, let's see. According to this article, he looks like an upstanding citizen. Sponsors little league ball, soccer, hockey and helps out with local charities.*

Okay, let's take a look at his record. Damn, nothing here. No arrests, no tickets, not even one for parking. Ha! I came close to changing that last one!

He smiled.

So far, nothing here indicates he could be a killer.

AJ picked up another sheet and smiled. *Wow. Look at this!* Before he could finish his thought, the door opened. Julie came in and shook off the abundance of water from her jacket and hat.

"What are you doing here?" he asked. "I thought you were off for the next couple of days?"

"Well, there's not a thing on TV and I knew you would be here going through all the Corbett stuff. Thought you might be thirsty and seeing as though we're both off the clock." She pulled a six pack out of her large purse and held it up. "Not only will this quench your thirst, it'll help loosen your mind."

Julie set the beer on his desk and as he reached over to open a couple, she hung her wet clothes on the back wall and pulled up a chair beside him. "So, did you find anything?"

"Sure did. Just as you came in," he said with a proud grin.

"Okay ... share!"

"It seems before opening up his restaurant, Mr. Corbett was in the armed forces where he did a double tour of duty."

"Oh yeah?"

PREDATORS AND PREY

"Yeah and that's not all." AJ stopped and took a short sip of beer. It was more a pause for effect than being thirsty. He set the bottle on the desk, enjoying the look of anticipation on her face before he continued, "Corbett was a sniper during his tours. No idea how many kills he made. It really doesn't matter. Trent Corbett's been trained in the same style of long-range shooting which has been our killer's M.O."

"Wow! It all fits. So, are you going this to the Feds with this?"

"No. Not right now. I think they'd blow it. Look, at the moment, I have an advantage. I've been to his restaurant, and he never saw me. He doesn't know I was even there. If he had seen me, he might suspect I was on to him, but right now he has no idea of who I am and more importantly," he paused for effect again, "he doesn't know I'm on to him!"

Chapter 19

It was Wednesday morning, two days since Chief Johnson showed up at Corbett's. Those nights were sleepless ones for Trent, who spent much of them running a multitude of scenarios through his mind as he tossed and turned the night away. Mornings found him completely exhausted and in desperate need of coffee.

Maya didn't stay over Tuesday night as she needed to be up extra early for work the next day. Trent didn't have to work till noon. Although he did manage to sleep in until ten, it wasn't enough to catch up on the sleep he lost in the hours before. Groggy, he climbed out of bed and headed straight to the coffeepot and flipped it on.

It was a still couple of hours until he needed to be at work. Two problems still ate away at him. The first, of course, was Johnson showing up at his restaurant. Was it a coincidence? The second was Maya. Sure, she hadn't gone to the cops about him ... yet. But would she? Although both thoughts randomly bounced around in his head, he felt there was a solution for one.

The ringing of his phone startled him out of his thoughts. He swore, then saw who it was and smiled.

It was Maya.

"Hi, Honey. Just called to see how you slept."

"Pretty shitty but, hell, that would be a lie because I don't think I slept at all."

"Sorry to hear that," she replied. "Is it because you missed me being with you?"

"No, it's not that." He thought about what he just said. "No ... I mean, of course I do. Always. I think I'm bothered by, you know, that visit."

"Have you noticed anything unusual, like somebody's watching or following you?"

"No."

"You're an alert guy and you haven't noticed anything. I think you're okay."

"Yeah, I guess you're right." A thought jumped into his head. "Stupid question. We still on for supper tonight?"

"Now, that is a stupid question. Of course. Silver Taps, as usual. Unless you have something different in mind."

"No. Silver Taps it is. Afterwards, I have an idea I need your help with."

"Really? What?"

"I can't tell you right now. Too many ears. I'll tell you tonight. Hang in there and I'll see you at supper."

The day couldn't go by fast enough for Trent. Although it was an ordinary day at work, everything he did seemed to take great effort and even after several cups of coffee, his mind remained fuzzy and unfocused. He was glad to see the closed sign go up and how cleanup was finished quickly.

"Off to meet Maya at Silver Taps?" Chelsea asked as she threw on a sweater and let loose her ponytail.

"You know it. How about you?"

"Oh, just curling up on the couch with my pooch to watch TV."

"Sounds nice and relaxing. Enjoy."

They said goodnight. After checking the security cameras and locking the door, he headed to Silver Taps. There were a few people in the place when he walked in. He nodded to a couple of regulars as he walked past them and sat at his usual spot at the bar. It was only a short wait before Maya joined him. She gave Trent a quick kiss before she sat.

Larry walked over and placed a small square napkin on the bar in front of her. "Evening, Maya. Having the Pinot again? Big pour?"

"No. Not tonight, Larry. Think I'll have a vodka martini instead."

"Martini!" Trent exclaimed. "I'd have dressed better had I known you'd be drinking uptown cocktails."

"Hey, leave the lady alone," Larry interjected. "She's always classed this place up, even with you sitting beside her and now she's taking it to a new level."

"Really?" replied Trent. "Ah, you're sucking up to her as you make more money from it than you do a glass of wine."

"Oh hell, I'm not sucking up, although you're right. I do make more off of one. You see, here's what's going to happen. Before you leave, at least one couple will come in and the woman will see Maya sipping happily on her drink. She'll think, 'Hey, I wonder what she's drinking. She seems to really enjoy it and it looks so good. Think I'll have one myself' So, please, Maya, whenever you take a sip, smile." With that, he turned and went to fix her drink. Trent noticed he was never asked what he wanted, but was sure when Larry returned, he would have a delicious new ale for him to try.

Trent set an elbow on the bar as he spun in his seat to face Maya. "So, a martini?"

"Yes. To celebrate."

"Celebrate? Celebrate what?" He hoped it wasn't an occasion he missed, like an anniversary of a first date or something which she thought he should know about.

PREDATORS AND PREY 107

She leaned over and put her lips close to his ear, "How you've asked for my help. If it's what I think it's about, then it means you trust me."

He nodded and gave her a quick kiss on the cheek. She smiled and leaned back. Knowing they couldn't carry on any further conversation about it in public, Maya took his hand and began telling him about her day. She spun around in her seat, with Trent doing the same when Larry returned with two drinks in his hand. He set a beer down in front of Trent and carefully placed Maya's martini in front of her. "It's stirred, not shaken."

"Oh. Now she's Ms. James Bond?"

"You, sir, are quite unrefined. You don't deserve such a lady."

Trent frowned.

"I'll tell you the difference. The taste is the same as when it's shaken but its presentation is clearer, cleaner and more inviting when it's stirred." He lightly tinged the glass when he was finished.

"Looks delicious!" Maya said as she took hold of the bottom of the glass by the stem.

"Wait till you taste it!" Larry had been in the business long enough to know not to hover over a client, so he casually left the two alone.

She took a sip, "Oh yeah! Larry definitely knows how to make a martini."

They talked a little before Larry returned with menus. "Sooo?"

"Perfect, Larry, Just perfect. This is what I'll be having now whenever I'm here. You never need to ask."

"Good to hear. I assume you're eating tonight. Ah jeez, look. A customer came in by himself and sat halfway across the room. Why the hell couldn't he sit at the bar like you guys."

"You could use the exercise," quipped Trent.

"Oh shut up," said Larry coming from behind the bar.

Trent's attention to what Maya was talking about quickly waned as he began to focus on the new customer. As stealthily as possible, he attempted to get a good look at him from the corner of his eye while looking to be interested in what Maya was saying. He tried to hear the man as he spoke to Larry, not caring what the stranger said, but to the sound of his voice.

"You're not even listening to me," Maya complained. She looked closer. "Hey, what's wrong? You're as white as a ghost."

"The guy who just came in. I think he's that Elm Grove cop." He saw Maya start to turn her head. "No, don't look," he said quietly as he squeezed her hand.

"Johnson?" she replied in a whisper. "Really? No!"

"I'm pretty sure, but I can't get a good look at him." He thought for a moment. "You saw his picture. Why don't you go to the bathroom? On your way back, you should be able to get a good look at the guy."

"Okay."

She slid off her barstool and headed for the washroom. Not having to go, she washed her hands, fixed her hair and returned to her seat.

"Well?" Trent asked in a low voice.

"I couldn't tell. He was looking down at the menu."

"Damn. So, what do we do? Leave?"

Larry returned, breaking up their discussion. "Do you guys want to hear the specials, or do you know what you want?"

Maya jumped right in, "I'll have the roasted mushroom pesto rotini. Trent?"

Her quick answer surprised him. He wanted to get the hell out as quickly and quietly as possible and figured she would, too. Obviously not. He looked at the menu to take a moment to calm down before answering. "I'm in a burger mood tonight. No tomato, thanks."

PREDATORS AND PREY

They handed the menus back. Larry had taken a few steps towards the kitchen when Trent called out. "Hey Larry, could you make it a double burger please?"

Maya leaned over and whispered, "Nicely done. Saying you want double the meat loud enough for the guy to hear in case it is Johnson."

He smiled at her, liking how she noticed his deception.

When the food came, they spoke quietly while they ate. Trent dropped his napkin on the floor and stepped down from his stool, managing to get a good look at the man.

"Shit, it is him."

"You sure?"

"What the hell's he doing here?"

"Are you sure it's him?"

Trent nodded. "Think he's onto me? This is too much of a coincidence. Maybe he's trying to force my hand."

"Look, just stay cool and eat."

Maya took a bite and then began chatting in a normal voice about growing up with her cousin. Trent marvelled at how normal her voice was. When he spoke, he thought he sounded forced and unnatural.

They declined a second drink when asked and as soon as they finished, stood to leave. Maya grabbed Trent's hand. The only direct way to the door was to pass by his table, so she made sure she was between him and the man as they approached. As they passed by, Maya let her purse strike the man's table. The man's beer sloshed in the glass but never spilled.

"Oh my God. I'm so sorry," she said, grabbing the beer. "Glad I didn't spill it. Would've been a shame."

The man looked up. "It would've been okay if you did. Of course, you would've had to buy me another."

"I would've bought you two."

The man laughed. "Glad it worked out. You two have a good night."

Trent sighed relief and said 'goodnight" back almost in harmony with Maya and they made their way outside.

"Well?" Maya asked.

"That was a hell of a dumb move. What if it was him?"

"So, it wasn't?"

"Thank God, no."

"You mean I missed out on having another martini, all because you had a bout of paranoia. My first one was fabulous."

"Sorry. It looked a lot like him. Close up, though, the voice was different. Still, if it was him, it would've been a dumb move for sure."

"Why? If it was him, then he's already onto you and would've seen you and me at the bar together. And no, we didn't look like co-workers or anything. We looked and acted like a couple, so he'd already be onto both of us. Now we know. It wasn't him."

Trent thought about it for a few seconds. "Yeah, you're right. Sorry about your second martini."

"Jerk!" she said with a smile. "Say, did you notice?"

"Notice what?"

"On the way out. I guess we were at the bar so concerned about the non-cop that you never noticed another couple come in and sat on the other side."

"So?"

"So, she was drinking a martini."

◆　◆　◆

When they were back at Trent's, Maya sat at the kitchen table while Trent grabbed a bottle of Pinot from the fridge. He poured them each a glass and sat on an angle from her. She took a sip, then looked at him in anticipation. "You said you wanted my help?"

"I do."

"Hopefully, it's about your next target. I think it's time and the sooner the better. I've been thinking and know who it should be."

"Before you do. Let me tell you mine.?"

"Sure. But I have to ask. Originally, you said you wanted to keep me on the sidelines. This will be the first kill after I told you I knew. Why the sudden change of heart?"

"Because I do trust you. Because I have a plan which'll need another person. You, of course. I'll make sure your identity's protected if anything goes wrong. I don't want you near the kill site-"

Damn, she thought.

"I will need you close by."

"Sure. I told you before I'm with you. Planning and anything else you need," she replied outwardly. Inside, she thought, *Maybe next time you'll let me be there for the moment.*

"Let me ask you. You said you have a target in mind. Who and why? I'm wondering if we came up with the same person."

"I didn't look at your list too closely when I found it that night. After doing my own research, I found there's a second person from 'the ten' living in Elm Grove."

"Ross Barker. I was thinking of him, too. So, why do you think it should be him?"

"I heard the shooter at the funeral, Olson, was from Lansdowne. Johnson probably came down to go through his house. Then he ended up at your place. So, I had to ask myself, why was he at Hayer's funeral in the first place? Why was he still following up?"

"Obviously, he's still trying to solve a murder of one of his townspeople."

"No. According to the news, the FBI's in charge of the investigation. Johnson, though, still feels the need to be involved. He wants to get to you before you get to the other member of 'the ten' living in his jurisdiction. He feels the need to protect Ross Barker."

"Okay, I can see where you're going with this. By taking Barker out of the equation, we've removed the reason Johnson has for looking for me. There's nobody left for him to protect. The Feds have all the resources so he'd leave the investigation to them and we'll have that fly out of the ointment."

"Exactly. Keeping ahead of the Feds is hard enough and will get harder. We can't also be worrying about a rogue lone cop also being after us. I think we need to move on this as soon as possible. What was your reason?"

"I'll show you." He went to his desk and returned with the laptop and hard drive, which he sat in front of Maya.

She leaned over as he brought up the file he created on Ross Barker. Before he had pulled the trigger on Howell in Elm Grove and left his first note behind, Trent copied as much information as he could from social media on all the ten.

Maya whistled and shook her head as she skimmed through Barker's file. "This is the first time I've seen all the stuff you pulled on these people. You must have figured they would be shutting down or upping their security on all their social media sites once they felt they were in danger. I'm proud of you for thinking ahead and for keeping it stored on a separate hard drive instead of on your work laptop."

She scrolled through the files and stopped. "Here's a term I haven't heard before ... *baited hunting*."

"It is what the name suggests. Guides string up meat in a clearing to draw out the animals the hunters are looking to shoot. You probably heard about Cecil, the lion who was shot by that loser Minnesota dentist. It's been said guides tied a dead elephant a hunter shot the week before to the back of a vehicle and dragged it from the wildlife park to an area where they had built a hunting blind. Then they waited for Cecil to follow the scent out of the park to where the scumbag hunter was waiting for him."

PREDATORS AND PREY

Looking at the file, Maya shook her head in disgust, "From what I see here, Barker's last kill was a leopard. His buddies scolded him and said didn't properly earn his 'Big Five kills' as baited kills don't count in their group. At the end of the string, he promises to go get one properly. What! His asshole friends say it's not a righteous kill, so he has to murder another. It burns my ass."

"I'm glad it pisses you off, as I need you with me on this. We're going to right that wrong. Like I said, I'll make sure you're safe and won't have to witness the act (*shit!* she thought). Your part is going to be big. Barker's birthday is a week tomorrow, which gives us lots of time to get ready. Plus, it's on a day that you start late."

"Why is my starting late important?"

"Because you're going to have plans that morning. We're going to make sure our Mr. Barker isn't alive to have himself any birthday cake."

Chapter 20

AJ was a morning person. The others at the station grew to accept his happy smile, humour and chatter when he walked in first thing in the morning. He felt there was too much to enjoy in life, like the morning he was currently witnessing. The sun breaking over the horizon gave an orange glow to the sky and a different colour texture to anything its beams touched. There was a slight crispness to the air. All was quiet except for the birds, which chirped and sang, occasionally interrupted by the sound of an engine of those driving to work.

Now, they missed his early morning happiness.

Although AJ explained to the Barkers, both husband and wife when they paid him a visit, that there was little he could do to protect them, he did promise to have a have a patrol car drive by their house as often as possible to show an increased police presence. Due to limited resources, it was the best he could offer. Instead of heading to the station first thing, AJ, instead, checked on the Barker house in the morning. He came to know Ross Barker left for work around 6:35 on weekday mornings. He did his best to be there when he did.

PREDATORS AND PREY 115

Usually, he arrived about ten minutes early and made sure he had a coffee and buttered, toasted sesame bagel for the wait. This particular morning was no different. As usual, he parked about four houses away on the opposite side and turned off his cruiser. He placed a paper napkin across his lap to catch the crumbs and seeds, then rolled down his window and sat enjoying the peaceful sounds of the world coming to life.

People were always on schedule in the morning. At night, they could be heading anywhere, however, on a work morning, most went through exactly the same routines before heading out the door. Only a small part of AJ's bagel was left and his coffee half finished when Barker came out the side door of his house and headed for the garage.

An unusual sound, a buzzing or whirring interrupted the morning's peace. Startled birds took flight from the trees around the home. Barker stopped and followed the sound to the front of his house. A children's quadcopter or drone came into view with a parcel attached to its underbelly. As the drone came closer into view, AJ could see the parcel was immaculately wrapped with what looked like an envelope stuck to it.

Hmm. Must be his birthday or anniversary, I guess, thought AJ, who smiled as he watched the drone hover over the front lawn for a moment before it slowly descended, landed and shut down.

Barker stepped over a narrow garden which followed the edge of the driveway and walked over to the drone. He picked it up, removed the package, and set the drone back down. The moment he stepped back, the drone started up and took off. Irene Barker, his wife, stepped out of the front door.

"Thanks, Honey!" Ross said holding up the gift.

"It's not from me. Maybe one of your friends is being creative. What is it?"

AJ heard the exchange, quickly clueing into what was happening. Immediately he began yelling as he hastily clambered out of the car, "Get in the house! Drop the package. Get in the damn house!"

It was too late. He saw blood fly from Ross Barker's side, followed immediately by the crack of a gunshot. A split second later, the report of another round filled the air. AJ winced at the sickening smack of the bullets colliding with Barker's chest. Barker's body lurched backwards, and he was dead before he hit the ground, never hearing his wife's terrified scream.

AJ pulled his revolver and scanned the area where he heard the shots come from. Although he saw no movement, he raced in that direction anyway, calling on his shoulder mic for backup as he did. AJ was in excellent shape which he needed to be as it was all uphill for him. After running through the backyard of the house across the street, he bounded over a chain-link fence without hesitation or missing a step into the next yard.

Quickly he crossed it and opened a gate leading to the front. As he sprinted up the side of the house, he saw a figure drop to the ground from the flat roof of the garage of the house across the street. It was a male with a bag slung over his shoulder, long enough to hold a rifle.

"You there!" he hollered, "Police ...Freeze!"

As he expected, the suspect fled into the backyard and when AJ reached it, saw him finish clambering over a six-foot wooden fence. AJ knew he could clear the fence much quicker and gain on the suspect. When he reached it, he jumped, bounced his feet off the boards, which propelled him over. In his haste, though, he momentarily forgot his training and fell into the shooter's trap. On the other side, he found the fugitive against the side of the building with a revolver pointing at him.

He jumped and rolled to the side. The gunman fired a second later, blowing dirt blew up from the ground in the exact spot where he'd been standing. AJ, lying on his side, returned fire. He shot twice and saw both shots strike the brick on the house. The gunman appeared around the corner in a crouched position and fired another three rounds. One struck the ground an inch beside AJ's head. Instinctively, he covered his head with his arms. The other two dug into a compost heap which AJ was laying beside.

When AJ looked up, the gunman had disappeared. He gained his feet and in a walking crouch, his weapon raised, he made his way along the side of the side of the house to the street. Looking left, there was nothing to see but a silver car in the distance turning a corner and disappearing out of sight.

"Shit!" he uttered as he bent over to catch his breath. One moment, he thought he had the gunman dead to rights. The next, he thought he was going to die. He kicked the ground, holstered his revolver and headed back to what he knew would be a gruesome scene at the Barker home.

Trent's plan had worked. After he dashed to the front of the house, he turned and saw Maya there waiting for him, the trunk open. He threw the bag and himself into the trunk, hollering for Maya, "Go. Go!" As she sped away from the curve, the truck lid slammed down on him.

When AJ returned, the scene was what he expected. Ben Chambers, who had been close to the scene arrived before the paramedics and was covered in blood, having tried his best to bring Ross Barker back from the dead. Irene Barker was hysterical while a couple of women attempted to calm her. A small crowd of neighbours, now they felt safe, stood quietly by the driveway. A sheet covered the dead body.

"Where's the package?" AJ demanded as he crossed the lawn to where Ben stood. "A drone delivered a package and an envelope to him moments before he was shot. I want to see it."

"It's right there," Ben said as he pointed to the torn, blood stained present a few feet away.

AJ snapped on latex gloves, which he always carried and marked the area where the package laid. When he picked it up, he wasn't surprised to find it felt light and empty. It really was the envelope he wanted a look at. Carefully, he removed it from the package.

Inside was a neatly folded paper. Carefully he unfolded it and saw it to be a copy of a Facebook page showing Barker standing proudly with a long-barrelled rifle over a dead leopard. Like the others, a speech bubble was drawn above the leopard. It read: *You baited me so you could kill me. How did you enjoy being baited?'*

Chapter 21

Maya turned the corner, drove a half a block to a street which would lead her out of the neighbourhood and to a main thoroughfare. There, she turned left instead of right in case somebody was attempting to follow. Her thought process was if she was the one doing the chasing, she would think the fleeing car would turn right, as it was faster and easier than waiting for traffic to part. Luck was with her as there was a break in traffic, so she only needed to slow before turning.

After driving a few blocks, she turned into a plaza, pulled in behind the string of stores, and stopped between a couple of dumpsters. She pushed the button on the door to pop the trunk, and as soon as Trent was in the passenger seat, she headed back to the street.

"Are you okay?" she asked as she looked left before making a right. She saw him nod, still trying to catch his breath. "What happened out there? I had just brought the drone to altitude and sent it off when I heard all the shooting. Did you have to kill anybody?"

"Of course, I didn't. I'm out there to kill killers, not innocents."

"Okay, but what happened?"

Trent explained what took place up to the point where she picked him up. He shook his head and yelled, "Fuck! How in hell did he know I was going to be there?"

Maya thought for a moment before it came to her, "He didn't! Remember why we decided to take out Barker? So, Johnson would have nobody left to protect and would leave the investigation to the Feds. He knew when Barker left for work in the morning and was there to provide a police presence, thinking if he were there, you wouldn't strike. Well, he was wrong. Ha!"

"Damn, we should have thought of that. Maybe I could've maybe found a better spot further away."

"Well, thankfully, it worked out. Did he get a good look at you?"

"No. I never showed my face and made sure he kept his head down by ducking my shots."

"Did you hit him?"

"No. I told you, I don't shoot innocents, especially cops. I made sure he felt his life was in danger, though."

"You wouldn't shoot a cop, even to save yourself from getting caught?"

"No. I couldn't live with myself."

Damn. Those principles are going to get you into a hell of a lot of trouble, she thought. "Are you sure he never saw you?"

"Ya. I'm sure."

He became quiet and slouched in his seat, looking out the window, watching the world fly by as they drove in silence. She didn't know if he was always this way after he completed his task or busy trying to figure what went wrong. A hint of a smile came over her as she ran though her mind all she had heard, felt, and seen.

She knew she couldn't tell him. The plan placed him on a garage rooftop up a hill three streets away. A few blocks away from him and the house, in a secluded area, she would launch the drone and guide it by camera to the target

PREDATORS AND PREY 121

area. Once she saw the package was received, she would restart the drone, fly it off south towards a nearby lake, then head directly to the car to pick up Trent at a prearranged location. As the drone was unregistered, there was no way of tracking it to them if they ever found it. This, of course, meant she wouldn't be able to witness the killing.

Only she was determined there would be more to it than that.

Instead, she found a different park with a raised playhouse for the kids and a perfect view of Barker's house. She saw the bullets impact and Barker's body twist and crash to the ground.

Holy shit! I've never seen anything like it, she thought, trying to hide the joy on her face. *You'd be so mad if you knew, but I've never seen a man shot before. I had to witness it...and oh, it was so special.*

It happened so fast. The blood. The guy's head bouncing off the ground when it hit. It was all so beautiful. So much fun to see. Trent, thanks for bringing me. Oh, son of a bitch, my juices are running.

Trent looked over at her. She wore a small smile with her right forefinger pressed to her lips, which told him she was pleased she could be a part of this. "Thanks for following through with your part. I was in a jam and could only pray you'd be there."

"Of course. We laid out the plan, and I had to follow it to the letter for it to work." She checked the mirror out her side window. *Okay, so I did a little more.*

"When I heard all the shooting, I wasn't sure what to do. I figured you would need to be able to find me once you got away, so my only move was to be where you wanted me to be." She saw a what looked like a quiet country road ahead. "Should I turn here so you can stash the gun bag?"

"No need. I already did it while I was in the trunk. One thing. I'm glad I listened to you and bought this. I never knew silver was the most popular car colour. We blend right in, like my old one did."

When he brought his new purchase home, he put in his garage where they could go to work on it. They pulled out most of the springs and padding inside the rear seat, accessible only through the trunk, where they built a secret compartment. The job was completed perfectly, as anybody looking inside the trunk would never notice the Velcro seal, which kept the back of the seat in place. They didn't want to be pulled over for a reason not related to a shooting they committed minutes before, only to have the police find the rifle and ammo sitting in the backseat or trunk. It was another great idea from Maya.

They drove to Northcote City. Originally, the plan was to drop her off at the bus depot to catch a bus back to Lansdowne so she would be to work on time. He didn't want to take any chances after the shootout, though. It was quite possible there were many closed-circuit cameras placed around the depot and he didn't want his car spotted in any of them, so they decided it was best for her to get out a few blocks away to be safe.

"See you at Silver Taps after work," he said, giving her a kiss before climbing into the driver's seat.

She held his face between her hands and said joyfully, "You bet." Then she kissed him intensely, before walking towards the depot.

Trent, as they planned for his part of the alibi, drove across town to Jackson's Tableware and Restaurant Supply, to select plates, bowls, cups and saucers for his diner. He'd been meaning to replace what he currently used, so his trip to the company was more than only filling a need for an alibi. Although their plan went off the rails somewhat and he'd been shot at for the first time in years, everything ended well. A man who deserved to die was dead. His restaurant would be receiving new dinnerware and, ironically, he could write off the gas he used that morning as a business expense.

Chapter 22

AJ sat in the outer office of his precinct. When Agent Johnson from the FBI entered, AJ took a seat behind his desk, hoping to keep a good distance between them. The agent, though, had other ideas. Instead of remaining across the desk from AJ, he wheeled the old wooden swivel chair around the desk to the side so he was close enough their knees almost touched.

I know what you're doing. Invading my space to make me feel uncomfortable and intimidate me. Hell, that's not going to work. For the next five minutes, he answered the agent's questions before a deep sigh escaped him as he was about to answer another.

A scowl came across Agent Johnson's face. "What? As a peace officer, you know I need to ask these questions. I'm merely trying to get a clear idea of what happened and how."

"I sighed because you've asked this same question a couple of times before. Look, I know interview tactics. Wear down the suspect. Get him to contradict himself. Change his story. Break him down. Except, you damn well forget,

I'm not a suspect. A witness? Yes. A participant? Most definitely. But I'm not a suspect and, hell, I shouldn't be treated like one. I was chasing a criminal who just committed a murder. Shot a man right in front of me. So, back off!"

The agent folded his arms across his chest and leaned back in his chair, "I ... we ... don't think of you as a suspect. I was wondering why you were there at the Barker residence so early in the morning, precisely at the moment he was gunned down. Just wondering if you knew something?"

"Okay. Once again, from the top. Ross Barker was part of the '10'. He lives in my jurisdiction. We all have an idea this serial killer would be coming for him at some point. We didn't know when, where or how and we sure as hell don't have the manpower to provide him 24-hour protection. I could have a car there when he left for work and raise our presence around his house by doing a number of drive-bys. Our hope was our increased presence might be enough to keep this killer away."

"Sure worked well."

"Hey, I don't need your bullshit. What the hell has the FBI done on this case, given all the vast resources you say you have at your disposal? I'll tell you. Nada, nothing. So keep your fucking smart ass comments to yourself."

Agent Johnson leaned forward. "Look, Chief. We want to find this psychopath, and I know you do too. So. You say that while chasing him and exchanging gunfire with him, you never saw his face?"

"No. He had back to me while he was running and I was too busy ducking shots to have a look."

"Really? I've got a gut feeling you're holding back. There's something you know about this whole damned affair you're not telling us."

It was AJ's turn to lean forward, which he did so he was inches away from Johnson's face, "Just what are you accusing me of?"

"Nothing ... nothing at all. Make no mistake, I believe you're a good, honest cop. But you're small town. You've had little training to handle a case like this. If you're holding back and I think you are, you'll find out quickly how deeply over your head you are. You'll be putting yourself or others on your force in danger. Oh and if I find out, I'll have your damned badge, Chief, and any others who are withholding information up on charges."

Both men snapped back quickly in their chairs as if it was choreographed. A moment later, the precinct door swung open and Julie walked in. She concentrated on shaking the excess water off her hat and coat. "Jesus Christ, it was beautiful one moment and then the sky opened up. I was a block away when it happened. It's pouring out now."

She looked up and saw the two men glaring at each other, enraged. "I can come back."

"No, it's okay, Julie. Agent Johnson's just leaving, aren't you?"

The agent stood, reached in his pocket, pulled out his business card, and held it out. AJ made no move to take it. "You already gave me one when you came in. Gave me another the first time we met. I don't need a third. I don't lose things."

"Here, have it anyway," Johnson said with a sneer as he tossed the card onto AJ's desk. The agent walked over to the door, put on his jacket and looked outside, "Sure is miserable. Wish I thought to bring my rain gear."

Julie came to his rescue, pointing to a tall bucket beside the coat rack, "Grab an umbrella. We keep them here for people who come in and find themselves in a downpour when they're about to leave. They happen quickly around here."

"Thanks. That's what I like about small town precincts. They know their community and tend to friendlier, more people-oriented." He reached over and pulled a green umbrella from the bucket.

"Johnson," AJ said with a deadpan expression. "It's not a gift. It's a loan. We expect it back."

Agent Johnson nodded, stepped out the door, popped open the umbrella and disappeared into the downpour.

"What on earth was that all about?" Julie asked as she poured herself a steaming cup of coffee.

"The FBI thinks I'm not telling them everything. They think maybe I knew in advance about this morning's shooting and didn't tell anyone."

"That's ridiculous! If we knew or suspected, we would've let them know. We're not about to risk the life of a citizen. You know, I hate to ask, but I guess you didn't tell him about being at Corbett's."

AJ sheepishly dipped his chin like a young boy whose mother caught him in a lie. "Decided to keep that nugget to myself."

"Then don't be so pissed. It looks like he was reading you right."

He lifted his head and tapped the side of his fist lightly on the desk. "Yeah," he said with a sigh. "It's that I can't exactly tell them about it now or they'll be all over me for suspecting Corbett and not informing them before. Now a man's dead and if the FBI finds out, I could be charged. Definitely would lose my job."

"Remember AJ. It's not only you. Ben and I know too. Guess we were all too arrogant to think we could get this guy ourselves."

AJ looked at her and nodded. After running his chase with the subject through his mind one more time, something didn't seem right. He looked at Julie, then at the floor, then up at her again. "He has an accomplice."

"He does? How do you know?"

"Because, after we exchanged fire, I wasn't long following him to the front of the house and already, he was gone and his car was far down the road."

"Are you sure it was his car?"

PREDATORS AND PREY

"Silver and shinier, but yes, it was his, and he must have been in it, although I didn't see him. On that street there wasn't anywhere for him to quickly get out of sight." He thought for a moment more. "There has to way a way for me to get us off the hook for this and get the FBI's attention on Corbett."

"That would be good. How'd we go about doing that?"

He looked at his desk and thought for a moment. Then his head popped up, and he pointed towards Julie. "I know. First, could you double check all the records and see what Corbett drives. I never got the license plate, but I'm sure that was a new car I saw. Wouldn't it be fabulous if it belonged to his accomplice?"

AJ drummed his fingers on the desk for a moment before he continued. "I need a good reason to go to Lansdowne, one the Feds can't question. That way, I can stop into Corbett's for a bite. Hopefully it's on a day when he's working so I can see him. Then I can go to the Feds and tell them I was at his restaurant for lunch and recognized him as the man I was talking to the day of Howell's murder. Same build as the suspect I had the shootout with too. Hey! What a coincidence!"

"Sounds like a decent plan."

"You know, I've let this become personal. I feel, and this is stupid, guilty about how I let Corbett get away the first time, even though I shouldn't. And it's bothered me. As much as I would love to be the one to nail this bastard, it's best for all of our careers if we dump this shit on the Feds and leave them to it. Then we can go about our daily business and monitor their progress from a safe distance."

◆　◆　◆

Trent met Maya at Silver Taps after work as planned. She ordered what was now her new "usual", a vodka martini, while he went for an ale, a hoppy IPA.

"Everything good at work?" she asked.

"Yep. Put it all out of my mind before I went in. Nobody would know the difference. How about you?"

"Hell, I was the only one in the office. The others were doing inventory. Nobody knows whether I was early or late getting in."

They exchanged looks and grinned. After they ate, they ordered one more drink, like they usually did, before heading back to his place. It was important on a day such as this not to change their routine. It wasn't long before they fell into bed exhausted from the day's events, where they drifted off into a long, deep sleep.

The next day went quickly and smoothly. Trent worked the noon to eight shift again and was delighted when he arrived home to find Maya on the couch with a glass of wine, wearing one of his sport tee-shirts and apparently nothing else. An empty glass and a partially drained bottle of Pinot waited for him on the coffee table in front of her.

He sat beside her and poured himself a full glass and set the bottle on the table beside him so the coffee table was clear. They tinged their glasses together, enjoyed a sip and snuggled closer together while he grabbed the converter and flipped on the news.

"I don't think there will be anything new about us tonight," surmised Maya. She took a sip of wine and stretched her bare legs across the coffee table. It wasn't hard to notice Trent watching and admiring them as she did. She enjoyed enticing him and hoped she was right about them not being on the news, as she had something far more pleasurable planned.

"Sure hope not. Something new could only mean they might have something on us. Fingers crossed anything they talk about is only a rehash of yesterday."

Before Trent started his quest, he never bothered with the news. To him, it seemed the news never changed. Now that his pseudonym, the Predator's Predator, a moniker

PREDATORS AND PREY · 129

he absolutely loved, had a chance of making the broadcast, he tuned in and skimmed the news channels each and every night. He enjoyed it even more, now he had someone to talk with about it.

Trent flipped the station to a national network. Quickly, he turned up the volume. On the screen, an earnest looking reporter stood in front of a crowded scene of flashing lights which came from patrol cars and ambulances.

"*Tonight, in a Pittsburgh suburb, three men are dead following what can only be described as an attempt to copycat a Predator's Predator murder. At roughly eight-thirty PM, Donald Peterson, sixty-four and his thirty-nine-year-old son Frank, were shot inside of Donald Peterson's garage where they were cleaning their rifles for an upcoming African hunting expedition.*"

"Wow!" exclaimed Maya. "People are trying to follow your example."

"Not sure if I like this or not."

The reporter continued, "*A witness said the two men were working in the garage with the door open when shots rang out from across the street. One apparently struck Frank Peterson in the leg. His father, Donald, returned fire with his rifle before being hit with multiple shots from the gunman. The witness saw the gunman step out from behind a tree. He looked as though he took a bullet in his left shoulder as the arm was immobile and the shirt in that area was a deep red colour.*

"*The yet unidentified gunman dropped his rifle, pulled a handgun from the back of his pants, and walked up to the garage. Frank Peterson managed to sit up and draw his own weapon. They both shot multiple times and when it was over, all three were pronounced dead at the scene.*"

"Shit!" Trent muttered under his breath.

"*Among items found belonging to the dead gunman were two Facebook images showing the father and son with their last kills. Each, we're told, had a caption on it, similar to what has been found at the Predator's Predator killings. Police believe this is a copycat killer and the real serial killer is still at large.*"

Trent turned off the TV, and the two sat in silence for a couple of minutes. Maya was bursting to ask him how he felt, but seeing his face, thought it best to remain quiet and let him speak first.

"Son of a bitch!" Trent finally uttered. He took a long gulp of wine, tilted his head back so it rested on the back of the couch, and closed his eyes. "The jerk got himself killed."

He opened his eyes, returned to his previous posture, and looked straight ahead. His words came out calmly, which surprised Maya. "I don't want copycats. They might not have the same motive. They might only want an excuse to kill.

"I love the protests in the streets, on social media and in the press. I want the disdain and harassment to be so great, safari sellers will be too afraid to sell, trophy hunters too worried and scared to even consider a trip to Africa. I want the government to pass laws.

"Killing the killers is my quest. I don't want others to die for this cause."

"Me too," was all Maya could think to say.

Chapter 23

Connie Stapleton, Chief of the Springhurst Police Department, shut the cell door behind the prisoner whose hands were cuffed in front of him and led him to the main office area. She held up her hand, signalling the man and women on the other side of the counter who stood up when they entered the room to stay where they were.

"Hold your wrists out," she tersely said to the seventeen-year-old prisoner. He did as ordered. After she removed the cuffs, she signalled for the young man's mom and dad to come around the counter while the boy unconsciously rubbed his wrists. He hadn't been cuffed long enough for them to even suffer a mark.

"I'm glad you both could come," she said to the couple. The man shook her hand, and the mother gave her son a hug. "I've known you both for quite a few years and have watched Billy here grow up."

"It's Bill!" the teenager retorted.

The father stepped forward and pointed a finger in Bill's face, "Chief Stapleton is giving you a break so shut your mouth and be grateful."

"That's alright. If he wants to be called Bill, I should address him as such. I do apologize, Bill." The Chief continued. "Back to the matter at hand, it was a two-hundred-dollar pair of runners that Bill put into a hundred-dollar backpack and attempted to walk out with both from the store this afternoon."

Billy's mother scowled at him.

"Now, he's been a good kid for as long as I've known him. I thought instead of putting him in front of the courts, which would get him a criminal record, it would be best to call you to come get him. The store didn't like the idea, but I pushed and they went along with it. My guess is both of you could probably provide more personal punishment and guidance for him."

"Yes. We sure will," the mother replied. "First thing in the morning, I'm hauling him down to that store to apologize then-"

"Mom!"

"Don't you 'Mom' me. You're going down there to apologize and see what you can do to make it up to them."

Bill closed his eyes, bowed his head, and sighed. Connie broke into a grin.

"It's raining, so put on the jacket I brought for you and get your butt to the car," the mother continued. "We've a lot to talk about when we get home, but before we go, you thank the chief. She's giving you a bigger break than you realize."

Bill took a small step towards Connie, "Thank-you, Ma'am."

Connie put a hand on his shoulder, "You're welcome. You made a mistake and I hope you learned from it. I'm giving you a second chance, so don't blow it. Next time you'll go up in front of a judge."

The boy nodded. His mother placed a loving hand on his back, picked up her umbrella and led him towards the door. The father shook Connie's hand again and thanked

PREDATORS AND PREY

133

her before he left. On the way out the door, five wet people rudely pushed by him, obviously anxious to talk to the officer.

She recognized three of them right away, Walter Mathews, Ed Simpson and the always immaculately attired Rebecca Farnsworth, wearing a fashionable and probably expensive rain jacket. All three lived in the Springhurst area and all were part of the '10'. She had a hunch they'd be paying her a group visit and stepped up to the counter.

"Good evening, everyone. How can I help you fine folks this on this rainy evening?"

It was Walter who stepped forward to act as spokesman for the rest, "Chief, I believe you know three of us here. Let me introduce the other two. This is Spencer Maling and Samantha Edgars, both of Parkview Gardens." Each nodded when their name was spoken.

"May we come around and speak to you in your office?"

"No. I don't see any need for it. There's nobody else here. Now, how can I help you?"

"You must know why we're all."

"I'm really not in the mood for games tonight. Yes, I'm aware of your situation. I also know the FBI has spoken to each of you regarding their investigation, so please tell me, what do you want?"

"Alright, I'll get straight to the point. We demand some form of protection from your department. After all, our friends have been murdered and we have to believe we're on this maniac's list, maybe even the next to be targeted. We want to know how you propose to protect us."

"You're asking for personal protection from my people for each one of you. You must be aware police departments don't offer personal services. On top of that, we have only eight officers on staff to look after this town twenty-four seven. There are three of you who live here. It's hard enough to guarantee we do a twice day drive by."

"What do you suggest?" asked Rebecca, trying to soothe the tone of the discussion from the abrasive way Walter started it. She went in wanting to speak for the others, instead Walter, as usual, jumped in to take control.

"Ms. Farnsworth-"

"Rebecca, please," she corrected.

"Rebecca," Connie confirmed. The woman was always dressed in such fine, expensive outfits Connie found it difficult not to be formal with her. "In a normal situation, I would suggest bodyguards-"

"Bodyguards, my ass!" Walter declared, leaning over the counter. "What the hell-"

"Walter. Hush your mouth for a moment and let the Chief speak."

"Thanks, Rebecca. Like I was saying, in a normal situation I would recommend you all hire personal bodyguards, however, this is not a normal situation. This man kills from long range. As you've all heard, yesterday when your friend, Mr. Barker, was killed, an officer was there watching him and there was nothing he could do to stop it from happening. He almost apprehended him in the chase after-"

"Almost!" Walter huffed.

"Yes, almost, and he was almost killed in the process, too. Mr. Mathews, you don't seem to appreciate the danger the officer exposed himself to in trying to apprehend the suspect."

"Maybe we need people who know how to handle a gun to look after this. Perhaps we need to look after this thing ourselves."

"If you or any of your group raises a gun in any way except self defence, I will surely put your ass in jail and have you charged."

"While the killer walks!"

"Look, I will not have you shooting somebody who might be innocent. You have the right to protect your life, if threatened. Not to go on the offence."

PREDATORS AND PREY 135

A lengthy quiet followed as the two glared at each other. It was finally broken by Rebecca who, again, spoke in a calm manner, "Walter. We came here for help. Your attitude is not helping, so please, no more out of you. Chief, do you have any suggestions at all?"

"The FBI is handling the investigation. They're well-funded. They have six people dedicated solely to capturing this maniac and have all the tools to do so." All five shifted nervously while she spoke. "My advice is to be extra careful. Change your routines. The times you leave for work. The time you come home. If you eat your lunch in the same place every day, change it up. Go to different places at different time. Those who've been killed so far were shot while going about doing what they do each and every weekday and at the same times. This killer is methodical. He observes, then finds the best place to hide and wait. He knows eventually you'll walk into his crosshairs. All because of your day-to-day routines."

Connie knew they needed to hear something positive from her. "I'm as concerned as you are. Yes, the FBI is working the case, but there might be something we can do which we haven't thought of. So what I'm going to do is to call Chief Johnson in Elm Grove, he's the officer who was involved in the shootout with the suspect and Chief Freemont in Parkview Gardens and the FBI for a meeting. Perhaps we can come up with a way to finally apprehend this murdering bastard. Sorry to swear. I know it's unprofessional, but this bothers me terribly too."

Spencer Maling stepped to the front of the group and turned to face them, "I think the Chief is making an excellent suggestion. Samantha, Chief Freemont can give us an update on what took place."

"And I'll update all three of you," Connie said to her three residents. "So, is there anything else?"

"No, I don't think so. You've been quite helpful," answered Rebecca, who seemed to have taken over speaking for the group. It made Connie happy, as she never did enjoy speaking to Walter for any reason. "I think we're done here. Now, how about we go for a cocktail or two?"

They all nodded in agreement, thanked Connie, and left. It still was pouring rain and Connie was happy she didn't have to go out on patrol on such a miserable night. She needed to make a few calls before her shift ended. Then she could head home where her husband Glenn, an excellent cook, would have a fabulous hot meal waiting for her, as he always did when she worked late.

Chapter 24

Following the afternoon meeting between the FBI, Springhurst, Parkview Gardens and Elm Grove police departments, AJ stayed behind to talk to Connie. Not only were they the same age, they were also long-time friends. Even though they never dated, they met in high school and ran with the same circle of friends. After graduation, they attended the state police academy together and helped each other through the program.

"What do you think?" Connie asked as she walked over to the coffeemaker. She held up her cup to see if AJ wanted one before she poured.

AJ shook his head before answering. "I never know what to think of those psychological profiles the Feds come up with. Hell, are they any use at all? I look at this one and think it could be applied to so dozens of people in our small towns and hundreds over in Northcote City. According to their profile, most of them wouldn't ever come up on our radar."

"You've been the only one who's been close to the suspect. Does any of it fit?"

"Well, he was too busy shooting at me to get a chance to know him. I have no idea if he fits the profile." AJ laughed as he held up the profile pages in his hand. "You know, there's something which has been bothering me about that firefight. Something weird. Something which doesn't fit."

"Really! What?"

"I agree with the Feds that he's had sniper training sometime in the past. He's too good at shooting long range and with choosing perfect locations to set up. I know the Feds said they're talking to the army, navy and marines, but he could've also been a sniper with SWAT or any law enforcement agency ... hell, even with the FBI! It'll take forever for them to nail down any solid suspects.

"But that's not the point here. The point is, he's so damn good with a rifle. Rarely misses. The way I see it, if he has military or police training, then he's also well-trained with a handgun. He was waiting for me when I came over the fence. Could've killed me as I was still in the air or after I hit the ground ... But he missed! So here we have a man who hits his mark from a thousand feet and misses me at close range. How? Why?"

"You're thinking he missed on purpose."

AJ set his elbow on the desk and grasped his chin with his thumb and forefinger. "I kind of think so. Shit, I can't for the life of me think why. I was so close to nailing the son-of-a-bitch."

"But you didn't, plus he knew there was a car was coming for him. Maybe he only wanted to hold you off."

"Why? I could've got the license plate, his accomplice's description. Damn it, he's killed many times. Why not once more? Why not me?"

"Having some survivor guilt?"

"Oh, hell no. I'm happy to still be standing. It's the 'why' part which is baffling me."

"Well, you got me," Connie said. She looked down at her watch. "Look, it's three o'clock and my stomach's rumbling. Want to go get a bite to eat?"

PREDATORS AND PREY

139

"No thanks. I have other plans. Calling the meeting down here was really quite fortunate for me."

"Oh yeah? Why?"

AJ told Connie things he didn't bring up at the meeting. He explained how he stopped into Corbett's and saw a picture of the owner on the wall, recognizing Corbett as the man he had been speaking to right after Howell's murder. How he was unable to tell the FBI without being accused of withholding information regarding a crime. How he needed a good excuse to visit the restaurant again, before going to the Feds with his suspicions.

Connie whistled after he was done. "God damn it, AJ. That's quite the pile of shit you're sitting on. And you're right, the Feds would have your ass if they ever found out."

"It's the reason I'm heading over there now for supper. Now I have the excuse to be there."

"I'll join you."

"No, you can't. If you and I were going out to get a bite to eat, it would be here in Springhurst. I practically drive through Lansdowne on the way home and, you know, I was famished when I drove by."

"Okay. Let me know how it goes and hey if you need anything ..."

"I know," he broke in. "We've always been there for each other."

As planned, he pulled off the highway into Lansdowne and found a place to park a couple of blocks away. It was a much nicer day than the last time he was there, and he enjoyed the afternoon walk. The restaurant was about a quarter full when he entered, not bad for a weekday, he thought. He sat in a booth on the side which faced the door, so he enjoyed a clear view of the entire restaurant.

Like the time before, it was Chelsea who came over to serve him. She spoke with a sincere smile as she poured his coffee. "Well, afternoon, officer. It's nice to see you back. You probably don't remember, but my name is-"

"Chelsea. Of course I remember you," he replied. *Did she blush a little?*

"My goodness, did you really? Or did you read it off my name tag?"

"Never noticed you're wearing one."

"You're so sweet. Well, are you here for a meal or another piece of our bumbleberry pie? You loved it so much last time."

"Oh, the pie was unforgettable and I've got a big hunger on. In fact, don't even worry about the menu, I'll have what I had the last time, a-"

"Yes. A chicken club and, of course, pie for dessert," Chelsea interjected.

"Wow, I'm impressed. You'd make a good cop with a great memory like yours."

"No. I hear cops have even worse hours than we, plus they don't get tips." She spun on her heel and headed for the kitchen.

AJ watched as she walked away. She was fun to talk with and good looking, too. Probably grew up in Lansdowne and never left, he thought. A huge part of him wanted to ask her out, however, if it worked out that Corbett was the man they were looking for, it could complicate things. He turned away from watching Chelsea and saw Trent Corbett walk through the restaurant's main door.

Trent's day was going well, or so he thought. Once inside, he turned to ensure the door was closed properly behind him. When he turned, he was dumbfounded to discover the Elm Grove cop he managed to avoid the first time around, sitting five booths in front of him. He forced a smile and walked over.

"Evening, Officer. I'm Trent Corbett, the owner of this little place. It's nice to see one of our finest here. Have you been looked after?"

AJ stood and shook his hand. "Hi. Chief Avery Johnson of the Elm Grove police and yes, Chelsea's taking good care of me. It's actually my second time here. I stopped in last week and enjoyed it so much I just had to come back."

"Did you try our bumbleberry pie? We're well known for it."

"Sure did and I must say if I lived in this town, I'd pack on twenty pounds because I'd be having a slice every day."

"Great. I'm glad to hear it. So, what brings you here all the way down from Elm Grove?"

"I'm passing through on my way back from a meeting. I made sure to skip the snacks they set out, so I'd have lots of room when I stopped in here for dinner. They had some of my favourite's there too. That's how good of an impression your place left on me."

As much as Trent wanted to stay at the table to see if he could somehow find out what the officer knew, he felt it would be too unnatural to hang around. He couldn't come up with a reasonable excuse to remain. "Your food should arrive shortly, so I'll leave you alone and get back to work. I'm sure Chelsea will look after you quite well."

"Mr. Corbett, if it's not too much to ask, why don't you join me for a bit? You might be the owner, but I'll still buy you a coffee. After all, you do have to make a living."

"Nonsense. I'd be happy to join you. Don't worry about the coffee," Trent answered as he slid into the booth across from him. He smiled and added, "As a businessman, I can write it off."

Chelsea arrived and set the plate of food down in front of AJ. She expected Trent to get up and leave. Instead, she was surprised when he asked her for a coffee. With a little annoyance, she headed back to the coffee station.

She hoped to strike a conversation with the officer and hopefully give him her number or get his. With her boss hanging around, she could do either. She returned to the table, set the black coffee in front of Trent and with a

142   GORDON K. JONES

genuine smile, turned to the good looking cop, "If you need anything, anything at all, AJ, just holler and I'll make sure you're looked after."

"Will do, Chelsea."

"Oh and your pies on me today." She placed her hand on his shoulder as she spoke.

"No. No, Chelsea. It's on the house," Trent countered. "After all, we do appreciate the job all you officers do, no matter what town you're from."

"Thanks, Mr. Corbett. Thanks, Chelsea. Much appreciated."

Chelsea shot him a glowing smile and headed back to the kitchen. AJ smiled inwardly. *Oh, she likes me. If I asked her out, I know she'd say yes. Hell, I just can't. I shouldn't. Hey, what if she asks me out? Then she would be the instigator. Then ... oh hell, I don't know.*

Trent also caught Chelsea's smile. *Damn it, Chelsea. What're you doing?* He hoped his exterior didn't betray his irritation. *I don't even like him being in our town, let alone coming in here because he likes one of my staff. Oh Jesus! What if they start dating? Shit, I don't need this!*

AJ had a feeling their getting along rattled Trent somewhat and he hoped to keep him off balance. "I like her. Great personality. Good looking too."

"Yes. She's definitely an asset for us."

Both were quiet for a moment. AJ felt Trent's uneasiness. "Say, weren't you the guy I was going to give a parking ticket to a few weeks ago up in Elm Grove?"

"Excuse me?"

"Yeah. You must remember. It was the same day Charles Howell was murdered. I was about to write you up a ticket but you arrived back at your car just in the nick of time."

"Oh yeah ... Geez, I had forgotten all about that. Yeah, that was me. Sorry. I didn't recognize you."

AJ's gaze never moved from Trent's face as he spoke. "Well, as much as we're trained in facial recognition, for me, it's always been in the eyes. There's something about a person's eyes I can never forget. I can't say how, but if I see a person's eyes once, only once, I can pick them out years later. It's always been like that, ever since I was a kid. A person's eyes are as valuable to me as his fingerprints. It's how I recognized you."

Trent sipped on his coffee as the chief spoke. Although AJ's tone was friendly and unthreatening, Trent felt there was something more to it. "Hmm, interesting."

"You know, sometimes it feels more like a power. I've met people before, only for a moment or two, and then recognized them years later, only by their eyes. It's uncanny," AJ said in the same friendly tone as before. His voice became a little lower and slightly more serious. "So, tell me, what were you doing in Elm Grove that day?"

Trent wasn't entirely unprepared for the question. "Scouting mission. I got it in my head to maybe expand. Figured I could open up a few places in small towns where there was little competition. Maybe eventually become statewide. Thought I'd start by looking around in Elm Grove. Not too far away. Not too close to Lansdowne. Perfect really for my first satellite store.

"The problem, however, was there were already two places in Elm Grove. Both locally owned. I started thinking about how I'd feel if an out-of-towner moved in to take away my business. And would the community accept an outsider coming in? Things I didn't think of before. So, I gave up on the idea and was about to head home when I ran into you."

AJ took a bite of his sandwich. Either Corbett's explanation was too long or too polished. He didn't know which, however, something didn't sound right to him. It also came out too quick. "Sounds reasonable. Locals protect their own, unless it's a big box store which moves in. They slash their prices as they can afford the losses. Then everyone goes running to them instead of where they used to shop until the all the small businesses are closed up and

144 GORDON K. JONES

the business core looks like a ghost town ... Um, sorry for the rant. I've seen it happen too often."

"No problem. I agree with you."

"I imagine when you run a place like this, you over-hear people talking. You know, about things we, the police, wouldn't. Have you heard any whisperings around about the shootings we've been experiencing? Even a rumour. It's surprising where rumours might lead."

"Does this mean you don't have any leads or suspects?"

AJ leaned in closer in an effort to invade Corbett's space. His voice lowered and again, took on more of a serious tone. "Oh, we do. Nothing I can disclose. Every little thing helps, though. And I thought since we're chatting ..."

"I'm sorry. Nothing comes to mind. I wish I did," Trent replied, leaning away from AJ so he rested against the back of his seat. He wished there was something he could say which would send the cop off in the wrong direction. Nothing came to him except the desire to escape the close-ness of AJ inside that booth. "I'm sorry. I need to get back to work and your meals getting cold. It was nice meeting you. I hope you stop in again. Best of luck to you."

"Thanks. Nice meeting you too, Mr. Corbett. Please keep your eyes and ears open for me and if you do hear anything, anything at all, let me know," AJ took his card from his pocket and handed it to him.

Although he felt he couldn't get away from the table fast enough, Trent concentrated on crossing the floor at his normal pace. Along the way, he saw Chelsea, with a wide smile, cutting an extra-large piece of pie that he knew would be going to the Chief's table. He reached his office, closed the door behind him, and leaned back against it, gasping for air. Once he calmed down, he settled into the chair at his desk.

After absentmindedly staring at his laptop's dark screen for a long while, he left his office and took a quick

PREDATORS AND PREY

look around the restaurant. He saw Chelsea cleaning the Chief's now empty booth. His shoulders relaxed, and he smiled a weary smile. He headed to count the till and to move most of the funds to the safe. As he turned to head back to his office, Chelsea came up to him after depositing the dirty dishes in the racks.

"Hope you didn't mind me cutting the officer such a large piece of pie? He loved it the last time he was here."

"Of course not. I promised him a slice on the house. The size you gave him was a double, so make sure you pay for one of them."

There was a silence before a grin broke out on Trent's face. Chelsea hit him in the shoulder, "Damn. You almost had me going there."

"Hey, I'm a big fan of the law. I can't afford to comp a whole meal but dessert, sure."

"He was quite interested in that old picture you have by the front door The one with the news article of our opening. Asked me a whole lot of questions about it."

Shit, thought Trent, before he replied, "Really? Well, that's good. It means he likes the place. Hopefully he'll send some of his police friends our way."

"His empty plates tell me he likes this place a lot," she beamed. "He seems to have taken a liking to me too."

Trent gave her a questioning look. "Oh yeah?"

"Yeah. Before he left, we were talking, and he asked me out. Told me it would be to someplace nice." What she didn't say was that it was her who gave him her number and when she did, he said, "I could wait and call, but here's a better idea. How about supper this coming Sunday?" She felt Trent may not appreciate his staff hitting on customers. Better to have it sound like it went the other way.

"Really?"

"Yes. And of course, I said yes. He's good looking, funny and charming. I can't wait. It's been a long time since I've been on a date. Sunday can't come fast enough."

146 GORDON K. JONES

Trent placed a hand on her arm and forced a smile, "That's great. Good for you!"

"Then, before he left, he told me how he loved my eyes. In all my life I've never been complimented on my eyes, but there he was. Telling me how beautiful my green eyes are. I think I blushed. Hope I didn't, but I'm pretty damn sure I did."

After she left to serve another customer, Trent took the cash he held back to his office. He closed the door and dropped the loose bills on his desk. "Eyes! What's with this fucking cop and eyes? 'Oh, I can remember a person's eyes for years.' The bastard's fishing, trying to throw me for a loop. Get me to say something I shouldn't. Shit. Maybe I should've killed the son-of-a-bitch when I had the chance."

AJ climbed in his car, feeling his visit couldn't have gone any better than it did. Not only did he manage to plant some seeds of unrest in Corbett's head, seeds which could grow and force him into a big mistake, but he also came away with a supper date. He certainly felt there was chemistry between the two of them.

Oh yes. It was a great visit.

He pulled out his cell phone and gave Connie a call. There was no hello, no small talk when she answered. Only AJ speaking rapidly. "It's him. God damn it. I knew it was him. The guy I was talking to the day of the murder. Hell, I even got him to admit it was him I was talking to. Now that I've seen him up close, I know he's the guy I shot it out with. Something in the way he moves. I can't put my finger on it but, damn it all, I know it's him."

"So?"

"So now I need evidence. Solid evidence. Can't make an arrest merely because he was in the area of a murder and my gut feelings. It's enough, though, to start going at him hard."

Chapter 25

Trent was not in a pleasant mood when he arrived home. He shut the side door hard after coming through, kicked off his shoes and stomped up the stairs to the kitchen.

"Great, you're home. There's something interesting on TV which ..." She paused for a moment when she saw the look on Trent's face. "Hey! What's up? You look pissed!"

"Let me ask you. Can you recognize a person just by their eyes?" Trent asked, his voice slightly raised. He held one hand over his face and the other over his forehead to demonstrate. "If this was all you saw of me, could you pick me out?"

"Trent, what the hell are you going on about?"

"Well, there's a chance I might have been made."

"Made? What do you mean? What happened?"

"That cop was back in the restaurant today. You know, the same guy from Elm Grove who was there before. We talked. It seemed every word out of his mouth was said to throw me off. He went on and on about how he could pick any person he's met in the past just by their eyes. Damn, I think he suspects."

"You already had a great reason prepared as to why you were there that day. Did he ask you why? Did you use it?"

Trent nodded.

"So why are you so worried?"

"He could've seen my eyes when we were having it out in that backyard."

"Come on Trent. You're being paranoid. You said you were a fair distance away from him, plus the man's being shot at. He's too worried about being killed to have any time to spend gazing into those lovely peepers of yours."

"Yeah, you may be right. Shit, that conversation, though. He was digging, kept chipping away at me, trying to find a crack."

"Sit down for a moment," Maya said, pulling out a kitchen chair for him. She took a bottle from the cupboard and fixed them both a stiff rum and coke. "So ... did you say anything you think you shouldn't have? How'd 'you think you came off with him?"

Trent took a big sip and savoured its flavourful bite while he ran the conversation with the cop through his mind before answering, "Ya, I think I did okay. Held my own. There's nothing I said which would give him any reason to suspect me."

"Good. Then stop worrying. He has nothing to follow up on. Nothing to report to the Feds who we are the ones we have to worry about now. Of course, if he does tell them, you'll know it as they'll want to talk to you right away and you handle it the same way you did today. Besides, it's probably the last you'll see of that cop."

"No it won't be!"

"What? Why?"

"Because Chelsea's all hot on him and they're going on a date Sunday night. If this thing works out, he'll be around town a lot. Like I fucking need that!"

"Okay. Okay, let's think for a moment," Maya said as she sat down kitty corner to him at the table, "I guess

PREDATORS AND PREY 149

there's nothing you can do to screw up their little romance before it gets started."

"No, not a thing. I could screw around with her shifts, but it might raise the cop's suspicions of me and I don't need that. Remember what we discussed. Nothing can be different in our lives. We carry on like we always have and nobody will be the wiser. And besides, we're closed Sundays. Shit, what if by talking to Chelsea he becomes aware I'm away from the restaurant every time a hit's made?"

Maya drained her glass while they both sat in silence and pondered the latest developments. "We were going to take out Simpson in Springhurst next week. Maybe we should maybe lie low for a month or so."

"No, I don't think so. Doing nothing might raise his suspicions."

"Yeah, you're right. Damn, what to do ... how about some travelling, a mini holiday so we can do something in another state?"

"Good idea. Problem is, I always let the staff know when I travel in case they need to get hold of me and now this cop has ears on us."

"Maybe we could deflect. Say we're going somewhere and head somewhere else."

"If that cop's watching me and I'm away, he'll be sure to check for any hunter murders while we're gone and report it to the Feds."

"You know, we're not going to solve anything tonight. How about I fix us up another drink and we go watch some TV? There's a show which came on as you got home. We might find it interesting."

"What's it about?"

"A news network is hosting a live debate about the ethics of trophy hunting and whether it should be banned outright. We've missed about twenty minutes of it so far."

"Sounds good."

Trent grabbed some ice from the freezer while Maya mixed the drinks before they retired to the living room and

150 GORDON K. JONES

flipped on the TV. They discovered the discussion they tuned in to had become quite heated.

"Would you like it if somebody was shooting your cat or dog purely for the pleasure of killing," hollered a man on the right of the screen.

Before the entire sentence was out of his mouth, a debater from the other side jumped up and began shaking a pointed finger at the man as he attempted to yell over him. *"That's different. They're domestic animals and well looked after, thank you. Probably better than many of you self righteous assholes look after your own!"*

"Okay everyone. Let me interrupt here," interjected the immaculately dressed blonde hostess as she held up both her hands in an effort to stop everyone from talking. *"The discussion has become a little out of control, and I need to restore some order before we continue. I want to warn you again this is a live show and to watch your language."*

Trent laughed, "Ha! I love it! No way she's keeping control of this group. Look at them. They're all steaming, ready to explode."

The camera zoomed in on the hostess, who took a moment to look down and read from her notes. *"African nations are concerned as the Predators Predator murders have severely cut down on their tourism. They claim the drop in the hunting trade is affecting their economies. As a result, safari money is being taken away from villages who need it for food, fresh water and other necessities. Would the pro side like to comment first?"*

A large, stout man stood up from his seat and made his way to the dais, *"Yes, thank you. The cutback on game hunters travelling to Africa and spending money has caused enough concern that a contingent made up of representatives from hunting nations on the African continent has arrived here to discuss the situation with our government. Look, what we do as hunters is perfectly legal. We cull herds according to each country's standards so the animals don't become overcrowded and starve."*

PREDATORS AND PREY   151

A chorus of loud outrage erupted from the other side with the statement, which almost drowned him out, causing the speaker to raise his voice until he too was shouting. *"We pump millions into their economies. A few years ago, it was estimated at about two hundred million. This is money those governments need for infrastructure. Money the people need to help their villages to survive and prosper.*

The protest of his statements grew louder, so the man's shouts could barely be made out. *"We're not doing anything wrong here. Nothing illegal. Yet it seems we have to sneak around like criminals to do it."*

A woman from the other side stepped forward and addressed the man in a firm tone. *"Let me say how you're wrong, so wrong with your facts. First of all, the two hundred million spent on hunting is only a drop in the bucket compared to the amount of money the non-murdering tourist industry brings to the continent. Also, almost none of the hunters' money actually makes it to the communities where the hunting is taking place. It's the government and hunting companies who keep the money. It's a fact. Look it up!*

"As for your bullshit statement regarding culling the herd-"

"Might I warn you about language again," the moderator interjected in a raised voice, which was now the volume everybody on stage was using.

"Sorry," apologized the woman before continuing, *"As for your bullshit statement regarding culling. Sorry for my use of language. It's the only way to describe it. Bullshit. Your arguments say only older animals are killed. That's a bunch of crap as studies have shown there are only around twenty-five to thirty-five thousand wild lions left in Africa and hunters are reducing their total numbers by up to three percent per year. This is on top of the poaching which goes on. You're driving them to extinction and nobody over there is willing to protect them from you!"*

Another man stepped up to the pro side dais to speak and pushed the first man aside. The stout man stood

152 GORDON K. JONES

to one side, never returning to his seat, "*So does this mean you believe this Predators Predator is not a psycho but killing people in the name of conservation?*"

"*I believe that for whatever reason he's doing what he's doing, the end result is he's protecting those animals.*"

"*You condone what he's doing?*" yelled the stout man at the dais.

"*Doesn't feel good to be hunted, does it?*"

"*Fuck you!*"

With that, two men and a woman stormed down from their seats on the pro hunting side. Reaching the stage they rushed across it towards the woman standing on the anti-hunting dais which caused every man and woman on the anti-hunting side to charge to her defence. Punches were thrown. One man smashed a chair over a hunter's head sending him crashing to the floor bleeding profusely.

Trent and Maya laughed at all the chaos on the screen.

Security personnel ran onto the stage in an attempt to break up the fights. Instantly, they were overwhelmed when members of the audience stormed the stage. One camera turned from the stage to the audience, where it showed a number of arguments and fights taking place in the seats. Another camera angle showed the moderator with blood trickling from her forehead, being led offstage by a burly security guard.

Then the screen went dark and a few seconds later came back with the picture switched over to the regular network news studio. A man and a woman sat behind a news desk, obviously not ready for camera time. "*Oh shit!*" the man uttered as he dropped his earpiece onto the desk. The camera quickly focused on the female broadcaster.

"*I'm sorry. The network has decided to cut away and not show any more of the debate. We will provide you with updates from the scene when we receive them, but first, we'll take a break.*"

PREDATORS AND PREY

Maya turned off the TV and grabbed onto Trent, "Oh my God, just think, everything we watched. It was all because of you. You, Trent, you! It's what you wanted. You've lit a fuse in people all over the country. Got them all fired up and passionate about this. Christ, delegates are flying in from Africa because of you.

"That's how much of an effect you have on big game hunting. You've done such a great job. People aren't going over to hunt and it's hurting their economy. Nobody else has could ever have been able to do what you've done."

Trent stood up and began to nervously pace, "I know. We can't stop or take a break because of one cop. Gotta keep this momentum going! I'm not setting my gun down. Nope. No way. We're staying on schedule for our next one."

Maya gave him a squeeze. Only committing the actual murder was more exciting to her than planning one, "I'm with you honey."

Chapter 26

AJ came through the precinct's door, hung his jacket on the coat tree beside his desk, then skillfully flipped his hat on top of it. It was a successful afternoon. He had identified a major suspect in the Predator's Predator murders and done so in a way to ward off any way he or his staff could be accused of withholding evidence. In the process, he also managed to get a date with a vibrant, good looking woman. Yes, so far it was an excellent day.

He wore a satisfied grin as he took a seat behind his desk before Julie motioned to him from her chair at dispatch to come over. She put a finger over her lips not to ask why. He swung around in his chair and went to see what she wanted.

"I'll ask later how it went," she said to him in a low voice. "Right now, there's somebody in the meeting room waiting for you."

"Oh yeah. Who?"

"That FBI agent, Johnson. He showed up about ten minutes ago and asked to see you. Then he said he wanted some privacy and didn't want to be disturbed by anyone except you. I don't like him."

"Yeah, me neither. I just saw him this morning. I guess he never said what he wanted."

Julie shook her head. AJ sighed. He walked over to the meeting room door, knocked, and entered. The agent held a phone away from his ear. AJ took pleasure at how the agent looked so annoyed with his entrance.

Johnson held up a finger, then put the phone back to his ear. "I'll have to call you back." He set the phone face down on the table without a goodbye. "That was an important confidential call. You don't wait for permission to enter?"

"Not when it's in my station. I did knock to let you know I was coming in."

"Your girl out there-"

"Girl!"

"Sorry. I apologize. A female member of your staff-"

"You mean Officer. Have some respect. She's not a receptionist. Not a secretary. She's an officer and is damn good at her job." *Christ, this guy can get under my skin fast!*

"Sorry. You're right. I apologize." AJ doubted he meant it. "Oh, and so you know. I brought back the umbrella."

"Thanks. That's decent of you."

"Anyway. Your officer told me you hadn't arrived back yet from our meeting." Johnson smiled. "There were quite a few things I personally needed to tend to before coming here, and yet I still beat you. What took ya? Did you stop, do some shopping or something?"

"Wish I had the time," AJ answered with a false smile. "You see. Small town cops like us rarely go from 'A' to 'B' in a straight line. Too much ground to cover. Not that I have to explain myself to you, but I did a patrol around town before coming back to the office. All was quiet, you know, the way we like it around here."

"Sorry again. I complain about my workload, still, it couldn't be anything like keeping the peace in a town this size, twenty-four seven with such a small force."

"It has its challenges," AJ replied. He was trying to remain civil with Johnson and not let his dislike for him show. He closed the door before he spoke. "It's only been a few hours. What brings you here that a phone call couldn't cover?"

"After you left, I had a conference call with my superiors. It was suggested I come here so we could talk in person. I was going to wait till tomorrow but figured it best to get it out of the way now so I can get on with our investigation."

"Okay."

"We've found the drone we believe was used in the murder. Of course, it wasn't in one piece. We found it smashed against a tree. The serial numbers were removed so we can't trace it through the FAA. I doubt it would have been registered with them, anyway. We sent it off to our labs hoping to get maybe a partial print or some DNA. I doubt we'll find either. From what I've seen, he's too good for that."

"Well, thanks for letting me know. You couldn't have driven all this way just to tell me."

"You're right," the agent agreed. "First off, we want to thank you for all your input today. Your clear, concise account of the murder and the exchange of shots with the suspect were helpful. It's too bad you didn't get a better look at the suspect. We all understand how hard it is when you're under fire."

AJ bit his tongue. He wondered where the agent was going with this and at the moment felt a great need to keep his meeting with the number one suspect to himself. Depending on how the conversation went, he figured it would be easy enough to bring up before this session was over.

The agent continued, "My people feel you might be too, oh how should I put it, too zealous about wanting to catch this guy. Having shot it out with him would put this on a personal level with you. They also believe if you or your people were to go off with your own investigation, you may get in our way. I was asked to come here to confirm you'll be hands off on this case and let us handle this."

"You remember that two of the murders took place in my town."

"And we're going to bring whoever did this to justice. Look, we have as many people on this as you have on your entire force, plus a budget and equipment too big for your guys to even dream of. We're not asking for the Elm Grove PD to stay out of this, we're insisting. We do ask if you do hear or see anything of interest, you let us know. Other than that, you stay away."

"Sure will, Agent Johnson. No need to worry about us hick cops messing up your case."

"Look, officer. I know you don't like me. Many don't. It comes with the job, but I know you realize we're all after the same thing. You look after your town, we'll look after the murders and once this is over, I'll even buy you a drink." The agent stepped forward, shook AJ's hand, then headed to the door.

AJ followed the agent into the office area and took a seat at his desk. The agent grabbed his coat and headed around the corner to the door. "Till next time, Officer," he said, touching the brim of his hat to him before he left. AJ raised a couple of fingers in a half-hearted reply.

Julie stood up from her chair at dispatch, went over and leaned against AJ's desk, "Jeez, what happened in there? You look pissed."

"Bastard stinks of arrogance. Must be a job prerequisite. God, I hate people like him! He told me flat out the big shits want us locals to stay out of the way cause they're far more capable than we are about catching the Predator."

"So, tell me. I bet you stopped for lunch in Lansdowne."

"And you'd be right."

"Find anything good?"

"Oh yeah. The owner, Trent Corbett, well, he's definitely the guy I was talking to that day. Can't be entirely sure, though, if he's the one I shot it out with. I believe I managed to plant a seed in him which might force him into doing something to tip his hand. Something which might rush him, you know, have him make a mistake. One we can take advantage of. Really, I don't care if it's you, me or the Feds who end up getting him, I want this guy brought down."

"So why didn't you tell the agent about your lunch?"

"How do you know I didn't? You weren't there."

"Because I know you. I've known you for years. There's no way you would've told him."

"Yeah, you're right," he said with a smirk. "Now that we have a number one suspect, we can work together with Connie's people in Springhurst, plus the forces in Parkview Gardens and Northcote City to watch this guy. Together, we can nail this murdering asshole on our own. Those FBI fuckers think we're just a bunch of yokels down here. Well, we're going to show them we can get the damn job done and get it done without them."

Chapter 27

It was a sunny Friday afternoon. The air was still. Perfect shooting conditions. The place chosen to take the shot from was much closer than usual, so a good escape route was required.

Across the street from Spencer Maling's home in Parkview Gardens was a long park about a hundred feet wide, with a narrow stream running along the back of it. On the far side of the stream were bushes hiding the rickety wooden walls of a hut constructed by kids, imagining it to be a grandiose fortress or castle. For the moment, it was neither. Instead, it provided an excellent hiding place with great sightlines for an ambush.

As always, the key was planning and patience. Know when the target was due to arrive. Set up early but not too early to risk detection. Then sit and wait. It's where patience played such an important part. Once the deed was done, have a primary escape route and a backup one.

Maling usually arrived home from work around five thirty. Almost right on the half hour, the garage door began to open. Moments later, his Porsche pulled in the driveway and rolled straight into the garage.

160 GORDON K. JONES

Slowly a rifle barrel slipped between the gap of two boards of the makeshift fort, its sights set. The moment Maling stepped out of the car, a slight adjustment to the sights was made. As he closed the car door, a finger tensed against the trigger. Maling took a couple of steps to the wall, hit the door closer, then emerged from the garage. As soon as he did, a finger squeezed the trigger. Maling's body was blown backwards by the impact of a bullet slamming into his forehead above his left eye.

"Oh yeah! A head shot," Maya proudly muttered, even though she really wanted to shout it out as loud as she could. She pulled the smoking barrel back from between the slats and lowered Trent's rifle from her shoulder. Peaking through the opening, she watched Maling's sprawled resting on the ground against the rear bumper of his precious car disappear behind the closing door.

Although Maya had fired a rifle many times before, she was still surprised by the kick this one gave. It hurt like hell when she picked up the expended shell and she wondered if the rifle's recoil bruised her shoulder or worse. It was something she'd check later, as she needed to get going.

Before she left, she pinned the Facebook page to a wall, slid the rifle into its bag and dropped in the spent shell. Then she stopped and listened, surprised at how peaceful it seemed in the neighbourhood. It was as if nothing had happened. The crack of the rifle being fired, even with a silencer on it which never really silenced a shot, sent the birds into a hasty, noisy flight from the bushes around her. Immediately after, calm returned to the area. Only the sound of water rippling over rocks in the stream could be heard.

Hell, this makes getting away so much easier than I originally anticipated.

Carefully and quietly, she slipped along a footpath which ran through the thick trees to the road where she parked. She popped the trunk, tossed in the bag, then slid behind the wheel. With a huge smile, she took her time driving home.

PREDATORS AND PREY

Maya always loved reading about true murders. Helping Trent plan and secretly watch him execute one was a joy. Nothing, though, nothing could ever have the same ultimate thrill as being the one to pull the trigger. At the moment, she was euphoric! It was a day she would forever remember and cherish.

◆　◆　◆

The Friday supper rush was a little busier than usual at the restaurant, so Trent was out of his office on the floor helping. He was heading towards the counter with a load of dirty dishes, even though he was the owner, he wasn't too proud to assist with busboy duties, when he saw Chelsea standing, staring at the flat screen TV mounted on the wall. It was set to the twenty-four-hour news channel, and she seemed quite focused on it. It was unlike her to do so when the place was so busy.

"What's got your attention?" he asked as walked up to her from behind.

"Looks like that serial killer's at it again," she said, pointing to the screen.

"Really?" he replied, sounding more surprised than he realized he should have. Stopping beside her, he looked up. He wished the sound was turned on. On the screen were images of a crime scene. Flashing lights from police and ambulances reflected off the walls of a house, then the camera panned to the open garage. The caption underneath read; "*Predators Predator claims 8th victim.*"

"From what I saw, it looks to be a hunter down in Parkview Gardens who was killed," Chelsea commented. "One of those African hunters, you know, from that group which calls themselves the 10 or something."

"Wow! Have they flashed up what happened?" Trent said, attempting to sound casually interested, instead of confused and overwhelmed by the news.

162   GORDON K. JONES

"No, not yet. You know, I'm not sure how I feel about his guy. One part of me is cheering hard for him while another part can't condone murder," Chelsea replied, not taking her eyes off of the monitor. "I have no idea how I'll feel once he's caught. It's really strange."

Trent never took his eyes off the screen as he answered. "You're not the only one who's wrestling with the morals of this. It's quite the quandary. If they kill animals just for the sake of killing and we go out and kill them, aren't we worst by being judge and jury?"

"Maybe. Still, there's a big part of me which is cheering for him."

"Yeah, me too. I think I'll probably feel a little sad when they do get him (*damned right I will*) ... and you know they eventually will. (*Ha. No way in hell!*) Hopefully when all this is over, people will keep the pressure on and the government will have to act."

"I hope so."

Trent didn't want to keep up his acting. "Can you grab a couple of coffees for table 9. I have to do something in the office."

"Sure."

Chelsea headed to the counter while Trent dumped his load of dishes in the sink before making his way to his office. Once inside, he closed the door and opened his laptop. *Damn. Another copycat. At least this one didn't get themselves killed, but why in hell did he have to take out my next target,* he thought as he brought up the news channel to get their live feed.

"*Like the other murders, a note was found at the location from where the killer took their shot. Police are currently holding it as evidence, so we can't show it to you. We were told it was constructed like the others with a screen shot from a social media site. This one shows the victim holding up the head of a dead leopard he killed. A speech bubble coming from the animal reads; 'You bragged about bagging your 'Big Five'. Well, we have our Top 10 and you were on it!'*

"Son of a bitch. That's the message I made! No god damn way this is a copycat," Trent uttered under his breath in bewilderment. He could scarcely believe it. If it wasn't a copycat killing, then there was only one other person who could have done it.

Maya!

Chapter 28

Trent sat directly across the kitchen table from Maya and asked, "What in hell were you thinking? Jesus! You go and take my rifle, kill somebody and never think about maybe discussing it with me first?"

"I knew you'd say no."

"Fucking right I would've! We already talked about when our next kill would be. I said we needed to stick with your approach. Your approach! Plan well and never rush into anything. You sat there and agreed with me."

"Look..." Maya tried to interject.

"No, you look. We agreed how we were going to go about this, but then you get up this morning and say to yourself, 'Hey, I think it's my turn'. So you grab my gun and my note and go out with some half-assed plan, never thinking once of the consequences."

"Consequences! Like What?"

"What if you missed?"

"I didn't, though, did I? The bastard was dead the moment my slug hit him."

"What if you'd been seen? Shit, what if you'd been caught?"

PREDATORS AND PREY

"The place I chose was well hidden. So was the trail back to the car. The car was in an out of the way spot and I had an excellent primary and secondary escape route laid out. You know, I may not have had a great amount of time to plan, but I did my homework damn well and it went perfectly. As for being caught, if I was, then you'd be totally off the hook. I would've taken the fall for all of them."

Trent leaned across the table. "Was there anything you did which might suggest this job wasn't done by me?"

"Nothing. I made sure everything looked like it was done by your alias. Hey, I guess it's now our alias." She laughed a little. He didn't. "Even though I used my car, it's the same colour and similar in style as yours. Why?"

"I don't want this going down as a copycat killing. If it was, the trail might lead back to you. I wouldn't want that. I want you free of any blame. If, somehow, this all goes to hell, I want to be the one to be caught. I want to go down for all of them. I want them to take me alive. Think of the speeches I could make, the people I could rile up."

He took a breath and felt himself settle down a little. "After all, this was my idea and as much as you've helped me, should shit happen, I want you to be able to get on with your life and leave this behind. I want them to believe you never knew this side of me."

Maya reached over and placed her hand on his, "That's sweet. You are a man of honour Trent Corbett. Oh and don't worry. When they get the bullet back from ballistics, it'll prove it was fired by your weapon, which is why I used it."

Trent nodded and gave her hand a squeeze. He was feeling better and his voice became much softer. "So, tell me. What made you do it?"

"A couple of things. First off, since you found out I knew about you, I felt you never really fully trusted me. I was wondering what I could do to make you believe you could I was one-hundred percent with you. Doing what I did should end any doubts you had of me.

"Secondly, when you told me about that cop being in your place, it got me to thinking. You're worried he suspects you, which is bad enough. What if the date he has with your waitress goes well and he keeps on seeing her? He'll have somebody, unknowingly perhaps, on the inside ... Hell, maybe not so unknowingly? Anyway, by talking about her work life, it might allow him to match your time away from the restaurant with the shootings.

"I thought I'd throw a monkey wrench into that and the best way, I figured, was to drop one on a day you were working. Lots of witnesses for your alibi. I knew if I told you, you'd say no. I've fired a rifle before and was pretty good at it."

"You told me it was a long time ago. You know it's not like riding a bike and Christ, why a headshot?"

She put a hand to her mouth, trying to hide her grin. "Actually, I was aiming for his chest. The gun kicked harder than I expected."

"Oh shit."

"Not to worry. It still looks like a shot only a pro could make. When I scouted the place, I found this nice little fort to take the shot. Admittedly, it was a lot closer than the distance you shoot from, about thirty-five yards or so, but I was confident I wouldn't miss from there. That was my biggest fear. The rest went off perfectly, well, except for my shoulder. It hurts like hell!"

"You didn't have the stock pressed firmly against it, so when you pulled the trigger, the recoil kicked back into your shoulder. Come here. Let me have a look," he said as he stood.

Maya came around the table, unbuttoned her blouse and sat in his lap.

"I love the blue bra. The colour looks fabulous on you." He gently pulled the fabric of her blouse and bra strap from her shoulders to her elbow, which pinned her upper arms against her sides.

PREDATORS AND PREY

"Didn't know you liked bondage," she commented with a wicked smile. His only answer was a light kiss on her lips before looking down and gently touching the injured area. She jumped at his touch.

"Are you okay?" he asked, quite concerned. She nodded.

He took a closer look. Her shoulder was a multitude of colours, black, blue, plus a little yellow where the gun stock struck her. He gingerly ran a finger over the area, which caused her to shiver. "Does it hurt when I do that?"

"A little. Funny, it feels hot and cold at the same time."

Again he touched the middle lightly, which caused her to suck in her breath. There was one more thing he needed to do. He gently drew her blouse up till it was back in place, "Lift up your arm and hold it straight out to the side." She did it with little difficulty or pain. "Now rotate it up over your head as high as it can go." Even though it was a little more painful, she managed to do it.

"You're just bruised. Thankfully, there seems to be no damage to your rotator cuff. It'll need some rest, gentle stretching, ice and, of course, some love." He lifted her blouse carefully away and gently kissed the middle of the bruised area. "There. That should make it better."

He straightened up. "Tell me, what was it like for you? How did it feel deep down inside to pull the trigger, ending another human's life?"

"Orgasmic!" came her quick answer. "It was something I've always wanted to do but wondered if I could ever pull the trigger. I wondered if I could watch a man die because of me. I wondered how it would make me feel. Now I know. And it feels so good knowing he deserved it."

"Interesting. While in the army, I remember feeling empty after every kill, but when I began this, my feelings changed. I don't feel the same intensity about it as you did, although I do admit I get satisfaction from it. Maybe it's because I know these people aren't innocent. They're dying for good reason and I'm the one making it happen."

"Do you think I'm evil for wanting to kill?"

"No," he said, happy he answered quickly. *Oh shit. Is this going to become a problem?*

He knew he had to justify his answer. "In the army, especially as a sniper, you're trained to kill and feel justified doing it, as it's for your country and to protect your people. You're trained. It's a job and no more. Still, when I remember back to my first time, I felt much the same way as you did," he lied.

Before he could continue, she grabbed his head and crushed her lips hungrily against his. Her adrenalin and hormones were running through her hotter than they had ever been in the past. She reached to unbutton his shirt, but a bolt of pain shot through her shoulder. Trent winced at her sudden agony as she stepped back, pressing her hand against the injury. He saw her eyes well up.

"Maybe we should wait a night or two," he softly suggested. She dropped her head and nodded, her disappointment showing. He stepped forward and guided her into his arms, being careful not to press against the bruise.

Despite the throbbing, that night Maya enjoyed the best sleep she'd had for months.

Chapter 29

Discussing a local murder was not how AJ enjoyed starting his day. Usually, Saturday mornings consisted of having a coffee at his desk, then around seven thirty doing a foot patrol around town. It was a time of day when, except for the odd car, the only sounds which could be heard were birds, chirping and singing. He enjoyed the freshness of the morning air and the peace about him. Few people were ever out, and those who were, he knew. He found Saturday mornings therapeutic.

On this particular early Saturday morning, though, he was stuck inside at his desk, staring at two faces on his laptop. One was his good friend Connie, lieutenant of the Springhurst police and the other was Eric Green, lieutenant in charge of the Parkview Gardens PD. The three were discussing Spencer Maling's murder.

AJ flipped through the five photos from the emails he received from Eric. One was a long shot of the river and Maling's house in the same frame. Two were long shots of the garage and Maling's dead corpse and the others were of the little fort where the shot originated.

170 GORDON K. JONES

"What the ..." AJ exclaimed as he closed the screen they were on. "These are all useless! There's no close ups of the body or shelter."

"Nope," Eric answered with a sigh. "The Feds wouldn't let me get anywhere close. Had to rely on what they gave me. Not a damned bit of co-operation from them! They treated everybody around them like shit. Even our mayor!"

"Yeah, I've already dealt with them a couple of times. It's their show and the bastards never tire of demonstrating their perceived superiority over us."

A sound came from behind Eric, who held up a finger to whoever it was to give him another second, "Hey. The Feds might think this is their show, but it's our citizens who are being murdered. I still have one more potential target he'll be gunning for sooner or later. Samantha Edgars. Connie, I realize there are three up your way."

"Don't I know it," agreed Connie. "Damn, there might even be others we're unaware of."

"Okay. Let's all stay in touch. I'm outta here. We've got a three-car accident out by the highway," Eric said and signed off.

AJ and Connie stayed on. Connie was the first to speak, "So what do you think? Why was the Predator so close for this shot? All the others were done from a thousand feet or so."

"I don't know. Maybe it was the only place he could find to take a clear shot from. We need to get a good look at the area ourselves or we'll never be able to figure it out."

"Yeah, but Eric said the Feds wouldn't let him get anywhere close."

"Well, the Feds must have everything they need from the scene by now, so they won't have anyone posted. We should be able to get in for a closer look. See you there in an hour then?"

"You bet!

PREDATORS AND PREY
171

Connie called Eric to let them know their plan and an hour later, the three stood in the middle of a scenic country bridge which crossed a little creek. They stood silently for a moment. Their eyes swept the area on the lookout for anything unusual, anything which seemed out of place.

"Hey, isn't that the kid's fort the killer took the shot from?" asked AJ pointing to it as he leaned on the field stone wall which ran along each side of the century old arched bridge.

"That's the one," replied Eric.

"It doesn't fit his M.O, "AJ said, straightening up. Like a kid, he wished the three of them could sit on the wall, dangle their feet and talk about things. As they were all the head of law enforcement for their particular towns, the image, if caught on camera, wouldn't be flattering. "He loves long distance shots, and he's extremely accurate with them. It keeps him out of any potential trouble and makes it easy for a quiet escape. I'm honestly not comfortable with how close he was for this one."

"Could it be there was no other place he could get a clean shot from?" asked Connie.

AJ lowered the brim of his hat and placed his hand to his forehead to shield his eyes from the sun. He scanned from the Maling house to the surrounding area. "No, I already can see a couple of potential places he could have used."

"Wait. Are you suggesting this could be somebody else's work?"

"I'm not about to rule it out."

Eric was looking off of the bridge towards the little fort, "Why don't we go over and check it out. I'll follow the trail the killer likely took back to the road and you two take a wider route. The Feds are good. Still, they might have missed something."

They nodded in agreement. As the three reached the end of the short bridge, a black SUV pulled up and stopped.

Three men got out. Agent Johnson was one of them. He signalled the others towards the fort before he approached the three local officers. He slipped off his sunglasses before he spoke. "I see you couldn't stay away."

It was Eric who replied. His voice was firm and unwavering, "No, I couldn't. You see, the victim, Mr. Maling, lived in my jurisdiction and it's me, not you, who'll have to answer all his family's questions. I called in Chiefs Stapleton and Johnson from their districts to assist me. Unlike the FBI, we don't operate in a vacuum here. We assist one another."

Agent Johnson looked down and kicked a small pebble off the road with the side of his foot. "I think you have the wrong impression of what we're doing here."

"Pray tell. And what might that be?" asked AJ.

"We're here to capture or stop in any way possible this serial killer. I want to keep you guys out of it for a couple of reasons. The first is, we've run into local sheriffs before who've jeopardized our investigation. Now I don't think that would happen in this instance. You all seem like excellent officers-"

"Bullshit!" AJ said, covering his mouth with a fake sneeze. The agent flashed him a dirty look.

"You know, I really don't give a rat's ass what you think of me," Agent Johnson said with a little exasperation before he continued. "When we're called in on a case like this, we're aware of the pressures of performing the day-to-day duties of your jobs without the extra burden of having to be on top of an investigation of a string of high profile murders."

"If that's the case, why didn't you say so to begin with?" asked AJ.

"The first time you and I first met was right after you came away from a firefight with the suspect. Not the best way to ease into things. I admit I didn't handle our conversations well then or after that."

PREDATORS AND PREY 173

Connie jumped in, "Let's talk about this particular murder. The distance from the shooter to his target was much shorter than he usually takes. Think this could be a copycat?"

"I did until ballistics came back with their report an hour ago. The bullet has the same rifling on it as the others. This shot definitely came from the serial killer's weapon."

"Hmm, interesting," AJ said as he ran the news through his mind, "The body wasn't discovered right away so the shooter was able to make a quiet getaway. I gather there were no witnesses to the murder. Did anybody notice a vehicle parked around here which could've been used by the killer when he left?"

"Yeah. A neighbour noticed a grey or silver Chev parked about ten yards away from where I'm parked right now, down at the opening of the trail which runs through the trees along the riverbank."

Same rifle. Same coloured car. Damn, it was him,' AJ thought. "One more question. Why do you think the killer has murdered only one travel agent?"

"That's an easy one. My men and I have canvassed all the agencies in the area and they've all been honest with us. They're too scared for their own and their family's lives to sell any more hunting safaris. It was such a miniscule part of their business, so it was easy for them to give up. The Predator took out one, and it was all he needed. Now, guys, if you'll excuse me, I've got some work to do."

The agent slid his sunglasses over his eyes, touched the brim of his cap, and headed to join the other agents, leaving the three standing on the bridge.

"He was such a dick last night. I can't believe how straight forward he was with us right now," commented Eric.

"That's because he's got nothing. Just like the rest of us. After playing the big shit since he got here, he can't come out and ask us for help. He's hoping we have something to give him. He needs to solve this himself so he looks good to his people and can't have us locals getting it done instead. As co-operative as he sounded, he's running a little scared."

♦ ♦ ♦

"I know you probably don't want to talk about work," Chelsea said as AJ drove her home after their dinner date.

Although she felt an overwhelming need to know, she concentrated on not to asking about the latest murder during their meal. It worked out well, as she really enjoyed getting to know him instead. He was a gentleman with a great sense of humour and seemed to have as much of a good time with her as she did with him. Still, it was hard not to ask.

"It's okay. Go ahead," AJ answered. He had an excellent idea what it would be about.

"The man who was shot in over in Parkview Gardens on Friday? They're saying it's the work of the Predators Predator again. Do you think it is?"

"I can't say too much about it except we're working with Springhurst and Parkview Gardens to get this thing solved," AJ answered. He didn't want to leave it there as he liked her and wanted to see her again, but needed to follow protocol.

"Trent and I saw it on the news at the restaurant right after it happened. It blew me away."

AJ was dumbfounded. He thought for sure Trent Corbett was his man. He was finally convinced it was Corbett who took down Maling. Then, in one sentence, his number one suspect owned an airtight alibi. He needed to try to probe deeper without sounding like a cop. "I guess it would. It's not your everyday news for sure. I chatted with Mr. Corbett when I ate there last time. Nice guy."

"Oh, he's a great guy. Wonderful to work for. You know it's always such a shock to hear about someone being murdered so close to where you live, especially since there have been so many others."

She lowered her head and giggled softly. He liked her giggle, "I thought Trent was going to drop the dishes he was carrying when he saw it. God, he looked so shocked and pale. I'm not sure how he reacted to the other murders, but this one seemed to get to him. I don't know, maybe he came to Lansdowne to get away from all the big city violence and now this. I know all these murders are making me nervous."

"You can rest easy. This killer has specific targets in mind and unless you're a big game hunter, you're safe. You're not one of those, are you?" he added with a smile.

"Of course not, "she answered with another giggle as they pulled up in front of her house.

AJ was struck by how it looked like a scene from a Norman Rockwell painting. Chelsea lived in a small, old two-story home with a hedge which ran between her and the neighbour's driveway, a well-tended garden against the house's front wall and a white picket fence running across the front of her property and down the side of the lawn.

They both opened their doors at the same time. As Chelsea reached to the floor for her purse, it gave AJ a chance to make it around the car so he was there when her feet touched the ground. He extended his hand to help her out.

"Such a gentleman," she remarked as she took his hand.

"Mom did her best to raise me right," he replied, smiling as he closed the door behind her. She took his hand as they strolled to the front door. He heard a dog barking inside.

"Briley, It's okay. Be quiet," she said through the door to her Labradoodle as they stepped onto the doorstep. She turned to him, never waiting for him to make the first move. She put her arms around him and kissed him fully on the lips.

"Hmmm. I thought you liked me?" he said seriously in a deadpan manner and took a short step back.

"I ... I do. Why? What's the matter?"

"In the old movies when the girl likes the boy, she lifts her leg when they kiss."

"Oh. Okay. Let's try it again."

AJ pulled her to him and pressed his lips against hers. He glanced down and saw her leg come up. "Guess I wasn't paying attention the first time," he whispered in her ear after their lips parted.

"I guess you weren't." She stepped back, pulled the keys from her purse, and opened the door. This usually was where she would say goodbye but found herself not wanting the night to end. "I think we've put on enough of a show for the neighbours. Do you want to come in?"

She didn't have to ask twice.

Chapter 30

Trent took a swig of beer from his bottle and placed it between his legs, never moving his eyes away from the TV. The national cable news network was broadcasting a press conference put on by the African tourist commission regarding the loss of revenue due to the dramatic downturn of hunters who were travelling to African nations to hunt big game.

He pointed at the TV as he spoke to Maya, who was at their desk doing some research on his laptop. "Are you listening to this? Look at these assholes! They're standing there so dignified, saying people in their countries are hurting and starving because hunters aren't going over there as much and spending money. What horseshit! They're pleading poor even though hunting revenue is less than one percent of their tourist dollar."

The speaker on the TV continued, "It's estimated revenue from hunting sources has dropped as much as a third since the Predator's Predator rampage began. The United States, despite all their technology, all their resources, are either unwilling or unable to stop this mass murderer."

"Honey," Maya said with a smirk, "He's saying you're a mass murderer. Others call you a serial killer. Which do you prefer?"

"Animal Welfare Protectionist."

"Ha! Love it," Maya said with a little laugh.

She became quiet and placed her concentration fully on the laptop. She scrolled down the screen and back up before she swung around in her chair and called to Trent. "Hey, turn that thing off and come over here. I think I've got something you'll be quite interested in."

Trent pulled up a chair beside her at the desk. "What do you have?"

"A little background first. I was searching various American hunting groups and found a Facebook group page, Trueheart Conservationist Team. It's a closed group available only to people who've been accepted and authorized by the group's administrator."

"So? What's so important about this group?"

"Trueheart Conservationist Team. TCT. Also the first letters of a group you're familiar with, the Tyndall County 10. Now, most groups have a banner picture on their page showing what they're all about. You'd think a conservation group would have a banner picture of trees, blue skies, trees, anything like that. This one has no banner picture at all."

"Okay. I see where you're going with this, but you have no access."

"Not necessarily. Some friends showed me how they hack their way into private Facebook groups. I never thought it would actually come in handy until now. I got in and you'll love what I found."

She spun the laptop so Trent could see the screen better. In front of him was a picture of the Tyndall County 10 in a group photo together, each holding their hunting rifles in front of an inground pool, probably taken in one of their back yards.

PREDATORS AND PREY

179

"Wow! Holy shit! They thought they could hide themselves, but they didn't know about one talented Maya Livingstone being on the hunt for them. Great find!"

"Thanks. And look at this post from Bart Edward. He's using his middle name, Bartholomew, as his first name and his first as his last. Seems our Ed Simpson thinks this makes him hard to find on Facebook."

"Ha! Nothing gets by you. I love it, "Trent said with a single clap. "Okay, let's see what he has to say. '*Off to Africa on the 16th to bag an elephant to complete my big five and finally be known as a true Big Game Hunter.*' Ha! Not if we get to him first!"

◆ ◆ ◆

It was rare for AJ to have a chance to be in Lansdowne on a workday. After taking a prisoner down to the state's prison, he decided while on the way back to stop in at Corbett's to see Chelsea and have some lunch. Not only would he have a few moments with her, but he found it to be the best place to eat in the state.

The restaurant was busy when he arrived, however, most of the customers, except for two tables, had eaten and left by the time he finished his three cheese grilled cheese sandwich and side salad. He thought he was full until Chelsea came up behind him and set a good size slice of bumbleberry pie in front of him. This time, she had added a large dollop of whipped cream on the side.

"Damn, I don't know if I have room for this," he declared.

"Really? Remember, I've seen you eat before, especially our pie," Chelsea replied as she slid into the seat across from him.

"I meant the whipped cream. I'll always have room for the bumbleberry," he said, which brought a soft laugh from her.

AJ dug out a piece with his spoon as, when it came to pie, there was no need for forks. He ran it through the whipped cream and slid it into his mouth. As always, it was as good as it looked and smelled. Chelsea smiled and pointed to the small splash of whipped cream which ended up on AJ's cheek. He grinned and wiped it away. "Wow! Great lunch, great dessert, plus I get to sit across from a fabulously beautiful woman. I knew stopping in here would work out for me."

"You know, AJ, if we didn't have customers around, I'd give you something else to sweeten your lips."

"Damn, too bad. I guess we'll have to wait till Saturday night then."

He looked up and saw Trent standing outside the front door talking with a slightly heavy-set woman with dark brown hair with purple and red streaks. Chelsea turned her head to see who he was looking at.

"You won't get in trouble sitting with me, will you?" he asked.

"Oh no. The only people here aren't in my section. He doesn't mind us having short visits as long as it doesn't get in the way of our job. Interesting that she's out there with him. We don't see much of her."

"Who?"

"The woman he's talking to. His girlfriend, Maya. He's been seeing her for a while, but she's only been here a couple of times. She seems nice. Funny, Trent never talks much about his home life and, well, we all thought he was married to this place and didn't have much of a life outside it. Then he met Maya, and it surprised the hell out of us. She's so different than the type of woman any of us thought he'd ever be with."

"Really? In what way?" AJ asked, trying hard not to stare at them.

"I don't know how old she is. She seems to have a younger, more energetic spirit than he does. Not only that, she's much cooler than he is. Her hair, the way she dresses,

PREDATORS AND PREY

her attitude. He's kind of a serious guy and she seems a lot more fun. She's not at all the kind of woman I pictured him being hooked up with."

"They say opposites attract. Maybe it's true."

Damn it! I wish there was a way I could get a picture, he thought as he spoke. *How in hell can I do it discreetly? Think! There must be a way.*

Sandra called out for Chelsea, so she excused herself, saying she'd be right back. As he watched her walk away, an idea came to him. Casually, he pulled out his phone. Pretending to tap in a number, he subtlety snapped off four quick pictures before he put the phone to his ear and said hello.

After half a minute, he said goodbye and slid the phone back into his pocket. Outside, he could see Trent give Maya's hands a squeeze before he headed inside and she walked off, out of sight. *"Damn, I wish there was a way for me to follow her. These pictures better turn out. Oh man, I've got so many bells ringing in my head about this. Hopefully, they will jar something useful out of this brain of mine.'*

Chelsea made a point of going to Trent when he came through the door. She knew there was no problem with her sitting with AJ but was smart enough to say something to him about it, instead of him asking.

"I hope you don't mind me taking a few minutes to sit with AJ. My section was clear and we're pretty empty."

"Sure, no problem at all," Trent confirmed. *Of course it's a fucking problem.*

"Oh, and just so you know, I'm not putting the pie on his tab. I'm paying for it on my own. He sure loves it."

Again, Trent pondered why AJ happened to be in town. Did AJ consider him a suspect or was he really here because his job had him passing through town? Could it be even as something as simple as he made up an excuse to come see Chelsea? "So, what brings your boyfriend to town today? Is it work or is he really, really missing you?"

182 GORDON K. JONES

"We've only seen each other three or four times. Too early for him to miss me, or for me to consider him my boyfriend. Besides, he said he was coming back from taking a prisoner down to the jail south of here and was hungry."

"Hungry, yes. Hungry to see you. He's a chief. He could've sent someone else to take the prisoner, but decided to do it himself. Why? So he could see you, of course. Don't sell yourself short, Chelsea. You're quite a catch."

"Oh, go on," Chelsea giggled and excused herself to head back over to see AJ, who was starting to slide from his booth.

That's it Trent. Keep up the friendly, supportive stuff so she has nothing to complain to her boyfriend cop about.

"I guess it's time for me to hit the road," he said to Chelsea, doing his best to hide his eagerness to leave. He was dying to upload the pictures he took. Who knows what they may discover about Trent's girlfriend?

"See you Saturday then," she responded with a smile.

"You bet! I'm looking forward to it," he replied with a smile as he reached out and gave her hands a squeeze. He was almost to the door when he was approached by Trent.

"Everything was good, Officer?" Trent asked with a smile as he shook his hand.

"Sure was. Terrific, as always. You have a such a great place here. I never know when I'll be in the area, but if I know in advance, could I call ahead to pick up a whole pie for my staff?"

"Of course. We only need two hours' notice."

"Good to know. I'll do that next time I know I'll be in the area," AJ answered. This time, it wasn't a case of him keeping his enemies or suspects close. He truly loved Corbett's bumbleberry pie!

PREDATORS AND PREY

◆ ◆ ◆

Back at the station, he downloaded the pictures. Only one turned out clear, but one was all he needed. He ran a search through the state police database using the first name 'Maya' and Lansdowne as his parameters. It took no time to pull up what he was looking for.

"Maya Livingstone!" he said loudly to himself. Ben and Julie looked at each other, then at him. He looked back at the two of them and smiled, "Maya Livingstone. Apparently, she and our Trent Corbett are a couple. Just found out about her today."

"And?" Ben and Julie said in harmony to coax out the story they knew AJ wanted to tell.

"And I managed to sneak a picture. I knew her first name and ran it. Now I have a copy of her driver's licence, complete with her full name and address. She probably owns a car. I'll run a search for it next so we have her tags and know what she drives."

Julie walked over to his desk and looked at Maya's blown up license on his screen. "If Corbett is the killer, I wonder if she knows. Is she an accomplice, or being kept in the dark about the whole thing? I'll do the search and pull up anything I can find. It'll take me half the time it would you."

She headed back to her desk and, knowing her way around the police network better than anyone, it took under thirty seconds to find what she was looking for. "Got it. Originally she was from Connecticut and while she was living there gained her long gun eligibility certificate and a permit to carry a handgun."

"I love states who require licenses and permits. Makes our job a lot easier," AJ declared.

AJ smiled and was walking over to look for himself when Ben called out. "Her car's silver like his. Different brand and year but similar in looks."

"Hell, she's not only an accomplice. I believe she's the one who shot and killed Spencer Maling." AJ poked his finger against the screen. "Looks like we now have two murderers to take down. Hopefully, we can nail them before either one of them kills again."

Chapter 31

It was the first time Trent relied on somebody else to choose a sniper position for him. His restaurant, though, had issues which didn't allow him the time to scope out the area to choose a location with great sightlines to the target and camouflage. So, he hesitantly leaned on Maya to get it done. As much as he trusted her, as much as her planning had always been so meticulous, as much as she had been infallible so far, it still left him unsettled. He wasn't comfortable not being the one in control of the setup.

The area where Ed Simpson lived was a new higher end community. Only four homes were completely built and being lived in on the cul-de-sac. On the long road leading to it were three skeleton structures and another four, which were simply holes in the ground. From his research, he found the families currently living in the completed homes had moved in only three or four months before. Simpson lived on the edge of the cul-de-sac. The road leading in followed the contour of the valley. Simpson's home was built on the far side of the road, with the view from their front living room window overlooking the lightly treed slope.

186   GORDON K. JONES

When Maya and Trent first called up the area on Google maps, the area was so new the street did not yet officially exist. Only satellite shots were available. The houses were just holes in the ground or basement foundations running alongside a rough dirt road.

Maya spent as much time as possible before '*take down day*' scouting the area. As the images showed, there were mature trees, plus some saplings along the side of the hill. A rough dirt road set back from the top of the hillside would allow them hidden access to where they needed to be, plus an out of sight place to park. She felt the pressure to get every detail perfect, afraid Trent might dismiss the position she selected as unsatisfactory and lose trust in having her to do the pre-work for future shootings. It would disappoint her greatly if that happened.

After only a few minutes of her first visit to the site, she discovered what she believed to be the perfect spot. The sightline to the house was excellent and the sniper position well hidden. She broke out with a huge smile. "Perfect, Maya! Damned perfect! Trent's going to love what I've found for him here."

Her next task was to keep watch on any of Simpson's habitual routines, for it was those was those which would cost him his life. It was on her third evening when she confirmed the best time for Trent to take his shot.

Simpson arrived home each night around the same time. He would open the garage door from his vehicle as he approached. The door would immediately begin closing as he passed underneath. The plans for the house, which she managed to retrieve from the sales company's website, showed a door from the garage which went directly into the house, so he never needed to go outside after he parked.

A main floor office showed in the plans and after being home for ten minutes or so, Simpson would enter and stand beside a chair by the window. He would then reach

PREDATORS AND PREY 187

down and pick up a converter, straighten up, and turn on the TV. Same routine every night. Standing there with the converter made it the perfect opportunity to take the shot.

The following day, a half hour before Simpson was due home, Trent found himself more than a little anxious as he and Maya slowly drove along a crude, potholed construction road which followed the top of the ridge. He pulled the car around so it faced the way they came and parked far back from the edge so it couldn't be seen from below.

During their drive to the location, he'd been quiet. Jittery. Before they got out of the car, Trent turned to Maya, his fingers playing on the steering wheel. "Hey look, I'm sorry for being so out of sorts. You know, it's not that I don't trust your judgement. When I was with the forces, they always gave me the 'go ahead' to select my own lookout. This is the first time somebody ever did this for me. I truly understand the effort you put into this and, even though you've mapped it out for me in great detail, I won't be satisfied until I see it with my own eyes. I would never put this much trust in anybody else."

For a moment, he was overcome by this last thought. He leaned over and kissed her warmly. "Now let's go take out that son of a bitch!"

Maya led him to the spot, which was about thirty steps below the car. Poking out the side of the hill was an old sixty-inch-wide metal drainpipe set in concrete. The ground in front was baked hard and scattered with large stones. Over the years, the running water dug a hole in the dirt behind the rocks and stones which had been washed away from the pipe, forming a semi circular rise a few feet in front of the opening. Some low-lying foliage in front of the stones helped to seclude them.

Trent snickered quietly to himself as he placed his bag on the ground and sat down beside it. He pulled the scope out of his bag, scanned the area, taking more than a long moment to linger on the window, which would soon shatter as he took down his target. "Wow. Damn it, Maya. It's obvious there was nothing I needed to worry about. Shaded, sheltered, perfect sightlines, easy access to the car. Honey, you nailed it."

She smiled, dropped beside him, placed an arm around him, and pressed her soft lips hard against his. "Thanks. I hoped you'd like it."

The concrete wall framing the opening of the pipe gave them a backrest where they could sit hidden in relative comfort and wait. Trent assembled his rifle, aligned the sights and, as usual, checked the wind more than a few times. Maya knew how Trent liked things quiet while he waited, so silently she sat against the wall, her eyes closed.

Finally, they heard a car arriving on the street below. They both peaked over the short pile of stones and through the scrub to see. "That's him," Maya whispered. They watched the door to Simpson's garage open before his car reached the driveway and then begin to close the moment the car entered.

"Just like you told me. He's one efficient son of a bitch," Trent commented.

"Or scared," came Maya's interpretation. "It should be anywhere from five to ten minutes before he goes to into that room. His whole torso will be exposed for a nice clean shot."

Maya wished she ate before they left. She had been too nervous thinking about Trent liking the spot to do so. Now she was starving, and it was a rule never to bring any food to a shooting. A chocolate bar wrapper may accidentally be left behind, or a small piece of food could drop from either of their mouths, which could provide the authorities with DNA. It never hurt to be too careful. Still her stomach issued a loud growl, causing Trent to stifle a laugh.

They both sprawled on the ground and finally, after a wait which seemed like hours but actually was only a few minutes, they saw Ed Simpson walk into the room. Like he

PREDATORS AND PREY 189

did every day Maya had watched him, he picked up a converter and held it out toward the TV. As he did, Trent went to work.

Maya marvelled at how catlike he was. Even though they were on a bed of loose stones, when the time came, Trent moved silently and with little effort. After spreading prone on the ground, Trent quietly worked himself and the rifle into position. He lifted the weapon and adjusted his scope slightly. She noticed the butt of the rifle was hard against his shoulder and smiled. *There's where I went wrong before. Damn shoulder still hurts,* she thought as she raised her binoculars to watch.

She saw Simpson rise out of his chair and stretch. Instantly, she became aware Trent was no longer breathing. His crosshairs must be lined up with the target's back. A split second later, he squeezed the trigger. Sound and fire erupted from the barrel.

To their astonishment, the glass buckled on impact but didn't shatter. Although heavily scarred, it didn't appear penetrated.

Simpson spun quickly around, stunned, yet unharmed. Trent quickly let off another couple of shots with the same effect as Simpson dove for the floor.

"What the -?" he exclaimed as instinctively he rolled to his side, his words cut off by two bullets cutting through the foliage in front of where he'd been lying the moment before and ricocheting off the wall behind him.

He rolled over again, coming up against Maya's prone body. She was face down, with her hands covering her head. A bullet smashed the glass of the binoculars which she had held. The sounds of more bullets thrashing through the vegetation, whizzing by them, smashing into the concrete behind, completely unnerved her.

"Stay down," Trent urged, knowing whoever was shooting at them didn't have the angle. In vain, he tried to grab her. In a panic, she scrambled into a crouch and with her hands still covering her head, she rushed into the pipe while a hail of bullets tried unsuccessfully to take her down.

Trent looked over the rocks and saw a figure behind a tree holding a rifle. He let three shots fly. Two struck the ground beside the tree and the other plowed into the trunk. Not staying still, he rolled to his right and let another trio fly at a figure who was working his way up the hill. All struck the ground inches from his head. Before any of the two could recover, Trent scrambled into the pipe and fell against its side.

He found Maya on her knees in the middle with her hands covering her ears. There was no gentleness when he grabbed her and threw her against the wall beside him, so his body protected hers. Four shots sounded from beyond the pipe, two of them bouncing off the side wall while another couple careened off the roof of the pipe, above where Maya once stood.

"Trent! What the hell ya doing?" Maya retorted.

"What?"

"I watched you shoot at both of them and miss. I know you're a better shot than that. You could've dropped both of them easily."

"Just stay down!" Trent said with his hand on her shoulder and forced her down to a seated position with him. More shots rang off the ceiling of the pipe, raining dirt down on them. He never looked away from the entrance as he spoke, "I told you before. I won't shoot a cop. They're the good guys. We've got to figure another way out of this."

"Trent. What the -"

More shots pounded their enclosure. Trent looked down the tunnel, which took a turn to the right which he couldn't see past, "Do you know where this pipe leads?"

"Dead-end. Looks like it collapsed a long time ago."

"Shit!"

At once, all became quiet. No more shots sounded. Only the sound of voices could be heard. Maya, gaining her

PREDATORS AND PREY

composure, dropped to the ground and shimmied up to the entrance.

"What -?" Trent began before being cut off by Maya, who held up her hand a little, signalling him to be quiet. After a moment, she turned her head towards him. "Listen!"

He did. The men below were talking amongst themselves, but not in English. Their language was foreign, with heavy accents. There appeared to be three of them.

"They're not fucking cops. They sound African," Maya said, her voice shaky.

"Hired guns? Shit!"

Instantly, Trent was at the opening, crouched beside her. A bullet struck the concrete above the roof above bringing small chunks of concrete down on his head. He saw the flash where the shot originated from and brought the rifle to his shoulder. Maya backed away from the opening.

Trent squeezed the trigger and heard a man scream as he fell to the ground. *'Down one.'* he thought. At the moment, he didn't care if the man was dead or wounded, as long as he was out of action. *Now, where's the other two?*

He leaned out a little to have a look and immediately shots rang out. Being made in haste, they all missed. Trent saw a shooter in the open and fired. His shot too was hasty, only it didn't miss. The man pitched backward and rolled a few times down the hill.

Close by, he saw another man take cover behind a tree and took a couple of quick shots which embedded themselves into the tree trunk.

Kneeling inside the opening of the enclosure, he heard stones and pebbles tumbling down the slope above him. Somebody was working their way down from the top. Trent took two quick steps out from the safety of the pipe and pivoted to see a fourth man coming down at him, his handgun drawn.

Seeing Trent make his unexpected appearance, he stopped his approach and tried to raise his gun. He was

192   GORDON K. JONES

too slow. In a flash, Trent drew his own revolver and let off
three shots, all of which found their mark. The man fell to
the ground and rolled down over the edge of pipe. Trent
stepped out of the way as the body landed with a sickening
thud.

Not missing a beat, Trent pivoted to take care of
what he hoped was the last attacker. He saw the man scrambling down the side of the hill in a hasty retreat.

"Maya! You okay?' Trent asked as his eyes scanning the surrounding area. Nothing was moving except for
the leaves in the trees.

"I'm fine."

"Good. Let's get the hell out of here."

He took her by the hand and helped her step over
the dead body before they clambered up the slope to their
car. Maya jumped behind the wheel while Trent popped
the trunk and tossed everything into their hiding spot. He
climbed into the seat beside her. Both could hear sirens off
in the distance, getting louder as they approached.

"Shit!" Maya exclaimed. "Cops are coming. What're
we going to do?"

"I guess we drive towards the road."

Without question, she threw the car in gear. They
rumbled down the old bumpy old trail towards the main
road they knew the cops would be arriving on. The thought
made her uneasy. That and the fact Trent now was completely unarmed. It was only a short way before an old
tractor path appeared on their right, leading up over a rise.
Trent pointed at it.

"I have no idea where this leads, but anything is
better than the way we're heading."

Maya turned onto the trail and headed up the
hill. Surprisingly, it was much smoother than the road they
were just on. She began to speed up until Trent cautioned
her to slow down, as they didn't know where it might lead.
Once they cleared the top of the ridge, they saw a barn and
house off in the distance.

PREDATORS AND PREY

The trail led to a gate which opened onto a field. Maya stopped the car and was about to ask Trent what she should do when he jumped out, opened the gate and waved her through. He closed the gate after her, then walked beside the car as she drove across the field toward the next gate. It opened onto a field with about thirty cows grazing in it.

"Okay, go slow across this field. We don't want to spook them," he said, leaning into her window as he walked.

"You're concerned about fucking cows right now!"

"If they start mooing and running, it'll draw attention. Then, sure as hell, somebody will notice and catch our plate. Keep it slow."

She did she was told and when they came to the gate, Trent did as he had done before. He opened the gate, then closed it again once she was through. It was the last gate, so he climbed in. Maya guided the car down the laneway to the barn, then past the house. Trent kept an eye on the windows as they passed. Nobody showed at any of the windows. Once on the road, they headed home without incident.

Chapter 32

Trent was first through the side door of his house and up the stairs. He stormed through the kitchen, into the living room, where he angrily dropped his gun bag onto his favourite chair. For a moment, he stood there in thought before marching to the fridge.

During their drive home, Maya noticed he didn't say much. Instead, he stared at the road ahead. Either he was deep in thought about what went wrong or brooding. Maya had only been present for one of Trent's takedowns and from what she read in newspapers and saw on TV, he never before failed in any of his attempts. She knew nothing about his missions while in the army but thought not all of them could have run smoothly. The one thing she did know, this was the first time she'd been shot at and the first time she felt she might die. She was still terrified by the ordeal.

"We were fucking set up!" he announced to Maya, who followed him inside. She stopped at the top of the stairs and stared as he grabbed a beer from the fridge. After taking a healthy swallow, he headed into the living room.

PREDATORS AND PREY 195

She heard him drop onto the couch. "We were so damned lucky to get out of there."

"Luck had nothing to do with it. It was you who got our asses through this." She swung open the refrigerator door and pulled out a bottle of rum and a can of cola. She needed something much stronger than a beer at the moment. She spoke as she mixed a strong one. "Whoever they were, they sure didn't have your training or skill. You're right, though. It was a setup. Who the hell were they?"

"I have no idea, but they weren't there by accident. And that window? Bullet proof from a high calibre bullet? Hell, it was an ambush all the way." He paused when he heard the click of ice in a glass. "Hey, what're you making?" When he heard it was rum, he asked her to make him a stiff one too, drained the rest of his bottle and turned on the TV.

Maya pulled out a second glass and made him one as well as her own. She came in into the living room and handed him his glass. Before she sat down, she went to his gun bag to get his rifle for him, knowing he always liked to clean it right afterwards. Surprisingly, he waved her off.

"I'll do that tomorrow. Tonight, I want to get an idea of what happened today and figure what we could have done better." Maya noticed the business tone of his voice as he spoke. "You know, if they had set up anywhere else instead of spreading out directly below us, we would've been at such a disadvantage. For a fight like we had, it's always better to have the uphill position. The guy who hid above us? He had the right idea. Luckily I heard him. If they all had taken positions there, we'd be dead right now. Hell, that's something we don't want to happen."

After ten minutes, the local news came on. They hoped it might shed some light on how they'd been set up.

"*Today, around six-thirty, the sounds of multiple shots rang out from the hillside of the new upper end neighbourhood in*

Springhurst. Police have not yet spoken to reporters about what exactly took place. Rumours indicate there was another murder attempt made on an unnamed African game hunter, which was prevented by a group of men laying in wait. It's unknown who they are and why they were there. We'll provide you with more details when we receive them."

"Oh, for fuck's sake!" Trent retorted. "They said shit about what happened."

In a couple of gulps, he emptied his glass. He rose to make himself another, only to have Maya take his glass and gently pushed him back. She polished off her drink as she walked to the kitchen.

She fixed them both another drink, with it again being heavy on the rum. When she returned to the living room, she found him sitting with his head back and eyes closed. She wondered if he was replaying the scene through his mind to see what happened. No emotion showed on his face or in his posture. He opened his eyes when she walked up to him and thanked her for the drink. After taking an overly large sip, he set it on the coffee table.

"Trent," she said as she sat close beside him and grabbed hold of his hand. "You were in the army and I guess you were shot at many times. Probably found yourself in a few hellish predicaments. You had the advantage of being given the training to handle it all and I saw that in you today. I mean, hell, look at you now. A rock! Me? I've never been in a situation like that before and, Christ, I'm still shaking from it. How do you handle it?"

"The first time is the most terrifying. Then you start to maybe not get used to it but learn to shut out the fear. Stop thinking about all the things which could've happened." He noticed her tears, so he pulled her close and put both his arms around her. Holding her comforted him as much as it comforted her. They stayed that way for a long while, never speaking, feeling safe.

Her eyes were drooping when his soft voice opened them again, "Come on, bedtime. We're not going

PREDATORS AND PREY   197

to hear anything more on the news tonight, so let's go get some sleep." She agreed and when they fell asleep, they were holding each other as tight as they did as when they were on the couch.

Maya was awakened the next morning by Trent, who was fully dressed kissing her cheek. The smell of coffee brewing, potato pancakes and eggs cooking filled the air. He was glad that as a vegetarian, she still could eat eggs and enjoyed them as much as he did. "Hey, honey, wake up. The news is on in fifteen minutes."

"Really?" she said as she rubbed her eyes before awkwardly struggling to a seated position. "I was in such a real deep sleep right now. When we went to bed, I was out right away. I must have been exhausted."

"You had quite a day yesterday. Like you said last night, you've never been through anything like it before. Once you felt safe, your body and mind allowed you to let it all go and shut itself down for the night."

"Okay. Give me a few minutes and I'll join you. Breakfast smells wonderful."

"Well, it should," Trent said with a grin, "Or did you forget the business I'm in."

Maya climbed out of bed, walked down the hall to the washroom, where she cleaned herself awake. She threw on a change of clothes and joined Trent in the kitchen. They ate, grabbed their coffees and took their places in the living room in front of the TV, where they waited with great anticipation for the local news. Maya wasn't sure how long Trent had been up. His rifle was cleaned and leaning against the wall beside his favourite chair. She wondered why it hadn't yet been put away, deciding not to ask.

Finally, the news began with images quickly flashing by of scenes from the upcoming reports while a seriously toned voice-over gave the headlines, *"More details released regarding a deadly shoot-out in Springhurst yesterday with the Predator's Predator, plus, a new state tax package to be introduced today and-"*

198   GORDON K. JONES

"Deadly," Maya said with satisfaction, her voice rising over the volume on the TV. "Sounds like you got at least one."

Trent only nodded. His attention never roamed from the show.

The blonde female commentator was sitting behind a glass-topped desk with the video showing a man on a stretcher behind him, "*Yesterday evening, the Predator's Predator made an attempt on another known African game hunter, Edward Simpson, at his home in Springhurst. Unknown to the now famous serial killer and local authorities, a trap had been set to capture the man before he could kill again. The effort left two dead and one wounded in the ensuing engagement. Our Jim Campbell is at the scene.*"

"I knew it," Trent muttered. "I knew it was a fucking setup. Bastards!" He took a sip of his coffee and leaned forward toward the television as though the sound from it wouldn't have the strength to make it across the room.

Maya smiled and gave him a playful slap on the shoulder. "A fat lot of good it did them. You took out two of them and we got away. Damn, Trent, I'm so proud of you!"

Trent looked over in her direction with a faint smile. He realized it was his actions which allowed them to escape unharmed. He turned his attention back to the TV and held up a finger, signalling for quiet. He needed more details.

The news showed a tall, thin man with thinning brown hair holding a microphone, standing in front of what Trent recognized as Ed Simpson's home. "*It was an elaborate plan to draw out the Predator's Predator so he could be captured or killed. Authorities say Edward Simpson or somebody else in his hunt club had been contacted by a spokesman of an African group. Whether this group is part of the same African contingent which is here currently to discuss the same problem with government officials is yet unknown.*

"*Mr. Simpson agreed to be the bait in the trap. His nightly routine was laid out so he would end up standing on the*

PREDATORS AND PREY 199

other side of a window, providing an irresistible target for the assassin. The window was replaced with high-grade bullet-proof glass. Clues were left online showing he was about to embark on an expedition to Africa to hunt elephant. Four men then laid in wait for the killer to make his appearance. Investigations are ongoing as to whether these men were professional soldiers, mercenaries, or members of one of the African nation's covert group of operatives.

"As hoped and planned for, the killer arrived and his position was identified the moment he took his first shot."

"Bullshit! Then why did I manage to get off another couple?" Trent retorted loudly at the TV. "The sound from the first shot would've alerted them to the area the shot came from. It would be the flash from my second shot or third round which would give away our position."

"A firefight ensued. Two men who were part of the ambush were killed and another wounded. The fourth man in the ambush was not injured. No blood was found in the area where the Predator's Predator took his shot, so it's assumed he escaped unharmed. Shell casings were found in the area where he hid, something the police or FBI had never found before and may assist in helping to identify the killer.

"Authorities are also investigating whether the plan was to capture the Predator's Predator or kill him outright."

"Really?" Trent shouted at the reporter on the screen. "Hell, it's God damn clear they wanted to kill me ... kill us. Capturing us was never an option." He looked at Maya. "Hopefully, the asshole who got away never caught a glimpse of you."

"Even though the serial killer never managed to kill the man he came to shoot, he left behind more than shell casings. Police also found what they call his calling card, a printed Facebook sheet from Simpson's profile page. Simpson's picture is in one photo and a picture of an elephant is above it. The comment below Simpson read: 'Going for number 5 of 5'. Above it was a speech bubble. Inside was a poem from the elephant. 'Try to kill

me for tusk, try to kill me for game, you'll only end up in a casket, with yourself to blame.' We'll have more details for you as we get them."

Trent flipped off the TV, leaned against the back of the couch, took a sip of his coffee and glared at the blank screen. "Simpson, God damn it, I'm sure as hell not done with you!"

Chapter 33

Jim Campbell was a reporter for a local television network affiliate in the same area where he grew up. He'd been at the station for years, mostly by choice. Many felt he never left for another station with a larger viewership and industry advancement, as he was comfortable in his position at the station and enjoyed living in his hometown.

The truth was, he stayed at the small station because he was scared, maybe even terrified, of moving to a large network. He feared the stress of moving, the stress of fighting his way to the top and, most of all, the fear of failure. It wasn't until he was older when he was able to realize this, something he finally came to terms with and could accept. Not begrudgingly, though. Life was good for him.

The appearance of the Predator's Predator gave him some stature. The entire network counted on him for his reports, as the country craved more and more about the rising string of murders. He received more face time on air in the past few months than he ever had in his entire career. Jim Campbell was fast becoming a familiar face nationwide. The thought played on his mind how this story could move him up to the big leagues, something he wasn't sure he wanted.

Sunrise found him one of the first people to arrive at the Simpson house the day after the shooting. It was reported Ed Simpson and his family wouldn't return home until around noon after spending a night under protection at a hotel. It not only gave them a safe place to unwind, decompress and sleep, it allowed the police to continue their investigation around the home without interference.

Jim knew to expect a crowd of reporters and onlookers. Everyone he talked to at the scene, police, witnesses or neighbours, didn't have any new information to offer. He needed more than fluff pieces on how the neighbours felt. The examinations of the shell casings and the letter were being handled by the FBI, who already were being stalked by a mob of TV, online and newspaper reporters.

There was one advantage he enjoyed over the rest. He knew Ed Simpson casually enough to call him by his first name. Although in different grades, they had attended the same high school. He hoped it would give him an edge. All he could do in the meantime was enjoy the bright sunny morning and watch as more reporters, film trucks and the curious invade the normally quiet neighbourhood. He was experienced enough to know this was a story in itself worth reporting.

Finally, after doing a couple of "on the scene" reports, he watched the crowd part as a couple of patrol cars came into view and pulled into the drive. Ed and his wife, Sandra, holding a young infant in her arms, climbed out the back of the second car. Immediately, the crowd surged forward but were held back by the numerous police detached to stop such a trespass.

Questions were shouted from reporters. Once out of the cab, Ed gently put his hand on his wife's arm to guide her towards the house. She didn't move. Instead, she stood like a statue, clutching her child to her chest, overwhelmed by the mass chaos at the end of her drive.

PREDATORS AND PREY

A reporter shouted a question. She stared at him, transfixed. "Mrs. Simpson. Could you describe in your own words what you saw, what you felt yesterday when your husband was shot at?"

Seemingly in a hypnotic state, she turned towards the reporter, causing the crowd's excitement to heighten. An officer took a few quick steps and helped Ed turn her and lead her towards the house. As the enthralled crowd screamed at her, the officer and Ed did their best to shield her and the baby, until they were safely inside with the closed door shutting out most of the noise.

While the family were moving towards the house, Jim, who stood at six foot three, made sure he kept his place along the side edge of the lawn, hoping to be seen by Ed. While others shouted for "Mr. Simpson's" attention, he would call out "Ed". The move paid off as once Sandra was safely inside, Ed stepped back out with the officer and leaned over close to his ear. Ed stopped for a moment before entering to look back at the pandemonium he was leaving, then walked in and closed the door behind him, which instantly created quiet calmness.

As Ed stepped back into the house, the officer motioned for Jim and his cameraman. They made their way past the wall of police, much to the annoyance and anger of the reporters left behind. The officer opened the door for the two of them and closed it quickly behind them.

He could hear Sandra, who must have been in the baby's room at the top of the circular staircase. Jim glanced around, thinking how well financially Ed and his family had done over the years compared to him. Not that he carried any complaints or jealousies. He was quite happy with where he lived and how much he made. It was merely something he couldn't help noting.

Ed walked into the foyer and shook his hand. "Jim, thanks for coming in. It's bat shit crazy out there. A bunch of vultures wanting a piece of our flesh. Bastards. I hate them. How can we get them to go away? Right now, we're wore out and still rattled from yesterday. We need some rest. Look, I'm happy to give you an interview, but could you get the others to go away?"

Jim saw how exhausted he looked. "Why don't you go grab a water, have a shot or whatever you need to gather yourself together. There's no rush."

Ed, as he couldn't see through the stained glass in the door, pulled back the lace curtain from the long, thin window beside it and looked out at the crowd. They all began to shout and point. Cameras went off. He frowned and wearily closed it. "So tell me, what's the consensus out there? Is it true what I'm seeing all over the media? How so many people are cheering on this madman. What's the word on him not being able to kill me yesterday? Are people happy or sad that I'm still alive?"

Jim thought about it for a moment. "Let's go to the back of the house, away from the ears." Ed took him into the kitchen. "To be truthful, what I'm hearing it's about fifty-fifty. Just so you know, I'm on the side of the ones who's happy you're still here."

"Fifty-fifty. Holy shit. Really?"

"Yeah, sorry. Many are angry, accusing you of hiring foreign assassins to ambush on an American citizen on American soil. It doesn't sit well with the government or people on the street. It's burning people's butts."

"Foreign assassins! What about the fucker who tried to kill me? He's the assassin. The police and FBI don't seem to be getting anywhere!"

"Nobody knows that. Just because they're not tipping their hand doesn't mean that behind the scenes, they maybe getting close."

"I doubt it. If that were the case, he never would have been able to sit on that hillside to take a shot at me. Too many of us have been stalked and murdered. Damn ... and people feel sorry for the lunatic responsible because somebody took action to protect themselves."

Ed paused. Whatever energy he had when he came in quickly drained away from him. His head drooped. "Those reporters. What should I do?"

"You know they're not going away anytime soon.

Right now, they're doing their level best to listen in with shotgun mics. It's why I suggested coming back here out of range. They're out there trying to do their jobs. If you didn't invite me in, I'd be one of them.

"The best thing you could do right now is to speak to the cop in charge. Tell him to announce you're going to hold a press conference tomorrow and will announce the details later. I know people who'll help set one up. It'll help to appease the press and should disperse most of them." Jim didn't mind offering the advice but would be damned if he was going to lose the interview because of it. "Why not do that right now, then let me interview you?"

Ed nodded his head and went to the front door. As soon as he opened it, an instant barrage of questions were shouted at him. He told the officer at the door what he wanted and in five minutes, the officer in charge of the scene made the announcement with a bullhorn. Although they wouldn't leave as long as Jim was in the house, they calmed down.

It was time for the interview Jim craved. As he walked with Ed through the elegant living room to his study, the camera kept rolling. Ed kept explaining his movements on that day in great detail. The study was decorated the same way Jim had imagined. Oak bookcases crowded one wall, with a slat water aquarium on a shelf of the middle one. A large, flat screen TV hung on the opposite wall. By the window, facing the TV, was a deep, comfortable looking leather wing chair.

He showed Jim how he was standing by the chair to entice the sniper. When asked about the bulletproof glass, he only said he was advised the best would be installed. He demonstrated how he was standing when the first shot came and where he dove to when the bullets struck.

"Holy shit, even though the window stopped the first one, when the next couple struck, I was out of faith. I could picture the window shattering."

"The fact you had bulletproof glass installed indicates you were involved in this plot to, hmm, let's say, capture the Predator's Predator. Any comment?"

"Any comment! Yes, I have a comment. There's a murderer out there hunting our people down. Why not have bulletproof glass installed?"

"Is this the only window it was installed in?"

"Can't comment. I've been asked the same thing by the police and told not to talk to reporters about it as I'm under investigation for conspiracy to murder."

"Off the record, I gather you're going to say you knew nothing about the armed men."

"You know, this is fucked up. Somebody tries to kill me and I'm the one under investigation. Can you believe it?"

"Okay. Keeping in mind you knew nothing of these men, why don't we head outside and show me the window?" Jim asked. The idea was to do it as much as for his live report, as it was to rub his scoop in the nose of the big network reporters. He knew camera shutters would be snapping away in a frenzy and not only Ed's picture, but his own too, would adorn the cover of many a newspaper and magazine. "It'll give those reporters something, then maybe they'll disperse until your news conference."

Ed agreed and led him outside again to the noise and shouts from the reporters being held outside the property line. When they reached the window, Ed rapped on it with the back of his hand and remarked, "Yep, this baby saved my life."

"Can I get a picture," Jim asked.

"Sure can," Ed agreed and stepped up in front of the window.

Jim's cameraman swung the video camera off his shoulder and pulled a DSL camera out of his side bag. The

PREDATORS AND PREY

sun reflected perfectly off the window, making the scars of the closely spaced bullet strikes sparkle. Jim hoped his partner could capture it all perfectly. He had a hard time keeping the serious reporter on his face as he was drowning in the fame the moment would provide. Not Ed's moment. His moment. Jim was surprised at how much he was enjoying this.

Ed pointed to the bullet scars which saved his life the day before. Jim took a spot by the other side of the scarred window, still close enough to be in the shot while the photographer bent down for a better angle. The moment the camera clicked, Ed's head jolted backwards. Blood sprayed from the back of his skull and splattered against the window. His body bounced off the wall and collapsed ungracefully to the ground. A split second later, the sound of a single rifle shot echoed across the valley.

Screams came from the crowd. Some people scattered. Others dove to the ground. Everyone expected more bullets to fly. None did.

Jim also hit the ground and covered his head. After a few seconds, when no more shots came, he turned his head to look over at the bloodied face of the corpse beside him. He grimaced and looked away quickly. Right then, he knew he could never be a war correspondent. Sitting up, he instinctively looked towards the hillside.

It was green, still and quiet, as if nothing dangerous could ever come from it. The constant screams and commotion told otherwise.

Chapter 34

As soon as Trent saw Simpson's body drop, he eased back the barrel of his rifle from the ridge of dirt and stone which ran along the edge of the roadway above the same spot where he made his original attempt from. Although it didn't have the same excellent sightline to his target, his skill and experience allowed him to get the job done. He wore a look of satisfaction as he remarked quietly to himself, "Wrong side of the glass today, loser. Guess you figured I wouldn't be back."

Remaining on his belly, he pushed himself away from the edge until he was sure the angle of the hill would keep him out of view from below. He rose to a crouched position and scrambled to the car. Having left the trunk open, he quickly placed his gear in the car's hiding spot and climbed into the driver's seat. He closed the door as quietly as possible, then pulled away slowly to not raise any dust.

Even at a crawl, it didn't take him long to round a bend, knowing it would take a minute or two for police to carefully make their way up the slope where he would already be out of sight. He sped up and drove to the main road, which would take him to the highway. Trent

PREDATORS AND PREY 209

looked back, happy to not see another car, police or otherwise, coming from the Simpson's house.

He relaxed once he was on the highway, blended with traffic. *It's like we figured. Everyone would dive for cover, wait a minute or so till they felt safe, then try to figure out where the shot came from. Worked to perfection.*

When he arrived home, he drove straight into the garage and closed the door behind him. He left his gun bag in its hiding spot in the car, not wanting to be seen with it in the daylight so soon after doing the deed and headed through the side door of the house and up the stairs.

"Wow! You nailed him right in the centre of his forehead," Maya squealed as he came into the kitchen. "They were reporting live from the house when Simpson came outside with the reporter. You killed him on TV. Live!" She laughed. "Damn. It was spectacular!"

Trent wasn't sure if he was pleased or wary of her excitement.

She already had a beer in her hand, so he opened the fridge, grabbed one for himself and headed to the living room with her following behind. He eased himself onto the left side of the sofa and took a sip. Moments later, he found her sitting sideways on his lap, her arms draped around his shoulders.

"You gave me shit for taking a head shot when I did it. Then you go and pull the same stunt. We both figured you'd only have one shot." She kissed him excitedly, then leaned back a little so she could properly see him. "What a beautiful shot, though."

"I thought he might have on some body armour," he answered almost without emotion.

"No, you were showing off!" She laughed and eagerly kissed him again. Unlike the day before, she was having the time of her life. "And it was my idea too."

"It was," Trent agreed. "Full credit to you. Nobody, the police, reporters, nobody, expected me to show up today."

210 GORDON K. JONES

Once again, she pressed her lips hard against his. Then she leaned back and placed her hands on the sides of his face. "I so wanted to be there with you."

"Yeah, it was better you stayed behind. With all the people crowded below, I would hate for them to have seen the both of us. Seeing me would be bad enough. I never want them to find out I have an accomplice."

"I know and I think it's sweet, but I'm in as deep as you." Again, she kissed him long and passionately. "I know they won't show it on TV again, but if you want, you might be able to see it online before the authorities block it. I figure there were lots of cell phones out there recording."

"No!" His voice was stern. "I don't kill for the thrill. I'm doing it for a reason."

"I know. I'm sorry."

"It should be on the news. I need to know if I was spotted or filmed at all. I know they'll say if I was."

She took the beer from him and set it on the coffee table alongside her own. As she did, she undid the upper buttons of her blouse. Turning back, she placed his hand on her breast and her lips on his.

"The news will be on later," she said. She placed a hand on his hip, the other on his leg and rolled him over so they were side by side and for the first time, they enjoyed each other in a place other than in bed.

Chapter 35

AJ adjusted his shirt and jacket as he strode up the sidewalk to Chelsea's front door, hearing Briley announce his arrival before he was halfway there. When he reached the top step, he was surprised when the door was flung open with Chelsea, launching herself into his arms and strongly pulling him against her body as she kissed him hard.

"I'm so glad you're here," she half sobbed on his shoulder.

"Why? What's the matter?"

"Not a thing now." She took him by the hand and led him inside. After closing the door behind them, she pulled him in tightly. "I ... I was so worried." Again, her lips came together with his.

"I saw the news at the restaurant right after it happened," she whispered into his ear as she held onto him for all she was worth. "I've been watching the updates since I got home from work looking for you. Were you there? Did you see it happen? My God, it had to be a horrible thing to witness."

AJ could feel the anxiousness in her body and pulled back a little so he could see her face as he spoke. "No, I wasn't. At the time it was going down, I was giving a speeding ticket to an unhappy, argumentative driver."

"Oh, thank God." She pulled him in tight again. "I never thought of you ever being in danger. The idea of you being so close to where people are shooting ... jeez... you know ... we live in small towns where nothing much bad is ever supposed to happen."

"Chelsea, you never need to worry about me. I'm not about to get myself killed out there. Remember, if a tough situation does arise, we're trained to handle it," AJ said with a reassuring smile.

He thought it best not to tell her it about being on the news awhile back after having shot it out with the killer. He knew she was probably aware of the altercation but didn't know it was with him. "The best way I've discovered about not being shot is to be in an entirely different town than where the shooting is taking place." She giggled against his shoulder, "Like today."

She took him by the hand and led him into the living room. As she did, he briefly ruffled the hair on the labradoodle's head before his furry friend pranced over to his bed to chew on some rawhide.

"It must have been an awful thing for the people there to see." She squeezed his hand.

"Oh yeah. You know, I really shouldn't have joked about it now. After all, a man is dead and his damned killer's still on the loose."

"Still, you're here and that's what matters." She never let go of his hand as they sat on the sofa. If anything, she held it tighter. "You know, it's been a hectic week for both of us. If it's alright with you, why don't we stay in tonight? We'll get comfortable, order in a pizza, have some wine and watch a movie. What do you say?"

"I'd say it's a great idea," said AJ, immediately bending over to take off his shoes. He carried them to the front door and placed them on the shoe rack. When he returned, he found Chelsea sprawled across the sofa, leaning on its cushioned arm with her feet curled behind her and her legs not much hidden by her dress. It was a picture worth admiring. "Do you know how beautiful you look right now?"

She smiled shyly and tilted her chin down slightly. He sat and rested his hand on her calf. She placed her hand over his and gave it a squeeze. Of the many things she enjoyed about him was he wasn't afraid to give a compliment. He knew how to make her feel good.

"So, you must have been busy at the diner these past few days?"

"Oh, it was. Yesterday someone called in sick and another took three days off for a family emergency at the last second. It was Trent's day off, so we had nobody there to cover. Then today, another girl was off sick and Trent called in unexpectedly before the place even opened, saying he wouldn't be in. So, there we were, down three people for the Saturday morning rush."

AJ perked up with what she innocently recounted. It seemed too much of a coincidence that the man he pegged as the main suspect had the day off when the first shooting took place, then called in at the last moment the following day when Simpson was killed. Perhaps it was time for him to call the FBI, explain his suspicions, and leave it all with them. Or would he be putting him and his staff in danger of being accused of withholding evidence?

It was something he would need to think about hard before acting. Plus, there wasn't anyway he could jump up and leave at the moment without a good explanation, leaving out the part where he suspects the owner of her restaurant. Sometime in the future, when they had enough evidence to put her boss away, the subject would come up. Damn, it would be a hard thing to break up over. He knew he would need to convince her he started dating her because he liked her, not to gain information on Corbett's comings

214 GORDON K. JONES

and goings. Even though it was the truth, he knew it might be difficult for her to accept.

"That's too bad," he said after snapping his brain back to where he was, instead of where it wandered. "I guess your feet have been run off these past couple of days. Hmm, have you ever had a foot massage?"

"Only short ones when I go for a pedicure."

"How would you like one now?"

"From you?"

"Sure. Lay on your back and place your feet in my lap."

She did what he instructed her to do and rested her head on a cushion. He placed a cushion across his lap, then placed her leg on it. He slid his hands over the top before he began. She smiled as he began to gently caress the top and sides. A groan of pleasure escaped her when he began massaging her soul with his thumbs.

"Oh my God, it feels so good!" she exclaimed with her eyes closed as he began to work on each individual toe. "Once you're done with them, maybe we should head upstairs where you can work those magic fingers of yours on other parts of my body ... just ... just don't rush what you're doing now!"

"Don't worry. There won't be any rushing, here ... or upstairs either."

◆　◆　◆

AJ swung open the precinct door and headed straight to his desk. He didn't say a word. Not removing his jacket, he set his to-go cup of coffee on his desk, dropped into his chair and sighed. Julie's eyes followed him all the way. "AJ. No hello, good morning, no anything?"

"Sorry. Good morning."

"Good morning, right back at ya. Say, you look tired. Must've had a busy night. Hey, weren't you out with

PREDATORS AND PREY   215

your lady friend from Lansdowne? Guess she didn't let you sleep much."

"Jeez, Julie. Can't a guy come in tired without being harassed?"

"I'll take that as a yes. Good for you. It's been awhile."

"So, busy night?" he asked, to change the subject.

"Nothing special. What brings you in here on your way home?"

He ignored the inference, "I think it's time to call the Feds. Found out something yesterday they might want to know."

"Finally. What is it?"

AJ explained what Chelsea had told him about Trent. He also told her of the conversation the three of them had with the Feds on the bridge after the Maling murder. How they seemed much more receptive to working with the local police. She agreed he was doing the right thing.

"Damn, AJ, I'd love for us to nail the son of a bitch ourselves, but you're right. It's best to let them handle it."

He pulled agent Johnson's card from his wallet and dialled. Johnson answered right away. There was almost no small talk after the initial 'hellos'. AJ decided to inquire right away about the Simpson murder. Julie flipped on the TV news as he spoke. Everyone who worked at the station was used to talking on the phone with a lot of noise and commotion in the background, so it never disturbed him.

AJ spoke in a friendly manner. "I wasn't there at the scene yesterday and, like everybody else, didn't expect another attack so soon, what with so many FBI, cops and people around. I figure if you found the bullets from two days ago, they would be too damaged to get much from, still, what about the bullet from the murder scene? I know you'd get it to ballistics right quick. Anything come back yet?"

"Nothing yet. You may not be aware, it's not like a TV show. It can take some time and the labs have their hands full."

"Yeah, I know the usual timeframe, but I'm also aware this is a high-profile case and probably your department's number one priority. They'd drop everything to give it a look see."

"Look, Chief. This crime is out of your jurisdiction and-"

"I damn well know it is. Remember, this psycho killed two of my residents plus shot it out with me? So don't tell me it's none of my business because it sure as hell is!"

"Chief Johnson. As I was saying, this is out of your jurisdiction and yes, we're aware of your history with the suspect. You have to understand, though, we've decided it's in the best interest of the public and in apprehending the suspect, that we'll no longer be providing details to local law enforcements."

"What! That's bullshit!" AJ roared, which made Julie jump. "A few days ago, you were begging for our help. Now you think you might have this wrapped up, so you shut us out. Look, I don't care who gets the glory. I want him behind bars and my people safe. So, damn it, tell me what the hell you know."

"Sorry. Can't do that. We do have our own methods of solving these cases and don't need you or any local agency getting in our way."

There was a long silence as AJ attempted to settle himself down.

"You still there, Chief? Are we finished?"

"Hell no. We're not done. Alright then. Can you at least tell me if you have any details on those who set the ambush? Were they sent from Africa and was it with the involvement of their various governments? While we're at it, I'd like to know what Simpson's role was in all of this."

"Sorry again. We can't disclose any information while the crime's under investigation."

PREDATORS AND PREY 217

"Don't you be giving me the same line you give the press," AJ said in a raised voice. He heard Julie clap her hands and gave her a look. She pointed to the TV. He listened for a moment. "You can't disclose! Well, listen to this, you piece of shit!"

He held the phone up to the TV, then motioned for Julie to turn up the volume. It was Jim Campbell, with the report.

"Although no arrests have been made or suspects identified, we have an update on the men who set up the ambush on the Predators Predator two days ago. It's been confirmed the men were from three different African nations, South Africa, Namibia and Botswana. Inside sources indicate all three governments were possibly aware of this group of mercenaries and their mission. Sources say the funding for their mission may have come from more African nations involved in the trophy hunting industry nations than the three so far named.

"Before Simpson was murdered, he did reveal to this reporter he was not aware the men's mission was to kill the Predator's Predator. He was told by them their task was to capture him for trial. It was another man who originally contacted him with the plan and paid for the bullet proof glass for his window. He showed him how to set up a Facebook account to look as if he were hiding but could easily be found by the serial killer without suspicion. Simpson was promised full protection, a promise they obviously were in no position to keep."

AJ motioned Julie to turn off the sound. "Did you hear that? You can't disclose my ass!"

Only breathing could be heard on the other end of the phone. AJ could feel the agent's anger and surprise in his breaths as he tried to come up with a rational reply, "You know the report's totally unsubstantiated and might not be accurate. You can't totally believe a small-town reporter trying to get ahead."

"Hey! I know the guy. I trust him. I don't trust you and your 'can't disclose' bullshit. Go fuck yourself, Johnson!" AJ pushed the button on his desk phone to end the call.

218   GORDON K. JONES

He wished he had an old-time telephone receiver he could slam down in the agent's ear instead.

"Sounds like you decided not to tell him," Julie remarked. "Good for you."

"Uncooperative, arrogant bastard!" Anger and hate filled his voice.

Even though Julie rarely swore, she swivelled her chair around to face him and held up her coffee cup. "Fuck the Feds!" AJ's head jerked back in surprise.

"You got that right," he answered and holding up his coffee. "Fuck the Feds! We've got more than they do. Looks like us local yokels will have to nail this mother ourselves."

Chapter 36

Two police vehicles from Springhurst and Parkview Gardens sat parked in front of the Elm Grove police station. Chief Connie Stapleton of the Springhurst force and Lt. Eric Freemont, in charge of the Parkview Gardens Police, sat with their coffees in a corner office. The office had frosted windows facing the street so sunlight could filter in while peering eyes could not. In the office was a small oval table, chairs and a white board almost wiped clean. They were brought together by AJ, who now that he knew about Maya, was ready to present them with a plan.

The three were engaged in the usual small talk, which precedes any meeting. Finally, the focus was brought to the subject at hand with a question from Eric. "AJ, did you call the Coe Hill, Beaconsfield, and Brookfield offices? After all, they had citizens murdered by this lunatic too."

"I did," AJ answered. "They were told the same thing by the FBI as we were. Seems they were happy to do as they were told and let the Feds handle it."

Connie shook her head before offering her opinion. "Eric and I still have people we need to protect who'd be on his list. After what happened with Simpson, I agree with you. We should start being proactive. There's something I've been wondering about, though. You seem to have a beef with the Feds. Will it hinder anything we plan to do?"

"Nope," was AJ's quick and terse reply. "I tried to give them the same info I'm about to share with you, but they pretty well told me to fuck off. Not in those words, of course, although it felt like it. All the same, they shut me down and told me to keep out of it."

"Did you even try to tell them about your new info?" Connie queried with a smirk, already knowing the answer.

"Well, no … but in my defence, they never gave me a chance. I was too pissed off at the end to even try to tell them."

"They must feel they're really close."

"Maybe. I doubt it. Without the intel I have, they wouldn't begin to suspect Corbett plus they wouldn't know about Maya Livingstone." AJ passed them each a folder which contained her picture, driver's license and vehicle information. "Oh, did I mention how she and Corbett are a couple. I figured him to be a loner till Chelsea told me about her."

"Chelsea?" Eric queried

Connie wore a big smile as she explained. "I guess you don't know about Chelsea yet. She works for Trent Corbett at the restaurant and our AJ here has been doing some, let's say, undercover work with her on the case."

"No, nothing of the sort. Chelsea's great and I haven't pumped her for any info."

Connie put her hand over her mouth to unsuccessfully suppress a laugh.

"Pumped her for … ah hell no, I'm not going there," Eric grinned.

"Smart," stated AJ flatly. "Alright, let's down to business. Nine are dead. Seven of them part of the Tyndall 10. Thoughts?"

PREDATORS AND PREY

"I have two possible targets in my town who would be still on his list from the 10." Connie stated. As she spoke, she never lifted her eyes from the contents of the folder. "Walter Mathews, he's president of their group and Rebecca Farnsworth."

"It's interesting how he hasn't shot a woman yet," remarked Eric. "There are two women in the group. Both are still alive. I have Samantha Edgars, who lives in a condo in Parkview's town centre. He may have laid off her as all the other victims, save for the travel agent, have been killed at home and all lived in high-end neighbourhoods on the outskirts of town. Maybe living downtown put her at the end of his list."

Connie looked up. "What role do you think this Livingstone woman has in all of this? Is it possible she doesn't even know about his extra-curricular activities?"

"Oh, she knows," answered AJ. "Not only that, but I believe she was the one who pulled the trigger on Spencer Maling."

"Wow!" Eric exclaimed. "What makes you think that?"

"I'm eighty percent sure Trent Corbett is our man. Chelsea was with him at the restaurant the day Maling was killed, plus the distance he was shot from was much closer than usual, suggesting somebody else pulled the trigger. Everything else on the hit fits his MO. I'd bet a thousand dollars the paper, ink and printer used on the calling card left at the hut, was the same as the other ones which were left. Same with the rifling on the bullet. Damn, if the Feds were more co-operative, we'd know for sure. Oh yeah, she's in on this and damned well was the one who gunned down Maling."

"I can buy that based on the assumption Corbett is the Predator's Predator. Perhaps they planned it to throw off him as a suspect," agreed Connie. "So, where do we go from here? Still three left on his list. How do we figure who's next?"

"We can't," Eric stated.

"You're right. We can't. So maybe we should let them lead us to their next intended victim."

"You mean set up surveillance on the two of them?" Eric said with some disbelief. "You must have contacted the state police to help. I sure know you didn't ask our Fed friends."

"I contacted the state police but didn't go into details with them. They came back with the same old line. The Feds told them to layoff, and they were more than happy to comply. Personally, I'm getting sick of hearing it. Lansdowne has no interest in helping us either."

"So, it's up to us then?" Connie summarized.

"Sure looks that way," AJ answered. He patted his hand thoughtfully on the table. "I'd like this to be a twenty-four-hour thing, but without outside help, we're short of manpower to do so. Any ideas?"

"Do any of us have GPS trackers we could stick onto their vehicles?" Eric asked.

"Hell, we don't have the budget for that and until now, the need," AJ replied.

Connie drummed her fingers on Maya's photo, deep in thought. Then an idea struck her. "The murders have all been in the daylight and, like the rest of the world, they probably go to bed around the same time every night. Many of those nights they possibly spend together. We could cut out the night hours while conducting surveillance."

"What about when Corbett's working?" Eric interjected. "No sense in wasting manpower when he's at the restaurant. AJ, could you find out what his schedule is from your gal pal?"

"No. I don't want her suspicious of anything. If she suspects, she might act differently around Corbett, which could tip him off. After all, he knows about the two of us."

"How about this, then?" said Connie as she looked down and jotted something on the inside of her folder.

PREDATORS AND PREY

"AJ now is too noticeable around Corbett's. He's eaten there, talked with the suspect, and is dating one of his servers. We can't have him around there at all. Livingstone, however, has never laid eyes on him.

"Going on the assumption she's with him at each killing, she may be able to lead us to the next one. We can have AJ or someone from his squad have eyes on her each morning to see if she goes to work or not or if she ever leaves extra early." AJ and Eric nodded in agreement.

An hour later, all the 'ins and outs' were worked out for the surveillance. As they tossed their notes into their brief cases and stood to leave, Trent held up a hand. "So we're we all satisfied with what we have?"

The two nodded and vocally agreed.

"Okay. Great. We start tomorrow. Sure feels good to know we finally have a plan to bag these murdering son-of-a-bitches!"

Chapter 37

So far, seven hunters were victims as chosen by Trent. In total, nine had died. Maya was responsible for one kill and the dog-beater, although not on his list, deserved to die because, well, he was a dog beater. He noticed as time went on and his victim count rose, the difference he felt inside between the time a new target was selected and when his mission was completed.

Excitement filled his soul when a new name was chosen. The thrill of anticipation overcame him when the plan was finalized. On the day of the shooting, he was all business and after his bullet found its mark, he was left with a sense of satisfaction of a job done well and many animals saved.

On this particular night, the planning part of the process was completed while sipping on a Merlot. It didn't take long till they decided Samantha Edgars in Parkview Gardens would be next on their hit list. Samantha lived in a low-rise building, which made their upcoming task far more difficult than any they planned before. It was a challenge they both looked forward to meeting.

There was a thrill they both felt in their discussion on how to approach this new difficult endeavour. This excitement led to arousal, so the bottle was only half finished when they fell into bed for an hour of energetic, deeply satisfying sex. Afterward, they fell asleep naked, wrapped in each other's arms, while the remainder of the bottle of wine would have to wait until the next night to be finished.

When the alarm went off the next morning, they wearily opened their eyes. It was the first time they slept entangled with each other. Trent found it warm and comforting. Maya, on the other hand, had an issue. The thin sheet which covered her at the start of the night and been pulled partially off her.

"My ass is cold as hell!" she complained as she raised herself up onto an elbow.

"I'm nice and warm," he said with a chuckle. He grabbed one of her cheeks. "Oh shit, I think you've given me frostbite!"

She rolled onto her back, pulled the sheet and blankets over her, then turned onto her side and, with a laugh, snuggled her rear up against his side.

"Geez! It's like a block of ice." He didn't, however, move away. Instead, he turned over and spooned her.

After a few minutes, Trent lightly ran a string of kisses down her neck. It made her shiver. She moved her neck away from him and rolled over onto her back. "No time for that, Mister. I've got to get ready for work and you've got scouting to do."

"Yeah, damn it. I guess you're right." His voice rang with disappointment even though he found the scouting beforehand exciting. He also found her body and lovemaking thrilling and wished there was time for both.

It didn't take them long to grab a light breakfast and head out the door together. They took a moment to hug and kiss on the driveway before she climbed into her car and pulled onto the street. She waited while Trent brought his

226 GORDON K. JONES

car alongside her, facing in the opposite direction so their windows were side by side. They reached out, held hands for an instant before they drove off. Neither noticed a nondescript car following them.

It was about a half hour drive to Parkview Gardens. From their preliminary research, Trent knew Edgars lived in a penthouse suite at the top of a five-story condo. Google Maps showed there was no place where her assassin would have a shot from when she was home. He couldn't determine from the image on the screen whether there was a place where he might have a clear shot when she stepped out the main doors. Being downtown proved to be a problem in finding a decent place to hide, shoot, and escape from.

There was a treed parkette directly across from the condo, which was too close. He drove directly past the building, looking away from it, hoping to find a tall building or hilltop in the distance. There weren't any which suited his purpose. He crisscrossed the streets, heading away from her building until he was a mile away, and again, was disappointed. He wanted to stop and sit in the parkette to observe the building but was wary there might be store security cameras around which might show him entering the park. Knowing he couldn't be caught on any of them, he parked on the next street over, bought a paper, and took a walkway between buildings to the small parkette to sit on a bench at its back edge.

Connie was keeping a discreet watch on him as he drove. When she saw him park and enter a variety store, she knew where he would be headed, so she drove around and parked by Edgar's building. As suspected, she saw him enter the park from the rear and take a spot on a bench. Deciding it was best not to watch from her car, she walked to a coffee shop, bought a coffee and sat by the window, which held an excellent view of the park. Every minute or so she noticed Trent lower the paper, as if he were turning a page or getting a better look at an article.

Connie knew he wasn't reading.

She wondered how difficult it must have been in the past while following somebody to absorb oneself into the background. These days, all she needed to do was to play with her phone like everybody else. Just act like she's texting or playing a game while monitoring the park and she fit right in. No suspicion aroused by her quarry.

She took a sip of her coffee and felt her phone vibrate.

"AJ, what's up?"

"Calling to see how things are going. Where abouts are you?"

"I'm in a coffee shop in Parkview Gardens overlooking a beautiful little park. They make fabulous java here. How about you?"

"It's a dead end for today. She drove straight to work and hasn't left. At least now we know where she works. Might be good in the future to know where her office is. What's happening with our Mr. Corbett?"

"There's a few people in here, so I'll text you back."

Ending the call, she started tapping. "He drove straight here, then zigzagged the streets away from her building. Guess he found nothing. There's a small park across from the condo and now he's sitting on a park bench with a direct view of it pretending to read a paper."

She saw her quarry take a sip of his pop and look aimlessly around. Another text was sent. "Very good at hiding in public. Looks natural. Reading like its something he does every day. Anybody would think he's a local."

"He's had enough practice by now," came the reply.

Connie looked around and saw she was alone in the shop. Instead of texting, which she hated, she called. "Hey AJ. He's been sitting there about fifteen minutes. He's good. Some people have even acknowledged him as they walked

228 GORDON K. JONES

by ... hold on. He's on the move. I'm on him. Bye." Connie rose from her seat and headed to the door, a coffee in one hand, her phone in the other.

Back at her car, she laughed as she pulled a parking ticket off the windshield. *Wonder if AJ will split this with me.* She tossed it onto the passenger seat and called AJ on Bluetooth, "I'm heading around to where he's parked. How about you? What're you going to do about Livingstone?"

"I'm going to hang around till lunch to see if she leaves after half a day. Figure she won't, though. Looks like Corbett's doing the footwork today."

"Sounds good. Unless something big happens and I doubt it will, I'll call you after he's done and heading home."

She knew the way his car was facing when he parked it, so rounded the corner from behind as he was pulling away. Noticing he was headed for home, she ended her surveillance, following him for a while before pulling out and passing him on the highway. A smile and chuckle erupted from her as she glanced at him from through her rear-view mirror. *Ha. Guess you didn't find what you needed. But when you do, we'll be on you, asshole.*

That evening, Trent explained to Maya how shooting Edgars on her front doorstep wouldn't work. They decided on a different game plan.

The next day was Eric's turn to follow Corbett. He was disappointed to find Corbett left in the morning and went straight to his restaurant. The officer who relieved him at noon also found himself with a long and boring afternoon, as Corbett spent the entire day at the diner before heading straight home.

After Connie told him of Corbett's unhappiness with Parkview Gardens, AJ, in street clothes and in his unmarked cruiser, was pleased to see Livingstone leave Corbett's house hiding her streaked dark hair under a hat and instead, sporting a blonde wig. It was an hour earlier than

PREDATORS AND PREY

she left the day before, so he felt it safe to assume she was heading for Parkview Gardens with the intention of following Edgars when she left for the office.

He found he was correct in his assumption when she entered what could be called the downtown area and parked where she could view of the front door and the parking garage.

AJ pulled to the curb in a spot where he could see her car but wouldn't raise suspicion. It was something he didn't need to worry about though, as her eyes only moved from the building's front entrance to the garage and back again, over and over.

After a half hour of waiting, a car pulled out of the underground parking. He saw Maya's car start up. When she pulled out to follow, he did too. As much as he already despised, no, hated her, he appreciated the job Livingstone was doing in tailing her mark, keeping a safe distance back while always having her in sight, the same as AJ was doing it with her.

Edgars led the two cars she was unaware of in clandestine pursuit north until the buildings along both sides of the road turned to farmland and wooded areas. She turned right onto a paved road with planted cornfields running along each side. After a few minutes, a building appeared ahead, on the left side of the road.

It was a massively square three-story structure set far back from the road with a large colourful garden and a fountain which took away from the blandness of the plain grey building. Large letters were fixed atop of a huge boulder by the entrance spelling 'Quorum'. In smaller letters under was 'Components and Processors'. Edgars turned into the long drive.

AJ watched Livingstone drive past. Sensing she was going to return momentarily, AJ stopped at the side of the road and popped the trunk. He got out and walked behind it, hoping the scene he set looked natural. He watched as

230 GORDON K. JONES

Livingstone drove about a quarter mile past the laneway, make a U-turn and head back. She turned into the company's drive and drove towards the parking lot. Smart move, AJ thought, pulling in from another direction. As he waited for her to return, AJ surveyed the area.

The Quorum building sat alone in the country at the bottom of a fairly steep, treed hill on its east side. A field full of corn grew on the other side of a fence at the top of the hill and gently sloped away. After about a minute and a half, Livingstone's car returned to the road. AJ kept his head in the trunk as she drove by, apparently headed for home or work.

AJ didn't follow. Instead, he looked around and made drawings. If this was where they planned her death, only the hill would provide the assassins with good cover and sightline, he surmised. The hill, though, ran the entire length of the property. To make an arrest which would stick and keep Samantha Edgars safe, they would have to catch the two on the way to set up with his rifle and note in their possession. He looked up and down the road. Nobody had passed by him in five minutes. They could nail them on this stretch before they reached Quorum, and if they resisted, no civilian would be in danger.

It all sounded too easy. The thought unsettled him. Where was the hole in his plan?

Chapter 38

Trent sat on his sofa sipping on a beer while casually flipping the TV from one news channel to another. Before he met Maya, he would end his day by enjoying a beer after collapsing into his favourite chair. He hadn't used the sofa much before. Now the chair sat almost ignored as he spent most of his time in the living room, either at his desk planning, researching or sitting with Maya on the sofa. He guessed why he now enjoyed the sofa so much. It was not only comfortable, but if Maya wasn't there, he could feel her presence beside him. He looked forward to her being by his side soon.

He shook his head. *Wow! I've turned into such a romantic sap.*

It didn't take long for her to arrive from her afternoon of work, having taken the morning off to trail their latest target. Never stopping in the kitchen, she walked straight into the living room, tossed her jacket onto his former favourite chair, took a couple of running steps and jumped in close beside him. Beaming, she took his beer from him and pressed her lips hard against his. Then she laughed as she leaned back and downed the remainder of the bottle.

232   GORDON K. JONES

"I've found our next site," she announced. "Even has a wonderful hill overlooking it plus an excellent escape route. Shouldn't be hard to find a great place to set up."

"Terrific! Hold on a second. Look at this," Trent said as he pointed at the TV. The screen showed a reporter standing at what looked like the inside of an airport. He turned up the sound.

"I'm here at JFK International in New York, where a large disturbance has just taken place in the departures area of the airport. A traveller, Winston Varney, who had announced on Facebook and Twitter he was leaving today for South Africa on a lion hunting excursion, found himself confronted by an angry mob in the departures area of the airport.

"Apparently the altercation started when he was approached by a man and a woman as he headed to the baggage drop off."

The screen switched to show a man holding a white bandage to his head with one hand and clutching his ribs with the other while being tended to by a paramedic. "I was rolling my gear over to baggage when a woman stepped in front of me and wouldn't let me pass. I tried to go around, but she wouldn't let me. When I turned around to find security to help me, there was a man there blocking me. He grabbed me and wouldn't let go.

"Then I heard a spraying sound behind me. They let me go and I turned to find the original woman who stopped me had a red spray can in her hands. Later, I found out she sprayed the word 'killer' on the back of my jacket.

"Were you scared? Did you think that was the end of it?" asked an off-camera voice.

"No, I wasn't scared then. Mad, yes, but not scared. They let me go and I headed for the check-in desk when I saw a mob coming at me. They heckled, shouted and swore at me as though I was a damn criminal."

Winston stopped for a moment, dropped his head and seemed to wipe away some tears, "I heard somebody shout

PREDATORS AND PREY

how the Predators Predator should make me his next target. And then they all began to chant Kill the killer. Kill the killer!' That's when I became scared, hell, terrified. My guns were packed away. I couldn't get to them. I was defenceless."

He stopped to wipe his eyes again before continuing, *"I tried to break through but people kept grabbing at me, I'd fight and break free but there was always more to go through. Finally, I fell or was thrown down, I don't remember which. They kicked and punched and swore at me. There was nothing I could do. I didn't think they'd ever stop. Finally, security and the police came and rescued me."*

"Wow!" Maya exclaimed, never taking her eyes off the TV. "People are really taking your message to heart."

Trent nodded, his eyes never leaving the screen.

"Four people were arrested, and the victim was taken to the hospital for further examination. He sustained broken ribs and lacerations, but no other serious injuries. Needless to say, the victim missed his flight."

Trent muted the sound and looked over at Maya. "Feels good to know my message is being heard."

Chapter 39

Because of the security cameras surrounding the Quorum building, Maya once again donned her hat, blonde wig and sunglasses. Trent, meanwhile, wore a fake moustache, a wide-brimmed hiking hat with dark sunglasses. Together they didn't look out of place hiking around the treed hillside on such a bright, sunshiny early afternoon.

They weren't alone, which Trent was hoping for having planned to be there during noon hour. He hoped the company employees would be enjoying the gorgeous weather, and they were. His thought process was that if a security camera picked them up alone in the trees on the hillside, it would be suspicious. Now they were just two of many people enjoying a nice day.

Many were eating or sunning themselves on the lawn at the front of the building while a small group of about six ate their lunch together and chatted on the hillside or wandered the area. One couple, about twenty years old or so, were obviously doing some exploring of their own.

"I think they want to spend their lunch doing something other than eating," Trent surmised.

PREDATORS AND PREY 235

"How come we haven't done it outside? All the fresh air. Falling asleep afterwards with the warm sun beating down on us?" She took him by the hand.

"Sounds nice. We'll do that someday. Just not today." He squeezed her hand and guided her up the slope.

When they reached the hilltop. Maya told Trent to look toward the front doors, not wanting to point. "Executive parking is out front. Regular staff park out back. You can see where the Edgar's woman is parked, six spots to the right of the door."

"Gives me about ten, twelve seconds to take my shot. More than enough time."

Holding hands, they casually walked along the hilltop. It didn't take long to find a spot which met all their needs, one hidden by bushes with an excellent sightline to the building's front door. It was closer than Trent liked, however, the cornfield behind the spot would provide an excellent escape route. Satisfied, they started back to the road where they parked. Maya elbowed Trent in his side as they passed an area of small bushes and tall grass where they heard the sounds of the couple they saw earlier, well on their way to reaching their ultimate goal.

"Sounds like they're enjoying the warm sun," Trent whispered in Maya's ear.

She grinned. "We'll be having a much better, longer, indoor session tonight."

"Looking forward to it," he said, looking at her with a smile as she took hold of his arm with both hands. She gave it a gentle squeeze as they passed the now quiet bushes on the way to the car.

♦ ♦ ♦

Although they originally agreed to a daily conference call to share the results of their surveillance, AJ thought it best to meet in person this time as Julie discovered something which he felt couldn't be shared over the phone or in an online meeting. Once again, they gathered in AJ's corner office at the Elm Grove police station and were delighted to see him enter the room with a dozen fresh baked cookies and coffee from the local coffee shop.

He placed the cookies in the middle of the table and handed them each a marked cup, as he knew how each of them liked it. The cookies were a hit. Most disappeared before he even had a chance to sit.

He grabbed the remaining one and took a bite before he began. "You all know Julie." Connie and Eric both nodded. "Today was her turn tailing Corbett, and she came away with something quite interesting to share ... Julie."

Julie remained seated. "It started off pretty boring, really. I don't have to tell you how long a few hours can feel when nothing happens. Feels much better when you're led to something. Anyway, a little after eleven, Mr. Corbett and his girlfriend slash accomplice, Maya Livingstone, left the house together.

"Hmm, like the other morning," Connie observed, "Sounds like Livingstone doesn't spend much time at her own place."

"Better for us," said AJ. "Makes it easier to keep an eye on both of them."

Julie continued. "They drove off in her car. Eric and I did a rolling tail on them till Eric was called away. I continued on my own."

"Yeah, it was strange. I got a call from the station saying the Feds wanted to meet with me. Couldn't have my people tell them I was off working on something they expressly forbade me to do. I met them at the station and for some reason, they wanted any info I had on Samantha Edgars. I told them nothing of what I was doing with regard to her. Hell, they would have shit if I did. I told them about her community work and how well she was thought of around town. They left and, of course, warned me to say nothing to her and to stay out of it."

PREDATORS AND PREY

237

"Guess they'll want to see me next, then," Connie added.

"Count on it." Eric turned to Julie. "Sorry to cut you off. Please continue."

"The two went straight to the Quorum office and parked a little past the entrance. There's a wire fence which runs along between the driveway and the bottom of the hill, so they parked and entered the area from the roadway."

"Did you get a chance to follow?" asked Eric.

"No, I didn't. There was no way I could follow them without looking suspicious and I didn't want to spook them."

"Besides," said AJ, jumping in, "we don't want them to get to the point they're able to set up. We need to grab them before that."

The three nodded in agreement.

"They came out about a half hour later, got in their car and followed the same road eastward around a left-hand bend in the road. I gave them a good head start and when I rounded the bend, saw they were already turned around and parked. I believe this is where they'll park when they make the attempt.

"How far away from Quorum is it?" Connie asked.

"I figure it could take them a couple of minutes to cut through the field." Julie rose from the table and walked to the white board. She drew a square to represent Quorum and to the right of it squiggled lines to represent the hillside. Then she drew the road passing Quorum showing the left-hand bend. A little before the curve, she drew another line ending at the road. A magnet was placed to show where their vehicle was parked on the bend. "They'll be going through a tall corn field which will keep them hidden getting there and leaving."

"So far it looks well-conceived," Connie commented. "Of course, it's why they haven't been caught yet. They plan so well."

238   GORDON K. JONES

"It gets better when you think it through." Julie said, picking up a red marker and tracing the suspect's probable route as she spoke. "They shoot Edgars at the front door. People, if there are any around her at the time, duck, run or freeze. Everyone's too surprised to comprehend what's happened. It would be twenty or so seconds before anyone dared to take a look to where the shot may have come from. Corbett's a pro, so would likely have left the scene in those short few seconds. It would probably be a minute or so before anybody thinks of calling 9-1-1, which gives them a head start. Remember too, Quorum's located outside of town. Any 9-1-1 response would take five to eight minutes to get there, which gives them plenty of time to get away."

"Makes sense," agreed Eric.

"Now they can't be sure which direction police responding to the 9-1-1 would come from, but it would definitely be on the main road. Parking around the bend not only gives them a hidden escape route from Quorum, once they're back to their vehicle, they turn down this side road at the beginning of the curve." She drew a red dashed line along it. "It connects with many other sideroads which will take them anywhere they want to go."

"So, where does that leave us?" Eric asked, looking around. "And if I may ask, why don't we grab them when they pull onto the Quorum road like you mentioned before AJ? They'll have the weapons. The Feds have the ballistics. We have the surveillance. Slam dunk, we got 'em!"

"Two reasons." AJ stood and walked to the board. "One. We want to capture both with the evidence. If we pull them over on the way and they're heading to reconnoitre the area one more time and don't have their rifle, then the entire case blows up in our faces. We'll have tipped our hand. We won't have enough evidence to get a search warrant. They'll know we're onto them, so they stay clean and we never get them. You know the FBI will be all over us and could even nail us on obstruction of justice."

PREDATORS AND PREY

"But we know Monday will be 'go time' for them?"

"All we're going on right now is Chelsea mentioning to me how she believes they'll be busy Monday, as Corbett has it off. Nothing else. No way we can be sure Monday's the day which brings us to the second reason. Say we pull them over and yes, they have all his stuff in the trunk. There's still no hard evidence on her. We have him. Maybe not her. He could take the fall. Say she has no idea of what he was doing. Not enough evidence to convict or maybe even take her to trial. So, she walks, free as a bird. A victim of hitching up with the wrong guy.

"And that would be bullshit. She's not innocent or an accomplice. I know she's murdered too and I want her as much as I want him."

"So, what's the plan, AJ?" Connie asked before finishing the last of her cookie.

"We need them parked, out of the car, convictable evidence in hand but not yet in the corn field. There'll be four of us, so we should be able to nail both of them dead to rights. Eric, as this is your jurisdiction, could you schedule a couple of your cars to be in the area in case we need backup? Don't tell them why."

"Sure."

"It's a lot closer than I would like it to be," said Connie. "Are we going to warn Ms. Edgars?"

"No. As much as I'd like to, we can't. I don't want her doing anything out of the ordinary which might tip them off and have them abort. We're going to take them down the moment they pop the trunk and have the gun bag in hand."

"My man, Ben, will be parked on the main highway with a radar gun a mile from the turnoff. He has the plates and description of both their vehicles. He's diligent and observant. When he sees them, he'll radio us.

"Okay. First off I want all of us to use either our own vehicles or your unmarked patrol cars. That way if we're somehow spotted, it won't raise any alarms with them.

They all nodded in acknowledgement.

"Eric, you'll be parked a quarter mile past the bend."

AJ made an 'x' on the board to illustrate where he wanted him. "Connie, you'll pull into the Quorum laneway and wait. I'll be parked down the dirt road, out of sight. Julie, Your going to come with me. I'll drop you off across the road from where we suspect they will be parked. I want you hiding in the bushes. When they step out of the car, give us the signal. The moment they pop the truck, let us know and we converge quickly. Julie will be the first one they see when she comes out of the woods, so her gun will be drawn and raised. Then, before they can act, we come barrelling in, sirens wailing. This way, they won't have time to draw any weapons they have on them.

Eric stood and looked around the room. "If we screw this up, a woman may end up dead and we'll have the FBI all over us. It'll be our jobs. But more importantly, we'll have failed at protecting a woman we knew was in danger. That, I know I couldn't live with."

"I could go on about how Samantha Edgars lives under my jurisdiction and it's my duty to protect her. but I've met her a few times. She's a nice, likeable woman. Not that being likeable has anything to do with it. Still, having a chance to get to know her a little makes this personal to me. We have to nail these assholes before they can harm her.

"We just have to."

Chapter 40

It was late Sunday night and, as they usually did the night before putting their plan into motion, they stayed overnight at Maya's. People came and went all day Sunday on Trent's street, so nobody paid attention to the green plastic bag he carried to the closed garage where his car was parked. He even gave cheerful 'hellos' to those who saw him as he walked along with the concealed gun bag, which looked to others on the street as a bag of garbage.

Nobody would probably notice the two leaving the house extra early on the morning of the shooting, but, as everybody in his neighbourhood seemed to know each other, Trent didn't want to take any chances. Instead, they packed the car Sunday afternoon and enjoyed the rest of the day at Maya's. The people in her apartment building were content to keep to themselves, hidden behind locked doors, which made Trent and Maya much more comfortable when they slipped out early on Monday morning.

Trent always slept well the night before a kill. When he was with the service, he spent hundreds of nights sleeping in damp fields, the hollow shells of buildings, on rocks and the slopes of hillsides, knowing the next day, perhaps minutes after waking up, he would be taking the life of a stranger. Lying in a warm comfortable bed with a beautiful woman snuggled against him and knowing when he pulled the trigger the next day, it would be for a justified kill, made sleeping no chore at all.

It was different for Maya, who spent most of the nights before, tossing and turning or staring at the ceiling. She held no fear about being caught or killed, as they planned too well. Certainly, she felt no remorse for the person about to die. What kept her awake was the adrenalin which ran through her veins as she envisioned how the day would unfold.

She rolled onto her back and pictured the different ways Samantha Edgars' body might contort when struck by the fatal bullet. Would her body jerk straight back and slam the back of her head against the ground when she fell? That would be fun to watch. Or would it twist and pitch to the left or right and bounce and roll when it struck the ground? An image popped into her head with each one. She was too busy enjoying each vision running through her mind to be able to sleep.

The anticipation was as stimulating and satisfying as when the real thing happened. A large smile appeared on her face the more she thought about it. She loved the life she had fallen into and, by God, she loved Trent.

After a few minutes, she gave him a soft poke in the side. He remained on his back with his eyes closed and spoke in a groggy voice, "What's up? Can't sleep again?"

"I have a question, then I'll let you go back to sleep."

He opened his eyes, gave them a rub before he rolled onto his side to face her. "What's on your mind?"

She rolled over a little more on her side so she could see him better, "Um, I've been laying here thinking, wondering. What's the closest you've been to a person you've killed?"

PREDATORS AND PREY

"Huh?"

"In the army. I know you were a sniper, but did you ever have to kill somebody up close?"

He became fully awake. "No. I was always conveniently a long distance away. What I did cleared the way for others. Thankfully, I didn't have to do it often. Why?"

"You know I enjoy watching you complete your work. It's so wonderful to watch those people die, knowing they deserved to, and it's you who've made it happen. Well, it's intoxicating. You're making the world a much better place and I get to watch you do it. You know how I love that, right?"

"Uh-huh."

"Well, tomorrow we'll be much closer, so I'll have a better view." She rolled over onto her back with her hands clasped behind her head. "I find it exciting. Makes it hard to sleep. Too bad I can't be even closer."

He sat up. Even though he didn't like what she was saying, he spoke calmly. "It would ruin the message I'm sending. Those people, those murderers, are killing some of the most beautiful, most majestic creatures on our planet. The chicken-shits do it from far away so they're safe and the animals, hell, they don't stand a chance. I avenge their deaths by killing those predators the same way they themselves killed. If I send them to hell from close up, the message would be lost."

Maya sighed, rolled over, and rested her head on his shoulder. "You're right. You don't want to lose that message. It's too important."

She closed her eyes and slid back under the covers. Thoughts rolled through her mind. *Damn, I wish we could plan a kill where we're right there. Close enough to feel their breath. So close I could watch the light of life turn off in their eyes. So close, so close, I could feel their death instead of only witnessing it. Still, I'm damn lucky to be able to be as close as I am, I guess.*

244 GORDON K. JONES

Trent slid down beside her and kissed her tenderly. He could tell she was still restless, so he raised himself up on his elbow, resting his head in his hand as he spoke. "Big day tomorrow. Try to get some sleep."

"Don't know if I can." She reached up and excitedly pressed her lips against his. They never parted as she rolled him onto his back.

She placed a leg over him and was about to move on top of him when he stopped her. "Honey, we agreed. No sex the night before. I want to keep all my senses sharp."

"Are your senses sharp right now?"

"Oh yeah."

"Good. I want to be sure your senses are super keen for tomorrow morning, so I don't want you to have sex with me."

"I'm glad you understand." He closed his eyes.

Frustrated, Maya snuggled against him, put her arm around his chest and tried to sleep. In her head, the visions returned of the Edgars woman, blood bursting from her chest, her body twisting like a rag doll before it hit the ground. Then her thoughts were replaced by scenes of what the two of them would be doing together naked when they arrived home afterwards. It was those pleasurable thoughts which had her drift off into a wonderful sleep.

♦ ♦ ♦

AJ rested on his back, bathed in the light of the three-quarter moon flowing through the bedroom window. He breathed deeply and smiled. With each breath, he enjoyed the scent of Chelsea's hair. When he turned his head toward where Chelsea rested her head on his chest with her left arm spread across his body, her light fragrance filled his senses. His arm cradled her with his hand, gently caressing her soft skin. Both were completely naked with the messed-up blankets only partially covering them.

He realized how he was now spending most of his nights sleeping at her place. Not that he was complaining, especially as he laid there enjoying the quiet, caring moments which always followed their lovemaking. In fact, he had even become used to Briley's snoring from his bed across the room. He had been with snoring women before, had been accused of snoring himself, but never before heard a dog snore. Now he wondered if he could ever sleep without hearing it.

His eyes were about to close when he decided to check his watch to ensure his alarm was set for early that morning. He gently slid his arm out from under her and lifted it into the air to look. Chelsea raised her head and gave him a puzzled look.

"Whatcha doing?" she asked softly and gently poked him, "You're off till noon tomorrow, remember? I'm the one with the early shift."

"Sorry. I forgot to tell you I have an early morning meeting in Springhurst," he replied. "I'll probably be heading out as you're getting up."

Chelsea rolled her head off him and onto her own pillow. She then flipped onto her side, facing him. She ran her hand over his chest as she spoke, "That's rather unusual, isn't it? Having to be in so early when you're scheduled for later.? What's so important or can I ask?"

"Cop stuff," he said. He kissed her forehead. "Early morning stuff comes up every once in a while."

"So, you can't tell me?"

"You sound worried."

"Does this have anything to do with that murdering maniac?"

"No. The FBI has control of that situation," he lied, hoping he sounded convincing.

She kissed him lightly on his lips, "Good. I'm glad the FBI's on it and not you guys. They're making the big bucks. They can take all the risks."

"Why? Think we couldn't handle it?" he said jokingly.

"Oh, I know you could, but I hate the thought of you being in danger. When I first went out with you, I never thought I would be concerned about you and your job. Never mind, you having to deal with a serial killer. Then that man was shot on TV with police all around. If that wasn't worrisome enough, I discover you never told me about your shoot-out with the Predator's Predator."

"We already talked about that."

"I know. Still, I worry whenever you're on duty."

"Well, you have no reason to worry tomorrow. I'll be in a hot room pounding coffee and snacks, trying to stay awake. Civic law is boring as hell."

"You sure? You don't sound right." She kissed him tenderly.

"Probably because it's late, I'm tired and not looking forward to getting up early. It's going to be a long day and I need to get some sleep. You too."

"We haven't been together very long, but already I feel, you know, close to you. I love having you in my life and really hate for anything to happen to you."

"Yeah. I feel the same way. Life improved for me the moment I met you. Now, nothing's going to happen to me, okay?"

"Okay." She rested her head on his shoulder, held him tight, and closed her eyes. *I don't just love having you in my life. I love you. One day I'll say it out loud to you and know you'll say it back.*

As she lay beside him with her thoughts, his went in another direction. *Should I have brought in the Feds? There'll be four of us and two of them. Wish we had more people for the take-down. Hell, we'll have the drop on them. Back-up won't be too far away. This operation's been too well planned. Oh God, I hope we didn't miss anything.*

He fell asleep holding her as if they would never have another night together. It was the same way she held him.

PREDATORS AND PREY

◆　◆　◆

Trent had been laying awake for about ten minutes. He gently nudged Maya's shoulder. She stirred but never came awake. Softly saying her name, he nudged a little harder. Her eyes squinted open. She looked at him, then at the clock, and back to him again.

"It's three-thirty-seven. I was in the middle of a weird dream," she said, rubbing her eyes.

"I have an idea."

"You said you didn't want sex earlier, but sure." She rolled onto her side.

"No, it's not that. Another idea."

Maya rolled onto her back, disappointed. "What is it?"

"We were going to park on the road but we're right beside a cornfield."

"I know."

"So, farmers always have a couple of gates off the road so they can get their machinery in and out of the field. Instead of parking on the road, why don't we head down even earlier, find one, pull into the field and park totally hidden. Then we wait till its time."

"What if somebody sees us?"

"That's why we leave now."

Maya thought for a moment, turned onto her side and kissed him. "Trent, you're a brilliant man. Let's get ready."

Chapter 41

Julie sat on a large rock hidden from the road by a low hanging leafy bough and long growth rising from the ditch. She looked at her watch. Impatience was overtaking her. The takedown, she thought, should have happened by now, except the major participants hadn't yet arrived. There wasn't a car which passed by since she'd taken her spot.

She grabbed her radio, "AJ. Still nothing. Think it's planned for another day?"

"No. Corbett has today off. This has to be the day. Ms. Edgars hasn't passed Ben on the highway yet and probably won't arrive for another fifteen minutes or so. Maybe Corbett likes to set up at the last minute."

Julie raised her field glasses. She looked down the road towards Quorum, then scanned the fence line past where she sat and followed it towards the bend in the road. An open gate came into view. She adjusted the focus. In front of the gate was a culvert over the ditch. Behind the gate, corn stalks were bent and broken as something had driven over them.

PREDATORS AND PREY

She grabbed her mic. "Listen up, people. I think they parked in a field a little east of me on the bend."

AJ grabbed his radio. "Eric. Check it out but go slow. Everybody else hold position."

Eric started his car and slowly rolled along the gravel shoulder. A glimmer of light reflecting from the field caught his eye. He stopped at the culvert and jumped out with his revolver drawn. "I've got a car parked in the field. Nothing moving around it. Going in."

"No, damn it. Wait." AJ shouted into the mike. His tires threw up gravel as they spun to gain traction. In a few seconds, he was there. As he jumped out of his car, he saw Julie already standing on the culvert, gun in hand. Connie pulled up moments later. The only one missing was Eric.

"Shit. He went in," AJ muttered.

For a few moments, nobody said a word. Only the sounds of corn stalks rustling in the breeze could be heard. The tension which absorbed the three lifted when Eric appeared from the cornfield. "They're gone. I found their footprints. Should we try to track them through the field?"

"No. They probably followed the rows, which would take too long to track. Besides, they're probably already at Quorum, set up, waiting." He glanced at the faces of the other three and realized they were waiting for him to determine their next move. "Okay, Julie, you're with Eric. You guys park by the entrance to the drive and follow the hill in from there. One up top and one below. Connie, you're with me. We'll park at the back and follow the hill towards the other two. Let's go find these bastards."

"What if we spook them and they abort?" asked Eric.

"Let's make sure if they do, they can't use this," Connie said, drawing a knife from its sheaf. Then, after a couple of determined steps which took her to the side of the suspect's vehicle, she plunged her blade into a tire. AJ and Eric chuckled and followed her example.

250   GORDON K. JONES

"No sirens. Park quietly. Guns out and use extreme caution," AJ ordered. As he climbed into his car, he thought of Samantha Edgars. He was aware the situation had deteriorated and every decision he made meant the life or death of the woman they were out to protect. It was something she was totally unaware of as she got ready for work. She might even be on her way. He made another call on his radio as they pulled into the Quorum driveway. "Ben. We have an issue. Block the road into Quorum. Nobody gets by you. Nobody!"

◆   ◆   ◆

Trent and Maya's clothing were damp from making their way through the dew-covered corn. Once they exited the opposite side of the cornfield, they cut the fence, made their way through and up the short rise to the crest. They followed the top to where they planned to set up.

Maya took the wire cutters and proceeded straight down the hill from where they were to cut another opening in the fence for a quicker, easier escape. When she returned, she found Trent on his stomach, in position, having finished putting his rifle, tripod and scope together.

When they originally found the spot, it looked as if it could easily shield both of them. Now that she saw how he was set up, she realized there was only enough room for him and his rifle. Disappointed, she knew that as much as she wanted to, she couldn't be by his side when he squeezed the trigger. By crowding him, she might accidentally do something to throw off his aim. Instead, she went to find a better spot to view the event from.

She followed the ridge for about fifty feet where she found a place protected by bushes, which afforded her an excellent view of the building's entrance. She smiled, remembering it was the same place the couple they saw days earlier had their rendezvous.

PREDATORS AND PREY 251

"I found a better place to watch so I don't disturb you when it's time," she told him when she returned. "It's not far from here with a clear route to the hole I cut."

"You pulled it apart and made a good size gap after you cut it?" he asked.

She both loved and hated how he was all business on these days. No small talk till after it was all over and they were on the road, in the clear and heading home. "Of course. We've got a clear path through. Then we head for home and when we get there, I'll give you something else to be mighty satisfied about. Even better than I was offering last night."

"Let's concentrate on getting this job done first," he said without a smile or emotion before he laid back down and worked on adjusting his scope. She frowned and shook her head as she left.

◆ ◆ ◆

AJ and Connie drove slowly along the drive, looking like regular employees headed into the office. They parked at the rear, got out, and stood looking along the length of the hill. He didn't like how they happened to miss them on the road as planned. Because they did, the two were likely already set up and awaiting their quarry. The good news, though, was they were unaware Samantha Edgars wouldn't be entering the crosshairs of his scope.

He stood with his radio in hand, "Julie. Eric. In position?"

Eric answered. "Yup. I'm taking the top. Julie will walk the bottom. You ready?"

"Let's go."

"I've got the top," AJ said, then quickly turned and headed up the incline. Once on top, he drew his gun and signalled to Connie. She drew hers and began working her way towards the others.

252   GORDON K. JONES

They made their way quietly along the slope, taking great care to be as quiet as possible. Eyes and ears fully concentrated on the world in front and around them, all aware each one of them shared equal danger. They knew their lives depended on spotting Corbett first, before he saw them.

At best, there was only a fifty-fifty chance of that happening.

◆ ◆ ◆

After leaving Trent, Maya headed back over the crest and, for her own peace of mind, pulled the fencing a little further apart. On her way back to her lookout, she spotted movement to the extreme left of her. Like a cat, she dropped quietly to the ground and crabbed sideways until she was behind a small bush.

A man approached, dressed in a uniform of some sort and a protective vest, scanning the hillside. A two-way radio was attached to the top of his vest. She watched him carefully. *A security guard? Shit. Must be a rent-a-cop working his first day on the job by the way he's looking around. Fuck! He's going to see Trent and call it in.*

Quickly and silently, she stole her way to a large oak tree, crept behind it and waited. As always, when she came to a job, she came ready. She pulled out the small pistol she comfortably had tucked away, then thought twice about using it. The noise would alert everyone, and they would have to abort. She knew the amount of hell she'd have to pay if that happened.

She looked down and spotted a rock. *Too awkward to hold. Might drop it.* Reaching into her pocket, she drew out her knife. No, he could call out after she used it. She flipped the gun in her hand, deciding a good crack in the head would drop him quickly and quietly. He was almost upon her, so she shifted around the tree, her back pressed tightly

PREDATORS AND PREY

against its trunk, hoping the tree was wide enough to completely keep her hidden.

Staying out of sight, she held her breath as she heard him slowly pass. Stealthily. she slid around the tree, keeping it between the two of them. After she heard him take a few more steps, with great silent speed, she stepped out behind him.

Eric heard the soft thump of her footfall behind him and went to turn. It was too late. The butt of a gun slammed into his temple and, with a grunt, he collapsed.

Maya wasted no time as she dropped on top of his nearly unconscious frame and undid one of the Velcro straps on the top of his vest. She raised her knife and plunged the razor-sharp blade into the top of his chest. His eyes opened wide for a moment, revealing his sudden terror.

Straddling him with her other hand over his mouth, a muffled sound erupted from him. She listened intently. No sound or panicky cries for help came from below. She yanked the blade from his chest, swung herself off her victim while keeping her hand over his mouth. The man's leg was jerking in spasm, a sight which filled her with joy. A warm, satisfying feeling flooded inside her.

She eased her hand off of his mouth, lifted her head and looked around. Below she saw a woman with a radio attached to her belt, carefully and slowly walking while looking up towards her. It was clear the woman wasn't on a morning stroll. Maya ducked her head and slid to the backside of the crest.

Cops! I have to warn Trent!

She backed further down the side, then in a crouch, headed his way as quietly as she could.

Thinking she heard a sound coming from above her, Julie looked up. She didn't see a thing, including Eric. Nervously, she scanned the hillside and saw what could be a sprawled body. She raced up towards it, praying it wasn't who she feared it was.

GORDON K. JONES

◆ ◆ ◆

North of Trent's position, AJ made his way along the crest of the hill, each step taken with great care while his eyes scanned the area ahead and below him. The top of the hill didn't run level instead, rising higher as he went along. A deep gully forced him downward to the middle of the hill.

Then he saw it. A brief flicker of light coming through a patch of bush near the top. It was a type of reflection which could be a reflection from a mirror or glass ... or the scope of a rifle.

As Corbett had not yet spotted him and he was still a little north of Corbett's hiding place, AJ kept low and began to creep up the hill. He believed he was still far enough away he could make it to the top and hopefully swing around to approach Corbett from behind, to take him without firing a shot. Then he would radio for the others.

A snap from a stepped-on twig betrayed him and he saw Corbett's head pop up over the low bushes, looking in his direction. For a brief moment, neither man moved. Then, in a flash, AJ, hand on wrist, had his revolver pointed directly at him. He was thankful his quarry hadn't reacted and pulled his own trigger. It would be an exchange of gunfire AJ would surely lose.

"Corbett!" he called out. "We have the entire hill covered. Hands up, get to your feet and step away from your weapon."

He was relieved and somewhat surprised to see Trent comply. The man looked utterly defeated as he raised his hands and stepped out from behind the bushes. "Hold on and stop right there. Keep those hands raised."

With his free hand, he reached to his shoulder radio. "I've got the shooter. We're near the hilltop, about halfway along. Note, one suspect still unaccounted for and considered dangerous."

"Where is she?" AJ demanded of his captive.

PREDATORS AND PREY

"Who?"

"Your partner, damn it. I know she's here with you."

"AJ," he heard the radio crackle with Julie's panicky voice. "AJ ... anybody there!" He was too preoccupied with Corbett to reply.

"Alright, Corbett. Hands behind your head and slowly come my way," AJ commanded, not wanting to move from the firm footing where he stood. His eyes never left Corbett as he took careful steps towards him.

Unexpectedly, Maya burst out from behind a large pair of trees to the right and behind Trent, her gun raised.

"Trent! Run!" she shouted as she let go of three shots before AJ could react. One missed, one struck him just below his vest while the third nicked the side of his neck. He fell back against a tree, fully exposed to her next shot.

"NOOOO!" Trent screamed when he saw blood splash from the bullet strikes. He spun around. Maya was only a few feet behind him and was about to fire again. Instantly, he pulled his hidden revolver and fired twice, neither one missing. Her body jerked backwards, slamming hard to the ground with a scream.

With his handgun still raised, Trent quickly spun back around to AJ, praying the man wasn't seriously injured. To his horror, he saw the officer's blood covered hands clutching the wound as he slowly slid down the trunk of the tree. Trent was about to lower his gun as he took a step towards AJ to help when a woman appeared from below, her gun raised.

"Connie, No!" AJ muttered weakly before all went dark and he toppled to the ground.

"Bastard!" Connie shouted as she pulled her trigger three times.

Trent felt a scorching, searing pain strike him like a glowing hot poker being thrust into his chest. Then, more astonishing pain flowed as the other two struck as he stumbled and twisted before crashing to the ground at Maya's side. He felt his energy rapidly slipping away as he looked at her.

It was all the strength Maya could muster to roll her head to the side so she could look at Trent. "Oh God, Trent. Why? Why?" she gasped.

Even though he was fighting for each breath, he still managed to answer in a weak voice, "Cause ... because we don't ... we don't shoot innocents ... specially cops."

"But ... Trent ... I ... I love you."

"No ... you loved ... the thrill of killing. Same as ... the bastards ... we killed." he said meekly as more of a statement than an accusation.

Connie quickly went to AJ. She set her weapon on the ground beside her before pressing her hand against the wound in an attempt to stop the bleeding. She heard her radio go off and answered with her free hand. It was Julie, her voice shaky and panicked. "I heard shots. You all okay?"

"No, AJ's down. He's bleeding bad. Suspects down and immobile. Where the hell are you?"

"With Eric. He's been stabbed. It's bad. Real bad. I think he's going to die."

Connie let go of the wound and switched channels. "Two officers down! Conditions dire. Ambulances needed ASAP. Quorum Industries. I repeat, officers down and in dire condition. Respond immediately to Quorum industries." After explaining to dispatch where on the grounds they could be found, she returned to doing her best to stem the bleeding.

A moan escaped AJ's lips and his head fell to the side. Connie picked up her revolver, stood, walked up to the two fallen bodies, and fired twice. First into Corbett's body, then into Maya's. She holstered her weapon. If they weren't dead before, they were beyond rescue now.

She pulled her knife and cut off her sleeve. Dropping to her knees, she balled up the cloth and pressed it hard against AJ's oozing hole. Grief erupted from her, as it did Julie, as both worked hard to save their friends lives, while far off in the distance the faint sound of sirens could be heard.

Chapter 42

It was a busy morning as Chelsea said it would be. There still was another hour or so left in the breakfast rush. Not only was Trent not there, it was also busier than usual. Wondering if it was her imagination, she checked with Sandra, who confirmed she had, indeed, rang through more bills than usual.

The restaurant's TV was mounted on the back wall and, as always, was tuned into the local 24 hour news network. Normally, she would glance up to it from time to time in case there was anything interesting, but on this morning, it was too busy.

It was closing in on nine and she was walking toward the back with dirty dishes skillfully balanced on both her arms when she heard Sandra call out, "They got him. They finally got the Predator's Predator!"

Chelsea look up at the screen and never noticed the sound of the dishes she dropped smashing against the tiled floor when she saw the news scrolling across the bottom of the newscast. *Officers fall in deadly shoot-out with Predator's Predator suspect.*

PREDATORS AND PREY

259

"Oh my God… CHELSEA!"

"I see it. I see it" Chelsea reached into her pocket and hit AJ's number, which seemed to ring endlessly before going to voicemail. "Shit." As she frantically pounded his number again, she screamed to anyone who would listen, "Sound. Somebody, turn up the sound!"

She rushed to the screen. On it, a female reporter, microphone in hand, stood in front of the Quorum sign at the entrance to the drive. Behind her to the left was a three-story building. To the right of the driveway was a treed hillside. It was the flashing lights of haphazardly parked police cars and ambulances lighting the scene behind the reporter, which sent an eerie chill flashing down Chelsea's spine.

"Oh my God!" she gasped. "Where the hell's the damned sound!"

"Sorry," Sandra answered as she leaned over the counter, grabbed the converter, and pointed it at the TV. "I had trouble finding it."

"I don't care, Sandra. Turn it up. Sound! I need sound!" Chelsea shouted, at the moment not caring that Sandra was her manager. Sandra saw the state Chelsea was in and immediately cranked up the volume.

An off-camera voice of the news anchor trailed off with, *"Our Amy Bartley is at the scene. Amy."*

"I'm standing here in front of the offices of Quorum Component and Processors, where gunfire interrupted the peaceful countryside morning north of Parkview Gardens. It's rumoured but still unconfirmed, the man known as the Predator's Predator was killed in a gun battle with local police. Unsubstantiated reports say a female accomplice also died in the shootout.

"Unfortunately, the death toll may include local police involved in this multi jurisdictional action. Reportedly officers from Parkview Gardens, Elm Grove and Springhurst police departments all took part. Although not yet confirmed, we heard at least one officer may have died on the scene, another being gravely wounded. Both were rushed to County General Hospital."

260 GORDON K. JONES

Chelsea gasped. "NO! Oh God. No! AJ don't let it be you. Please, please, it can't be."

"Also not confirmed, the two suspects involved in the shootout were found dead on the scene. One of them, we're told, apparently being the killer known as the Predator's Predator. Again, none of this has been confirmed by authorities.

"The woman targeted by the serial killer was not involved nor at the scene. No names have been released at this time."

She hit her speed dial again and as before, it rang a few times before going to voicemail. A crash of the restaurant's door being flung open startled her and the rest of the diners, who turned towards the sound. Three men in black suits came barging in, holding up badges with an extreme air of authority. George, a local police officer, followed behind and joined them as they lined up by the entrance.

"FBI!" the first one in announced loud and firmly. The three let their badges drop, so they dangled from their necks. For a moment, the room went quiet. The eyes of the three surveyed the room.

"Everybody but staff can leave." When nobody moved from their tables, his voice and air of authority increased. "People, I mean now. You're done eating. I want you out. NOW! This place is closed until further notice for investigation."

Sandra quickly moved behind the counter, grabbed a tower of to-go containers in one hand and an empty dish tub in the other. As she carried them to the door, she called out, "You can all use these to put your food in. We'd appreciate it if you could put your empty plates in the bin I set on the table. Oh, if you have cash and care to pay, please leave it on your table."

"And do it in a hurry," commanded the agent.

Chelsea ignored what was happening around her and rushed over to the local officer, grabbing him by his arm, "George. Do you know if AJ was there? Was he killed, wounded? Oh please, I have to know."

PREDATORS AND PREY

261

"I don't know. If you-" George was cut off by an agent who stepped in, took hold of Chelsea's arm and gently tried to pull her away.

"What the hell you doing?" she complained, yanking her arm free.

The man who looked to be in charge, Agent Johnson, called out again. "Please! I want customers to leave and all restaurant staff to line up by the counter." He looked at Chelsea. "That means you too, miss."

Chelsea ignored the order, instead pleading with George for any news he might have.

"I said, staff against the counter!" Johnson ordered.

The agent, still with Chelsea, reached out to gently take her arm to guide her away. He was surprised when she slammed her elbow hard against his chin, sending him stumbling back.

"Let her be!" George hollered and stepped between the two. "She's upset. Her boyfriend AJ was involved in that shootout!"

George's words jolted her like a thunder bolt. Her hand went to her chest and for a moment, she found it hard to breathe. The entire place froze. Every eye was upon her.

Sandra rushed over and took the shaken Chelsea in her arms. Chelsea trembled and tears ran down her cheek. She turned her head towards the Lansdowne officer. "George. Somebody. Tell me he's okay!"

Silence. Awkward silence. She began to shake. Why wouldn't anybody say anything? They merely stood there, frozen, a mixture of pitying, concerned expressions.

The phone in her hand vibrated. She looked at it, confused. Again it buzzed.

"Chelsea. Answer it," Sandra said, bringing her to her senses. She nervously placed it against her ear. Barely she managed a weak 'Hello'.

"Is this Chelsea Henderson?"

"Yes?"

"This is Connie. I'm with the Springhurst Police department and an old friend of AJs. I'm at County General. AJ's been brought into emergency and I knew he'd want me to call you. It's serious. Can you get here right away?"

"Yes, of course." She dropped her phone into her pocket and headed for the door. An agent stepped in her way.

"Oh my God. AJ's in serious condition. Nobody dare try to stop me from leaving."

George stepped beside her and took her arm. "I'll drive you." He led her past the line of FBI agents and out the door. Screeching tires sent them off with the siren wailing.

Chapter 43

What would normally be a fifteen minute drive to the hospital, George made in seven. Along the way, he did his best to reassure Chelsea, whose worried hands shook as she constantly mumbled, praying for AJ's health.

George pulled up to the emergency entrance and let her out, then pulled away so he wasn't blocking the entrance. Chelsea rushed through the doors and was met by Connie, who recognized her from a picture AJ had shown her. Connie took her to a triage nurse who led her through a door with a sign above it reading, *Intensive Care*. Inside was a long, curved room with a counter on her left running the length of it. On her right were a dozen individual rooms. When Chelsea entered AJ's room, she saw him and gasped.

A face mask with a hose running from it covered his nose and mouth. The right side of his neck was bandaged. Various wires ran out from under his sheets to a bank of machines. Bags of fluids hung from poles around him. Some were clear, one looked to be blood. Monitors beeped and their screens scrolled. Horrified to see how pale he was, she rushed to his side and took his hand with both of hers. She blinked rapidly a few times so she could see through her tears.

"Oh AJ." Her voice was shaky and fearful. "My God, don't leave me."

A voice spoke from behind her. "Ms. Henderson. Could you come with me for a moment? The doctors have to come in."

She nodded, then placed a hand on AJ's cheek and lightly kissed his forehead. Then she placed her mouth close to his ear, her voice a soft, tearful whisper. "I wish I had told you before how much I love you. Now you might die and never hear me say those words. You have to pull out of this AJ so you can hear me say it. Promise?" She kissed his forehead again and, with her head bowed, left the room.

Two men and a woman gently pushed passed her as she was leaving and closed the curtains around the bed. Only steps away, Chelsea attempted to hear what they were saying. Before she could hear anything important or useful, she was reluctantly led away by a male nurse. She turned back to look and saw AJ's curtains being yanked back and his bed, monitors and fluid bottles attached, being wheeled away.

"No," she said. She took a step to follow but was gently grasped by the same nurse who had escorted her from the room. She turned to him. "What… what's happening?"

Fear enveloped her. "Tell me. Please! How bad is he hurt? Where are they taking him?"

"The doctor will be by in a moment to explain." He turned and walked to the end of the counter, where he conferred with a woman in a white jacket. She saw the nurse point to her before the woman nodded and headed her way.

"Ms. Henderson?" Chelsea nodded and listened intently. "I'm Doctor Kadner, in charge of Chief Johnson's case. At the moment, he's in critical condition, having lost a lot of blood from his wounds."

"Wounds!" she gasped, putting her hand over her mouth. "My God. He was shot more than once? How? I mean where? I mean ..."

"It's okay. Let me explain. He received two gunshot injuries. A minor one to the side of his neck. Fortunately, it struck the fleshy area at the base of the neck so there's no damage in that area to be concerned with. He did suffer a major wound to his lower abdomen. He was lucky. The officer on scene did an excellent job of applying pressure on the wound until first responders arrived, or it could've been much worse, even fatal. A person can bleed to death in five to eight minutes. He was quite lucky to be looked after so well until help arrived."

"Does he need blood? I have blood. You can use mine."

"He will, but there's an issue. His blood type is O negative, a rare blood type. Only nine percent of the U.S. population has it. People, like the Police Chief here, who have this blood type, can only receive O negative. We have a very limited supply, not enough for an operation which we need to perform. May I ask, what type are you?"

"I, I don't know." Chelsea said, visibly shaken.

The doctor called over a nurse. "Could you do a blood test on Ms. Henderson to see what blood type she is. We're looking for O negative, which would be a match with Mr. Johnson? Thanks."

Chelsea was led to a closet sized cubicle with just two chairs and a small table. She was asked to sit in the chair with a larger than usual fold down arm rest. The nurse left for a moment, then returned with a needle and vial to withdraw enough blood for testing. She winced when the nurse inserted a needle into her arm and watched as her blood filled the vacuum tube. With ease, he withdrew the needle, cleaned the area, and applied a bandage. He stood

266 GORDON K. JONES

and gave her a reassuring smile. "We'll know in a few minutes. Please just stay where you are until somebody comes and gets you."

Knowing there was nothing she could do but wait, she leaned forward, holding her face with her hands. For ten minutes she sat, suspended in a surreal world, her mind unable to comprehend what was happening and what may happen. She tried as hard as she could to remove the bad images, envisioning her hand holding his while he looked at her with his warm, disarming smile. Then the vison would change to being told of his death. Being at his graveside.

"Positive thoughts," she whispered quietly, hoping to shut out those images. "Positive thoughts. Positive thoughts. AJ, don't you damn well leave me."

"Ms. Henderson." The voice came from the nurse who took her blood. She looked up to find her standing directly in front of her. "Ms. Henderson."

She shook her head a little. "Yes."

"Chief Johnson is being prepared for surgery. We need you. Please come with me."

Chapter 44

AJ winced and swore as Chelsea carefully worked at peeling away the bandage covering his stitches. "Hold still. I almost got it. Jeez, you can take a bullet like a man but, my God, you're a big suck when it comes to having a simple bandage taken off."

"What the hell do they put it on it anyway, super glue?" He cussed loudly when she finally yanked the bandage fully off. A concerned Briley trotted over and licked the side of his face. AJ wiped his cheek, then gave the dog a pat. "Yeah, Briley. I'm okay. I think she was just taking some frustration out on me."

"I was as careful as I could be," she said as Briley flopped down beside the couch.

"I know," he said with a sigh. "And thank you. Damn it, though. It hurts."

"Hurts me to do it. Still, it needs to be done."

"Yeah, I know." He watched as she tossed the old messy bandage into the garbage bedside the bed. Her hand was warm when she placed it on his forehead, checking for fever. "You know, you're the prettiest nurse I've ever had."

She smiled and stroked his hair. "You're just saying that, so I'll be gentle with you."

"No, it's true. Do you know what else is also true? I've never had a nurse who was in love with me before."

She stopped her examination of the stitches and sat on the bed beside him. "I never said I was in love with you."

He smiled. "Yes, you did. When I was in the ICU. I was in this haze, not quite out. Not quite in the real world but I heard you. I was awake enough to feel your tears on my cheek. If anything, those say love more than any words. But yes, I definitely heard you."

She smiled and took his hand. "I wanted to tell you under more romantic circumstances."

"And you gave me your blood. Saved my life. The doc said it was possible I could have died if you didn't."

She smiled. "I wasn't about to lose you. And, of course, with my Chelsea blood in you, you'll always have to behave."

He pulled her to him, kissed her softly, then said in a whisper, "Yeah, I love you too."

◆ ◆ ◆

AJ was sprawled on the sofa when he heard Briley barking in the backyard to announce Chelsea's arrival home. They called to each other while she kicked off her shoes at the door before walking into the room. She took a spot on the sturdy coffee table in front of him, set her purse beside her, then felt his forehead. It was something she did a few times a day and whenever she returned from being out. "No fever. That's good. You're healing well."

"Eager to get back to work. Sick of just doing my exercises then laying on the sofa."

"I actually think you're beginning to like it. You enjoy having me running around waiting on you hand and foot," she said with a smile. "I hear Eric's back to work."

PREDATORS AND PREY

269

"Yeah, patrolling his desk till he's fully healed."

"And here you are, still laying about, watching TV."

"Bullet wounds are messier than knife wounds. Takes longer to heal."

She laughed as she slid off the coffee table and onto her knees. She placed her lips tenderly on his. "I love you. I'm so glad you're alive."

"Me too ... on both counts."

Chelsea reached around, grabbed her purse, placed it in front of her, and opened it. As she looked at AJ, her expression turned serious. "I have something for you. Um ... before I give you this, I need to ask you something."

"Sure."

"Well, ah, this has been on my mind for a while."

AJ had an idea what she was going to ask. He'd been expecting it for sometime.

She took hold of one of his hands with both of hers. "Did you already suspect Trent might be the Predator's Predator when you started dating me?" She paused and bit her lip, afraid of what his answer might be. "I mean, did you start dating me just so you could get information on Trent? You know, a chance to get closer to your quarry."

"The first time I walked into Corbett's and you served me, well, geez, I don't want to sound like a love struck teen, but yeah, I was immediately taken with you. Your looks, your personality. You had me the moment you came to my table.

"I saw his picture by the door as I was leaving and recognized him. I was speaking to him right before a nearby murder was discovered. When I came back the second time, yes, I wanted to have a chat with him but also really hoped you'd be there."

"Oh." Her tone was questioning. She let go of his hand.

"No. No. No. I know what you're thinking, and it wasn't like that. Yes, I suspected the man when I came in the second time. Damn, I really wanted to ask you out. I was afraid that in the end, after he was caught and all was going well between us that you'd question our relationship, just like you're doing now. Didn't want to use you and I never did."

He grabbed her hand. "That's why I never asked you out. Remember, it was you who asked me and, of course, I said yes right away."

"Because of the case?"

"No. Because of the chance to get to know you better. I never asked you anything regarding the case and never asked you to do anything to help me with it. I know looking back, it might look the way it looks. Please believe me, it wasn't. I wanted to keep the case separate from us. I just wanted to get to know you better and I'm damn glad you gave me that chance."

"You know, AJ, before I asked this, I told myself that however you answered, I'd still love you and want you in my life. As I asked though, I realized deep down, it would have hurt too much if we had started our relationship with you using me. There'd be no way I could've gone on with it. I'm so glad you explained it to me the way you did because now I have no doubts about us. Asking you out was the best thing I could ever have done."

She leaned forward, put her hand against the side of his face, then lovingly, tenderly pressed her lips to his. His hand reached out to the back of her neck as they extended their moment. Finally, her lips parted from his.

"Now, that surprise I have for you," she said softly as she removed her hand from his face, reached into her purse and pulled out a small box, which she handed to him.

He looked at it, then at her before he opened it. Inside was a small glass veil with a chunk of metal in it. "My bullet?"

"Sure is. I picked it up from the station. Don't know what you want to do with it, or even if you wanted it at all."

"Oh yeah. I want it. Thanks for getting it for me. Maybe I'll find something to hang it around my neck with, that is once it's healed. You know, for some reason, I was hoping to get it. Don't know why, but I feel it's a part of me now. Thanks, honey." It was a struggle for him to roll onto his side so he could awkwardly hug her.

He asked for help in sitting upright and after she managed to get him in a comfortable position, took a seat beside him. Gently, she patted the bandage on the side of his neck, happy he didn't wince when she touched it. She took his hand, holding it tight.

"I had visitors while you were out. Internal Affairs dropped by to have a talk."

"So, what happened?"

He felt her squeeze his hand hard. "Well, not surprisingly, the FBI are pissed we kept them out of the loop. I'm told I'll be disciplined for it, but because of the results, it shouldn't be more than having my wrist slapped. Would have been much worse for me if Eric had died. If Eric and I had both died, well, that would have been the end of Connie, Julie and Ben's careers."

"Would have been horrible for me if you had died. Instead, here you are, a hero. You all are. That's what everybody in town's saying."

"Sure don't feel like one. I don't know, maybe I did this out of pride. Maybe I should've let the Feds handle it. Eric was almost killed. Me too. Hell, I'm definitely not a hero."

"You were to me before this all happened. Now you are one everywhere."

Her smile quickly disappeared and her head dropped.

"What's the matter?"

"I heard Trent's body was released. He's going to be buried in a couple of days, apparently in an anonymous grave."

272   GORDON K. JONES

"And?"

"Well, there's something deep inside of me saying I should be there when they do."

"You want to be at Trent Corbett's funeral?" AJ said, astonished. He let go of her hand. "Trent Corbett. The serial killer? Trent Corbett, the son of a bitch who shot it out with me."

AJ tried to stand. He fell back, sighing. "He killed eight people and you want to go to his God damn funeral. I'd go, but only to pack the ground down tight over the son-of-a-bitch."

"You told me you thought he purposely missed you. You also said he shot the girl to protect you and was lowering his gun and stepping towards you to help when he was killed."

AJ took a moment to settle down and took a few deep breaths. He couldn't fathom why she would want to go to the murderer's funeral. "Yes, you're right. I was too weak to stop Connie and don't believe he ever tried to kill me. Hell, do you know what it's like to be shot at ... to be shot. He may not have pulled the trigger, but it was because of him I was shot and Eric stabbed."

"I know," she acknowledged. "Trent killed a lot of innocent people, I realize that. I also feel his death was warranted. But it's not the Trent I knew. I knew him as a great boss, a man who cared about his staff and people in general. I always felt he was a kind man and still feel that way. He was always good to me. That's the Trent whose funeral I would like to attend but ... I know I can't."

AJ reached out, took her hand and pulled her towards him. She followed his lead and, still kneeling on the floor, hugged him.

"He loved animals," she said tearfully. "I guess in his own sick way was doing what he thought was right to protect them. Nobody will ever see that. With all the good the man held in his heart, he'll only ever be known as the Predator's Predator, serial killer."

PREDATORS AND PREY

◆ ◆ ◆

A few weeks later, the hoards of onlookers, death mongers and reporters who came to Lansdowne began to taper off. Even those who flocked to Corbett's for photos and selfies with it in the background became less and less every day.

Chapter 45

When AJ returned to work, he knew he'd be riding a desk for a few months until he could prove to state authorities he was fit for regular duty. One day, when he looked up after hearing the precinct door open, he was surprised to find Samantha Edgars standing by the counter. She was there to thank him and Julie, having already stopped in to see Connie and Eric. As she was leaving, she stopped at the door. "If there's anything I can do for either of you, please let me know. You saved my life and those of my friends they didn't get to."

Without a thought, AJ quickly answered, "There is one thing. Give up African game hunting. Let those poor creatures live."

"Nice meeting you, and thanks again," she replied. She walked to the door, then stopped and looked back, "Chief. I do promise to think about it."

AJ chuckled when he thought back to it as he pulled into Chelsea's driveway. Things were pretty much back to normal for him, which made him happy. The surgery incision was mostly healed, yet it still annoyed him. Nothing

PREDATORS AND PREY

275

big or newsworthy happened on his or anybody else's watch, and he hoped it would remain that way. He had enough of action packed days and was glad to return to the slower way of life.

Even though he had a key and spent pretty much every night of the week sleeping over, except for those mornings when he started early, he still thought it proper to knock when he first arrived. He didn't have to wait long for Chelsea to answer, and when she did, her beaming smile was wider than usual. She kissed him fully, took his hand and led him inside, where he found a wonderful aroma wafting in the air, one he hadn't enjoyed since the restaurant closed. With the owner dead, it didn't reopen.

Bumbleberry pie.

She led him to the kitchen and placed her hand on top of what looked like a pie box. He prayed there was more than a slice in it. "So ... whatcha got in there?" To his delight, when she flipped the lid open, a whole pie was inside.

"Nice!" he said, slapping his hands together. Before she could reach for the knife on the table to cut the pie, he grabbed her and squeezed her tight. Then he eased off so he could see her face, "I thought you said Tony would never give up his recipe. Smells great. Did you find one online?"

"Nope."

"He finally gave you the recipe?"

"Nope."

"You asked him to make it for you?"

"Um ... kind of."

"Kind of. What do you mean 'kind of'?"

"Well, I've done a lot of thinking the past few weeks about what I should do now that I'm out of work. Then it came to me. The restaurant's always done well, plus it was the only one in town. There's no place for anyone to eat now so I said to myself, why don't I buy it?"

"You bought it?"

"Sure did. I managed to scrape together enough money to put a down payment on it, and now it's mine. Going to call it ... are you ready for this? Chelsea's."

"Wow! That's fabulous. I think you'll do great. You know, you could've come to me. I've got some money stashed away."

"I know I could've, but I wanted to do this on my own. I worked there for so long and wanted to feel, to know, it was one hundred percent, my place. Running my own restaurant has always been a dream of mine. And now it's happening. You understand, don't you?"

"Yeah, I do. Congratulations."

"Thanks. The first thing I did after signing the papers was to go over to Tony's and hire him."

"Excellent move."

"Well, I had to." She placed her hands on AJ's shoulders, kissed him, and looked into his eyes with delight. "It was the only way I could think of keeping you in Bumbleberry pie."

Also by Gordon K. Jones

9781772311228 - paperback
5.5"x 8.5" | 264 pages
$22.95
FICTION
9781772311235 - ePub
9781772311242 - PDF

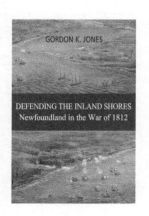

9781772310443 - paperback
5.5"x 8.5" | 164 pages
$19.95
NON-FICTION
9781772310450 - ePub
9781772310467 - PDF